STAY

ALSO BY VICTOR GISCHLER

STAY

VICTOR GISCHLER

Thomas Dunne Books St. Martin's Press New York

THOMAS DUNNE BOOKS.
An imprint of St. Martin's Press.

STAY. Copyright © 2015 by St. Martin's Press LLC. All rights reserved. Printed in the United States of America. For information, address St. Martin's Press, 175 Fifth Avenue, New York, N.Y. 10010.

www.thomasdunnebooks.com
www.stmartins.com

Designed by Steven Seighman

The Library of Congress Cataloging-in-Publication Data is available upon request.

ISBN 978-1-250-04151-7 (hardcover)
ISBN 978-1-4668-3805-5 (e-book)

St. Martin's Press books may be purchased for educational, business, or promotional use. For information on bulk purchases, please contact the Macmillan Corporate and Premium Sales Department at 1-800-221-7945, extension 5442, or write to specialmarkets@macmillan.com.

First Edition: June 2015

10 9 8 7 6 5 4 3 2 1

For my son Emery

ACKNOWLEDGMENTS

Props as always to my agent, David Hale Smith. Special thanks to my patient family. Much gratitude to the team at Thomas Dunne. Extra-special turbo gratitude to Brendan Deneen for his patience, support, and creativity.

PROLOGUE

Brooklyn, Six years ago . . .

He was currently going by the name Dante Payne. The two men with him also used aliases. They were dangerous men who'd been relocated to America. Like those who came to this country before them, they looked to start over and make their fortune.

And they were perfectly willing to take a few shortcuts. Certainly willing to break a few laws.

Laws had been invented to keep the rabble in line. To keep lesser men out of the way while people like Dante took advantage. Everywhere he looked in America, he saw weakness. If he were smart and patient, he would get what he wanted with relative ease. There would be occasional resistance, but it would be swept aside. Dante had experience with such things, knew almost immediately by the look in an opponent's eyes if he would fight or fold.

He browsed the back of the convenience store, hovering near a rack of potato chips and beef jerky. His compatriots stood next to a cooler of beer, dour and silent. The Korean behind the counter cracked open a roll of pennies to replenish the register.

Dante had done his homework, knew the routine, so they didn't have long to wait. The goombahs waddled in at almost the exact time every week. *Courteous of them to make it so easy.*

Mick Nastasi wore a deep purple jumpsuit the color of an old bruise. A thick gold chain around his neck. Rings. A fat man, the result of a soft life. Gray hair thinning. The big man with him was muscle, a sports jacket over a polo shirt. He had a half-eaten chocolate doughnut in his fist.

Nastasi went to the counter, smiled at the Korean, said whatever he usually said. This was routine business, not reason to suspect today would be different or special. The Korean smiled and nodded and handed the envelope with the protection payoff to Nastasi.

Dante's eyes slid to his men, and he nodded. They returned the nod then moved toward the counter and the two goombahs.

They struck calmly but without hesitation.

The first looped the garrote around the muscle man's head and jerked it tight, the thin wire biting deeply into flesh, blood squirting. He was dead before he hit the floor.

Nastasi turned, opened his mouth to scream, but the clear plastic bag came down over his head abruptly, muffling him. He was forced to his knees, hands pawing uselessly at the hands holding the bag over his head.

Dante stepped up to the counter, fixed the trembling Korean with an ice-cold gaze. "You don't pay these men anymore. You understand?"

The Korean nodded.

Nastasi began to kick and writhe in earnest, sucking for air against the plastic bag. One of Dante's men held the Italian's arms while the other one kept the bag over his head. Nastasi's desperate breaths fogged against the plastic.

Dante waited a moment before going on. He wanted the Korean to see Nastasi struggle for a few more moments. It would leave a deeper impression than anything Dante might say.

"You won't see me again," Dante told him. "You don't even see me now. One of my men will be along to pick up the envelope each week. It will be the same amount as always. Nothing will change. You understand this?"

The Korean nodded again, eyes flicking briefly from Dante to the suffocating man and back.

Nastasi had ceased struggling, hung limp in the grip of Dante's men. He nodded to them and they took the bodies through the back where a van waited in the alley.

Dante nodded at the Korean one last time then exited through the store's front door.

On the sidewalk out front, Dante paused and lit a cigarette. He squinted at the sky, exhaling a gray stream of smoke. It was a beautiful spring day, not too warm. A perfect time for new beginnings.

And his empire would begin here on this square block in a low-rent Brooklyn neighborhood. He'd decided to start with the Italians because they'd be the easiest. They'd become a cartoon parody of their former selves. A couple of families still ran rackets here and there, but they would be almost no trouble at all.

He would tackle the Tong next and then the Russians, who would be harder. There would be pushback, of course, but equilibrium would eventually establish itself. By then, Dante would have already set up several legitimate businesses through which to launder the money. In time, the legitimate businesses would stand on their own and he could separate himself from anything unseemly. Soon he would be on top again. He'd done it before.

And he'd do it again.

NOW

CHAPTER ONE

"Brent has Barbie's head."

David Sparrow had come immediately awake upon hearing Anna, his four-year-old daughter pad into the room, but he'd kept his eyes closed, remaining perfectly still. The ploy failed, and he felt the little girl climb onto the bed.

"Daddy."

He knew without checking the bedside nightstand that it was somewhere between six and six-fifteen in the morning.

"Daddy."

David doggedly stuck to his plan, lay like a stone, even feigned a convincing snore. Academy Award time.

"Daddy, Brent says he is going to flush Barbie's head down the toilet."

He felt Anna's soft hand on his face, a little thumb prying up one of his eyelids. "Daddy!"

Anna's honey-colored hair was disheveled from sleep. She wore a *Little Mermaid* nightgown and clutched a headless doll in one of her tiny fists. Lips curled into a snarl so cute it lost all possibility of menace. "Brent is being a monster again and says he will flush Barbie's head down the toilet unless I give him my Pop-Tart."

Brent. Eight years old. His new thing was seeing what could fit down the toilet. The extortion was a new angle.

David reached back, slapped his wife lightly on the hip. "You want in on this?"

Amy grunted from somewhere in the depths of the sheets and blankets.

"Right." David swung his legs over the side of the bed, sending Anna scurrying to the kitchen ahead of him. He stretched, heard something pop in his shoulder and reminded himself he needed to begin a regular gym routine again. A long yawn.

"I'll start the coffee," he told Amy.

Another grunt.

He shrugged into an olive drab T-shirt and followed Anna into the kitchen where she pointed the headless doll at Brent and made ray gun sounds. Brent held up a blueberry Pop-Tart as a shield.

"I'm blocking you," Brent said.

"Give me that head, Brent, or I'll melt your Pop-Tart."

"Give her the head, Brent." David took the coffee from the cabinet. Hazelnut this morning, he decided.

Brent groaned but handed over the head. Anna stuck her tongue out at him. They munched Pop-Tarts and drank milk. Friday was Pop-Tart day. They tried to go a little healthier the rest of the week.

As the coffee brewed, David boiled water for oatmeal. He was absurdly proud of his ability to time the morning ritual. The kids left the kitchen table to get dressed just as Amy entered and sat down. David set the oatmeal in front of her, slivered almonds and strawberries on top, a glass of orange juice and a cup of coffee on the side. She spooned oatmeal into her mouth as she opened her laptop and brought up her e-mail.

"Are you going to make your train?" David sipped black coffee from a Yale Law mug.

Amy shuffled papers into a briefcase that was so over-stuffed it threatened not to buckle closed. "Don't worry about me. Just make sure the kids are dressed."

I always do. David went down the hall, glanced into each child's room. Both were at different stages of getting dressed but basically on schedule. "Make sure you have *everything* in your book bag before you zip it up."

Anna: "Okay, Daddy."

Brent: "I *know.*"

David returned to the bedroom. Jeans, wool socks, hiking boots, a light flannel shirt over the T-shirt. Early April and it was warm enough to forget the jacket but not *too* warm. Usually his favorite time of year.

He met Amy at the door. "Keys, purse, laptop?"

"Got it all."

They kissed, lips brushing so fast, David wasn't sure he felt it, and Amy left.

"You monkeys dressed or what?" David shouted back through the house.

A little stampede down the hall, backpacks slung over shoulders. Brent's hair was almost combed. Good enough.

He hustled them through the side door and into the garage. He buckled them into the back of the Escalade, then buckled himself in. He turned on the local A.M. station, which reported traffic wasn't any better or worse than usual. Weather not a factor.

Ten seconds later he was on the road. Brent's school

was first. David eased into the drop-off lane, pulled up in front.

"It's Friday, buddy," David said. "Let's have a good day, so we can have a good weekend."

"I know." Brent climbed out, slammed the door behind him.

David watched him a moment before pulling away.

Next stop, preschool for Anna.

David parked and walked her in, kissing her on top of the head before releasing her into the swirl of children swarming into the building.

On the way out, he spotted the usual klatch of moms on the sidewalk next to the parking lot. Generally three to five of them, age range twenty-nine to forty-one. He paused and nodded to the four gathered in front of him.

"Friday again," David said.

The leader smiled, an athletic thirty-five-year-old in a tight yoga outfit. "How's Amy?"

David smiled. "She's good. Busy."

"Tell her she must come out with us for coffee some morning," said another one, frumpier, mom jeans.

"I'll tell her," David said.

"Uh . . . did you want to grab some coffee with us?" she asked tentatively.

"Next time. A lot on my plate today. You ladies have a great weekend." He tossed them a wave and headed for the Escalade.

He had no interest in joining the ladies for coffee but felt like it was about time he got an invitation. He chuckled at how petty that was and put the SUV into gear and headed home.

———

One more cup of coffee then he looked at his watch. Nine o'clock. He started cleaning clockwise around the house, living room, hall, bathroom, den, kitchen, dining room, living room. Then upstairs. Three bedrooms, master bath, kid's bathroom. He put the cleaning supplies away.

David checked his watch again. Ten fifteen. Not bad.

He bagged up the trash and took it out to the can on the garage side of the house. Without looking, he sensed the neighbor across the fence. If David could avoid eye contact and drop the trash into the can and leave again without—

"Hey, ho, neighbor! How's it hanging?"

David turned and smiled. "Hi, Mark. Doing fine. You?"

On the other side of the five-foot fence, David's neighbor Mark wrestled with a tangle of garden hose. He was a little pot belly on top of a pair of pale stick legs in Bermuda shorts. He jerked a chin at a younger, meatier version of himself. "You met my brother Gary?"

Gary was halfheartedly raking leaves into a small pile. He looked up for a split second. "Hey."

David nodded back. "Hey."

"You still out of work?" Mark asked.

David smiled. It wasn't easy, hurt his face a bit. "I'm not *out* of work, Mark. Just staying home for a while."

"Sure. What's it been? Like four months?"

"Something like that." It had been six.

"Hey, how about this guy," Mark said to Gary. "He gets to lounge around the house all day while the wife brings home the bacon." Mark winked at David. "Nice work if you can get it, huh, buddy?"

"Right."

"Well, things will look up sooner or later."

"Right." David tossed a wave and turned away before he could be drawn into further conversation. "You guys take care."

David circled back around to the front door and saw the mail had come. He took the wad of envelopes inside.

He sat at the kitchen table, a wastepaper basket next to him. He threw out the flyers. He opened the junk mail, glanced at it to make sure it wasn't important then ripped it all up and dumped the pieces into the basket. He made a mental note to buy a shredder. He wrote checks for the bills, stuck them into the provided return envelopes and stamped them, setting them aside for tomorrow's outgoing. He set aside Amy's mail. He opened and read a letter from Brent's school's foundation asking for money. He wrote a check for a hundred dollars, sealed and stamped the envelope.

David checked his watch again. Ten forty-two.

The house was quiet. Somewhere a dog barked.

In a little over four hours he could pick up the kids.

CHAPTER TWO

"The chicken okay?" David asked.

"Chicken?" Amy said it as if unaware what she'd been eating. She was forking food into her mouth absently as she looked at a file folder at the table. She looked at the chunk of white meat on the end of her fork as if seeing it for the first time. "Oh, yes. Fine."

Lemon chicken, rice, asparagus. A reliable go-to meal, maybe boring now. David made a note to take it out of the rotation. Maybe a pork roast. David decided to reevaluate the entire pantry. He'd been relying too much on starches.

Or was he simply inventing projects for himself to fill the days?

"I don't like asparagus," Brent said. "They look like wieners."

David frowned. "Brent."

"Green Martian wieners," Bent said.

"You're not supposed to say that Brent," Anna scolded. "You're in trouble."

"Just eat your chicken, Anna," David told her. "I'm the guy who decides who's in trouble."

Brent looked wary. "*Am* I in trouble?"

"Yes," David said. "You have to sleep on the roof tonight."

"Oh, ha ha, that's so funny I forgot to laugh."

"Both of you finish your milk," David said. "Are you done eating?"

"I am!" Anna said, throwing up her hands like she'd scored a field goal.

"I want dessert!" Brent. *Of course.*

"Tonight's not a dessert night."

"Aw, come on."

"It's free time," David announced. "Anna?"

"*SpongeBob!*"

"Approved." He turned to the boy. "Brent?"

"Minecraft!"

"*Gong!*" David shook his head. "No Internet and no video games. Let's change it up, okay?"

"Aw, *come on!*"

"You have a quarter million Legos in your room," David said. "Build something."

"Build what?"

"How about an Mi-24 Hind helicopter?"

"I'm going to build a pirate fort."

"Approved," David said. "Kids dismissed."

They pushed the chairs back and bolted from the room, slightly less noisy than dump trucks full of bowling balls driving over a rough road.

David gestured to the serving tray of asparagus. "Wieners?"

Amy lifted her head from the file folder. "What?"

"Nothing. Can I get you anything?"

"No. Thanks, hon."

She went back to the file folder with a pen, making notes.

She looked up again a minute later. "You okay?"

"What? Why?"

"You're quiet. I thought maybe you heard from the Army today."

"Oh." He shook his head. "No."

They'd sent him home to rest. They hadn't been clear exactly how much rest he'd needed or how long it would take. He'd stopped asking.

"I'm just thinking about building a barbecue pit out back," he said.

"Oh." Amy shrugged. "Sure. Whatever you like."

He thought about it for ten more seconds. How often would he use a barbecue pit? He had a cheap Weber in the garage he'd used maybe twice. Hamburgers and hot dogs. He thought he might like to try ribs, but nobody else in the family liked barbecue.

The idea that he needed to discover some hobby for himself seemed suddenly . . . tiresome.

David cleared the table and loaded the dishwasher.

The kids' free time evaporated, and David shooed them one at a time toward the bath, reminding Brent that soap and shampoo were integral elements of the process. Teeth brushed and final visits to the potty.

"Whose turn?" David asked.

"I've got the boy," Amy said. "You take the girl."

David gave his wife the thumbs-up. "Check."

He went to Anna's room where she was waiting for him under her Dora the Explorer sheets. She handed him two picture books in which the protagonist—a pigeon—was discouraged from driving the bus and staying up late. He finished reading, kissed her on the forehead, and turned out the light.

David made the rounds downstairs, turning off lights and making sure the doors were locked. No dishes left in the sink.

Back upstairs, he brushed his teeth and combed his hair. He considered shaving but generally preferred to do that in the morning. A little stubble wouldn't be a problem.

In the bedroom, Amy was already on her side of the bed, rubbing lotion on knees and elbows, her nightly ritual. She hadn't gotten as far as the face cream. She was still in bra and panties, hadn't slipped into the big flannel green monstrosity yet. Comfortable, she claimed.

He pulled the door closed behind him, locked it.

Amy looked up at the sound of the lock clicking. An easy smile came to her face. "Oh, yeah?"

David went to the bed, leaned down for a kiss. She returned it, lips wet and parting for him. One of her hands went behind his head to pull him down, a tongue snaking into his mouth with unexpected but welcome enthusiasm.

Now *this* was more like it. David had struck out a few nights ago, and Amy's schedule had been a whirlwind until today. This was something they *both* needed, he thought. It had been a long time coming.

Amy's hands went to his jeans, unbuttoning and unzipping. He pulled off his shirt. His pants and boxers came down and he stepped out of them. She grabbed his length and started working him. He climbed into bed next to her, and in a second they were entwined, kissing hard.

She was still tugging on him as he pulled her cotton panties down. He'd had big plans to slow-play this and make it last, but it had been awhile and he was driven by a fierce urgency.

David tossed her panties aside and positioned himself between her legs. He tried to maneuver himself in but it was awkward. He wasn't finding his way.

Amy reached down to guide him in. "Almost. Here, this way."

A knock on the door.

Are you fucking kidding me?

"Hey, the door's locked." Anna.

David composed himself, steadied his voice. "It's late, Anna. Go back to bed."

"I had a dream with spiders."

David felt Amy's hand against his chest. "David."

And that was that.

He rolled off her, grabbed his boxers and T-shirt. An unreasonable resentment rose up within him, and he shoved it back down. This was being a parent. This was part of it.

Amy was already pulling the flannel green circus tent over her head. She went to the door and opened it.

Anna ran past without pausing and jumped into the middle of the bed, sinking into the nest of pillows and the thick, down comforter. "I want to sleep in here."

"Of course, baby."

Amy and Anna snuggled under the covers.

"I think I'll go downstairs and watch TV for a bit," David said.

"You're still going with me tomorrow night, right?" Amy asked.

David sighed. "I won't know anyone."

"They're expecting you," Amy said. "And I need some good-looking arm candy to make those paralegal bimbos jealous."

A halfhearted smile. "Sure. Okay."

He switched off the light and left.

The dream had been gradually fading, becoming more obscure and coming less frequently, but tonight it was back in full force, vivid, so clear it was almost cinematic.

The streets of Damascus were littered with bodies. He could smell them. Buildings burned. Smoke. You couldn't see even halfway down any street there was so much smoke, black and thick and acrid.

Gunshots. Sometimes far away and other times startlingly nearby, echoing through the narrow streets. David couldn't always be sure of the direction. It was often difficult to understand who was killing whom and why. The sides hadn't quite been sorted out yet as various factions rushed to fill the power vacuum. Best just to shoot at everyone, or at least that seemed to David to be the prevailing strategy among the citizenry.

"Stay close," he told Yousef Haddad. "This wasn't the way we were supposed to come. I need to get my bearings." He checked the handheld GPS but wasn't getting a signal.

"We have to go back." Yousef's English was heavily accented but good.

"No." David had his orders. "A truck waiting in the suburbs will take us to a safe crossing at the Lebanese border. Then we make for the coast. We'll take a skiff south until we can get into Israeli waters. There's a trawler waiting to pick us up. We just need to be patient and stay away from the chaos."

Yousef stopped walking, which meant David had to stop also. He looked back into the man's resolute face.

"My wife and daughters are at my home." Yousef's eyes were hard. "If certain people discover I have fled, they will be raped by many men. They will be killed only after many hours of humiliation, and their bodies will be dragged through the streets and put on display as a lesson to others."

David considered what he knew of Yousef Haddad from the file.

The government hadn't sent David to rescue the man because he was a saint. Far from it. Yousef Haddad was a pivotal figure in the Syrian criminal underworld. As such, he had a finger in almost every pie, which made him the ideal informant, reporting on both government activities and insurgent movements. He'd provided names of faction leaders and endless details that kept the State Department and the CIA apprised of the situation on the ground. As long as Uncle Sam kept the cash flowing, Yousef kept the intel flowing.

So was it loyalty to Yousef that motivated the U.S. government to send in a man to fetch him out of the rapidly deteriorating situation in Syria? Partly. But it was also the fact that if he were captured by the wrong people and made to talk, it could be embarrassing for the U.S. government. David had been ordered to do everything possible to get him out.

Failing that, he had instructions to put a bullet in

Yousef's head. David wondered if Yousef suspected this. Probably. The man wasn't stupid.

"I have to go back for them," Yousef said.

If Yousef's file was to be believed, he had done much worse things to other men's wives and daughters. But every man loves his own. Yousef likely had no sense of irony about the situation.

"Another team has been sent for your family," David said. "They'll meet us."

"You know this for sure?" Yousef asked. "Are you in contact with the other team?"

"No. We'll have to trust them. And we don't really have time to debate it."

A moment stretched as the men took each other's measure. David became acutely aware for the pistol stuck into his belt at the small of his back, concealed by his light jacket. He felt sure he could bring it out fast enough if Yousef failed to cooperate.

The sound of gunshots the next street over decided things.

"They had better be there, government man," Yousef said. "When we get to the truck, my wife and daughters had better be there waiting for me. You understand?"

David nodded quickly and they set off again.

They were moments away from emerging onto a wide boulevard when a heavy machine gun chattered in front of them, kicking up chunks of asphalt and obliterating first-floor windows along the street. David had heard such weapons in action before, but it always sounded like all hell suddenly raining down on the Earth.

David and Yousef dove for the recessed alcove of a shop entrance. They pressed themselves flat against the cracked plaster.

A second later, a mob stormed past the entrance of the boulevard, young Syrian men in T-shirts and jeans mostly. Many wore scarves tied around there faces or ski masks. Some held clubs, others handguns. David glimpsed a couple of AK-47s in the crowd. Somewhere behind them the machine gun erupted again and bodies fell, the rest of the crowd picking up speed to escape, bodies pressed close, pushing and shoving.

Soon the crowd passed, and a split-second later, David heard the unmistakable creak and clank of an approaching armored vehicle.

It drove into view, opening fire again at the fleeing insurgents, the machine gun on top chugging lead and spitting .50 caliber shells out the side. It was a beat-up BRDM-2 but it was more than enough to chase off the poorly armed rebels. A troop of Syrian regulars with AK-47s followed at a crouch walk, using the armored vehicle for cover.

David squatted, motioning for Yousef to do the same. They'd wait for these guys to pass and then—

There was a flash and an explosive roar and a wave of heat. David put his hands over his face. When he looked again the armored vehicle was in flames and the regulars were shooting in multiple directions, including down the alley.

Yousef leaned in to talk directly into David's ear so he could be heard over the gunfire. "Molotov cocktail."

David nodded. That's what he'd figured, too.

The Syrian regulars tried to withdraw in an orderly fashion but the screaming mob that flooded in and around them finally convinced them to turn tail and sprint back the way they'd come, chased by the *pop* of handgun fire. Many went down with bullets in the back.

The wind shifted and the smoke from the burning armored vehicle filled the alley. David could feel the heat even where he was.

Two men emerged from the smoke wearing tattered jeans, sneakers, and T-shirts, scarves wrapped around faces. Both held AK-47s and were coming through the gray smoke at a crouch, eyes darting and anxious.

David drew the Glock .40, checked the magazine, and kept it low. He felt his back pockets, assuring himself the spare magazines were still there. If he and Yousef sat still and waited, the two insurgents might just walk right on by and—

The one closest turned, spotted them, his eyes going big as he raised the AK-47.

David didn't hesitate, raised the Glock two-handed and squeezed the trigger twice. The first shot bloomed high on the man's chest, the second more on target—square in the heart. He spun and fell in a heap.

David had already shifted his aim to the other who'd turned to run. Two more shots in the middle of his back, sending him sprawling forward.

He grabbed Yousef by the shoulder of his jacket and hauled him up. "Come on!"

They sprinted through the smoke, which gathered thickly around him now, stinging his eyes, getting into his throat. He coughed violently, wiped his eyes on his sleeve.

Water. David would suddenly give anything for a canteen.

Gunshots not too far away, seeming to come from every direction.

The smoke was so thick now he couldn't see the street around him. He'd lost Yousef. Some vague awareness reminded him he was in a dream. He kept the gun up, wondering what would come out of the smoke next.

Time and space shifted, and he was suddenly at the rendezvous point. There was that vague awareness of being in a dream, and yet David kept stumbling through the story, like an actor in a play, shoving Yousef into the back of a truck. The men in the back of the truck were holding Yousef as he struggled to get loose. The smoke swirled around them, cutting the scene off from the rest of the world, detaching it from reality.

"My family!" Yousef's shouts were desperate, edged with panic. His voice seemed like it was coming from the depths of some deep, black cave. "You said they would be here!"

"The other team has them." David hoped it was true. "You've got to go. Now."

Yousef thrashed free from the men holding him, jumped down from the truck. If he ran . . . if he got away from David . . .

Shoot him. Don't risk it. Shoot him now.

David brought he pistol down hard on the back of Yousef's skull just at the base. The man folded like somebody had flipped his off switch. David and the other men dumped his unconscious body into the back of the truck. Yousef was no longer David's problem.

He watched the truck pull away and fade into the smoke.

And then David was swimming. There was no world anymore, just smoke. He felt lost and weightless, the sounds of battle distant and tinny like they were coming from an old radio, and then—

David's eyes popped open. He'd fallen asleep on the couch watching TV. The Home Shopping channel was on the screen with the volume turned down.

Fuzzy morning light seeped in through the blinds. He stood and stretched, stumbled into the kitchen to start the coffeemaker and begin the day.

CHAPTER THREE

"Can you drive a little faster?" Amy squinted at the small visor mirror, opening her makeup case, the compact one she carried in her purse at all times. "We'll be late."

David allowed himself a quick glance at his wife before snapping his eyes back to the road. She was drawing a dark line under her eye with an eyeliner pencil. A *sharp* eyeliner pencil. If he needed to slam on the brakes, the pencil would go right through her eyeball. Since he didn't want to replay *that* conversation for the tenth time, he just said, "I'm doing the speed limit."

"You're worried about a ticket? Please." She switched to the other eye. "I'm the new Deputy District Attorney. I can fix a ticket." A sly smile.

David smiled, too, but he kept the Escalade at the speed limit. He'd estimated the travel time and predicted they would have twenty minutes to spare. No need to speed.

He glanced at the kids in the rearview mirror. Anna sat securely in her car seat, a dreamy expression on her face as she looked out the window. Amy and David had declared her potty training to have officially "taken" on her fourth birthday last week, a fact that made it a little easier for Amy's sister Elizabeth to agree to take the kids for the evening. The party for Amy in the city marked the first time they'd been out in six weeks.

He shifted his gaze to Brent, who had his head down into his brand-new 3DS, one of those handheld video games. David hated the blinking, bleeping noisy thing. He'd brought home a tennis racket for the boy two days ago. It had gone into Brent's closet next to the baseball glove, the football, and the roller blades. Brent would eventually get David's height. Maybe he'd try basketball next. Not hockey. David just didn't get hockey.

They were good kids, David reminded himself. They just weren't like David when he was their ages.

Who was?

He turned the Escalade into the neighborhood where Amy's sister had purchased a modest home six months ago. Her husband, Jeff, had been a department manager at Home Depot for six years and had finally been promoted to full store manager. The new house followed, and Elizabeth had quit her bank teller job to stay home with their eighteen-month-old son full time.

David pulled into the driveway. He saw the living room curtain pull aside then drop back again. David's eyes flashed over the lawn and front of the house. The hedges had been trimmed. There was an orange Frisbee under the back left tire of Jeff's Ford pickup. The gutters needed cleaning. There were tire indentations in the grass next to the driveway where someone had parked.

David climbed out of the SUV, opened the rear

passenger door, and scanned the neighborhood as he un-
buckled Anna from the car seat. The neighbors across
the street still had the old Chevy Impala up on blocks.
David couldn't spot any progress in the restoration.

Anna threw her arms around David's neck, pulled
him close to mash her cheek against his. "Daddy, I want
to watch the Dora DVD."

"I don't know if Aunt Lizzy has Dora, princess."

"I want spaghetti."

"We'll ask."

Amy and Elizabeth were already exchanging hugs on
the front steps. Elizabeth was a shorter, younger version
of Amy and still carried some of the pregnancy weight
on her hips. She smiled brightly at her sister, eyes gleaming and big, motherhood still a wonder to her. The sisters
were close, but Elizabeth's toddler and Amy's increased
workload kept them from getting together as often as
they wanted.

Jeff stood next to her, holding a beer in a Home Depot huggie. He was apple-cheeked with a patchy beard
and an all-American beer gut. Not for the first time, David felt a vague pang of envy upon seeing Jeff. Here was
a man who worked hard and made an honest living for
his family, but he was able to completely unplug on the
weekend. When he was home with his family, his job
was banished utterly from his mind, a cold beer and a
football game on the big-screen TV. He didn't deal with
demanding customers or unruly employees. No supply
problems or trouble with vendors. Not during family
time. Jeff could turn it off.

Turning off wasn't so easy for David. He'd been trying.

"Hey, David." Jeff extended his hand, and they shook.

"Good seeing you, Jeff." David noticed the fresh

sunburn on Jeff's neck, the dirt under his fingernails. He'd been working in the garden again, trying to get the tomatoes and pole beans up and running. There'd been loose talk of a green house.

Amy followed Elizabeth inside with the kids in tow. It was David's job to hang back and trade chitchat with Jeff. The intricacies of in-law diplomacy had become his specialty.

"How's everything down at the Depot?"

"Huge run on power tools." Jeff sipped beer. "I think everybody's getting the do-it-yourself bug all at once. Watching all those HGTV shows, I guess. Big sale. Moved a shitload of circular saws."

"Sounds like they keep you busy." David shoved his hands into his pockets.

"Sure." Another sip of beer. "What about you? Keeping busy? Around the house, I mean."

David smiled tightly. In the last three days, he'd replaced missing bricks in the chimney, fixed a dripping bathroom faucet, installed a ceiling fan in the den, painted the garage, removed a stump from the backyard, took apart and cleaned and reassembled the lawn mower, put up Dora the Explorer wallpaper in Anna's room, replaced a sputtering garbage disposal, changed the oil in the Escalade, and reread a dog-eared copy of *Ice Station Zebra*. So yeah. He'd stayed busy around the house.

David rocked heel to toe. "Oh, you know. The usual."

"Right." Jeff tossed back the rest of the beer. "Well, you know, it'll pick up."

Right.

Amy emerged from the house, Elizabeth right behind, the two sisters hovering in a cloud of chatter and family gossip. Glad-handing and cheek kisses and two minutes later, the Escalade glided north on the interstate into the city.

Amy checked her makeup again in the visor mirror, decided she'd finally achieved the desired effect, and shut the makeup case with a snap. She tucked it back into her purse.

They drove without talking.

"You're not going to do this all evening, are you?" Amy asked.

"I don't know what you mean." He knew exactly what she meant.

"The stony silence," she said. "You know this is a big night for me."

"I know."

"So you can warm up a little, okay?"

"They're your friends," David said.

"You're my husband, and I want you to share this evening with me. It's important." She flipped the visor down, checked her face again, flipped it back up again. "I mean, I don't ask a lot. I leave you alone to do your own thing. It's one night."

"I know. Don't worry."

"I just don't want you to do that thing where you make everyone you talk to feel irrelevant."

"If you can't say something nice, it's best to say nothing at all," David said.

"*That's* what I'm talking about. Don't do that. Talk about sports or cars or whatever guys talk about. Talk about women with big tits. I know you can be charming. I've seen you do it."

"I have no recollection of ever being charming."

"Trust me. We have two kids."

David grinned. "Okay. But it'll cost you. Later when we're home." He was still game even after the botched attempt last night. Maybe he'd get lucky. He was ever the optimist.

Amy giggled. "You drive a hard bargain, sir."

David parked in the underground lot below the government office building across from City Hall. They took the elevator to the top floor where a wide reception hall was decked out with white tablecloths and waiters in black tie.

Our tax dollars at work.

But it was all for David's wife—ostensibly—so why not?

Amy was immediately swarmed with the city's most prestigious attorneys and judges, all who'd come to pay homage to the new deputy district attorney. She negotiated the tidal wave of suits, gold cuff links, and Rolex watches with practiced poise. She'd spent ten years learning the ebb and flow of this particular shark tank, and tonight was the big payoff. Monday morning would bring a whole new set of headaches to go with the new job.

But not tonight. This was a celebration, and David reminded himself to act interested. He was the supportive husband. In spite of his wife's vote of confidence, he wasn't really sure how to go about being charming, but for her sake, he'd fake it.

He nodded and smiled automatically as he was introduced to various lawyers and bigwigs, and his eyes took in the room. A door behind the bar, probably back to the kitchen. Another door on the west wall with a red EXIT sign over it. A row of French doors leading out to a wide balcony. The small door to the side of the main entrance probably led to a utility room or—

"Stop that," she said quietly into his ear as she steered him toward a table with rows of champagne glasses.

"Stop what?"

"You're looking *past* everyone again. I bet you don't even know who I just introduced you to."

"Circuit Court Judge Myron Greenburg, Assistant D.A. Pete Howard, Gray Starling, senior partner at Starling and Doyle—"

"Okay, okay, stop showing off." She nodded to the waiter behind the bar to pour her a glass. "I have a present for you."

"Good. I like presents."

"That's the mayor across the room over there," Amy said. "I need to speak with him."

"And that's a present for me how?"

"It's a present because I'm not going to make you go with me to talk to him."

"It's like Christmas multiplied by my birthday."

"There's more." She reached into her purse.

"More is good," David said. "People say less is more, but I don't buy it."

She pulled out a cigar wrapped in cellophane, handed it to him. It was his brand, an ACID Kuba Kuba.

One of his eyebrows went up. "You know I limit myself to one a week."

"Special occasion." She grinned and gestured with her chin toward the balcony. "You can hide out there."

He kissed her on the cheek. "Say hi to the mayor for me."

"Yeah, right."

David unwrapped the cigar as he headed for the balcony, pausing to bum a book of matches from the bartender.

The night was cool and the balcony deserted in spite of the dazzling view of the city all lit up at night. Maybe all the lawyers and fat cats had grown numb to it. David went to the far end of the balcony before lighting the cigar. He didn't want any smoke wafting back inside and disturbing anyone. These days, one had to escape to the dark side of the moon to find a quiet place to light up. David was glad it was only an occasional indulgence. He puffed quietly, enjoyed the view.

Three minutes later, a pretty young woman in a bright red cocktail dress emerged from the reception, spotted him, and walked fast toward him, stiletto heels clicking on the tile.

She pulled a cigarette from a silver clutch. "Do you have a lighter?"

"Matches."

"That'll do."

He handed them to her. She lit the cigarette, stepping back, arms half crossing as she blew out a long silver stream of smoke. She watched the smoke drift away on the breeze, as if creating a gray cloud were the point of smoking.

"My dad says you used to be able to smoke anywhere. Like in *Mad Men*." She was maybe twenty-two, pretty in an obvious way, blond hair and blue eyes. "Now you always have to hunt around for a place. It's not fair really."

"Yeah." *So much for the dark side of the moon.*

"It's getting crowded," she said. "I think every lawyer in the state is in there."

"Yeah."

They chatted like that until she got near the end of her cigarette, David mostly nodding along. She was a recent college graduate, a law clerk. Her name was Wendy and her life story was an open book. Way too open. She was about to light another cigarette and launch into chapter two when her date arrived.

"Hey, babe, where you been?"

David remembered him immediately. Amy had introduced him as Carter Franks, a brand-new junior partner at a prestigious law firm across town. He wore an expensive suit and a bright garish tie pulled loose. Gold rings on the fingers of both hands. Manicured nails. A little gray was just creeping into his hundred-dollar haircut. He didn't have a hard look about him, but he wasn't in bad shape. Tennis or squash maybe.

When Carter spoke, he gestured with a large tumbler in his left hand, ice clinking and Scotch sloshing over the top. "I wanted you to meet some of the guys from the office. We're all thinking of heading to O'Malley's after the —"

He stopped abruptly, blinking at David. "Who's this?" He looked at Wendy, then at David and back again.

"We're just talking. He let me use his matches." Wendy held up the cigarette as proof.

Carter blinked again, focused. "Oh, yeah. The house husband."

David didn't bat an eyelash, but something in him tensed. Wendy took half a step back, like a field mouse suddenly aware she'd been standing in the shadow of a falcon without realizing it.

"Did he tell you about his sweet deal?" Carter asked Wendy. "He gets to sit home with his feet up while his wife slaves in the law mines. Talk about having it easy."

David smiled tightly, slowly brought the cigar to his mouth, sucked in smoke, and let it out smoothly.

"That's happening a lot, I hear," Wendy said, a clumsy attempt at diplomacy. "I mean, in this economy and everything." Her desire to be away from the conversation was so palpable, that you could slice it and serve it on toast.

"Yeah, but it doesn't hurt to marry up, huh, pal?" Carter winked at David. Like they were old friends.

David maintained the smile. "I guess I did all right."

"Sure." Carter slurped Scotch. "I'll be thinking about you on Monday when I'm slaving away at my desk." He turned to Wendy. "Don't worry about me, babe. I'm a provider. I got to make myself an attractive catch for girls like you."

He slapped her ass with a loud smack. She laughed nervously, trying to play it cool, but the embarrassment showed.

"Let's go." He took her by the elbow. "Seriously, come meet these guys." He tossed a condescending glance back at David as he departed. "Take it easy, pal."

"You too."

David finished the cigar, forcing himself to smoke slowly. When he'd smoked it down to a stub, he calmly tapped it out and placed it in a potted plant when he couldn't find an ashtray or trash can.

He cast a final glance at the cityscape. The view seemed drab now. Maybe it had never been very special at all.

He went back to the reception, face blank, walking slowly.

Amy found him immediately. "Well, I hope you enjoyed that smoke. I've just been talking to a couple of state reps who tell me . . . what's wrong?"

"I'm fine," he said too quickly.

She put a hand on his arm, squeezed, and David felt the tension leak out of him.

"I've talked to everyone I need to," she said. "Let's get out of here."

"It's your party," he said.

"And it's boring," she said. "Let's go."

He smiled his gratitude. She paused only a few times on the way out to exchange pleasantries. Soon they'd made their escape and were in the elevator heading down.

Amy's cell rang just as the elevator doors opened to the underground parking garage. She looked at the number and tsked. "I've got to take this."

She put the phone to her ear, used a finger to plug the other ear so she could hear the call better. They walked that way through the parking garage.

Amy spent a lot of time like that these days. Phone in one ear, finger in the other.

From the side David heard, "—talk to me like that, you bitch."

"I'm taking a taxi, Carter!"

He saw Carter and Wendy standing next to a sleek Mercedes three rows over. They continued to argue as David took Amy around to the passenger side of the Escalade, helped her in, and shut the door. Amy stayed on the cell the whole time, chewing over some tedious office matter with one of her assistants. He deliberately didn't look at Carter and Wendy as he circled back around to the driver's side and climbed in behind the wheel.

David cranked the Escalade. He adjusted the rearview mirror to look back at the scene and saw Carter grab Wendy by the elbow.

David opened the car door again.

Amy shot him a look. *Where are you going?*

He gestured, *It's okay.*

David approached Carter, keeping it slow and non-threatening.

"You've been nothing but a stuck-up bitch all night!" Carter was red-faced, spitting when he talked.

She was trying to pull away. "Let go!"

When David got within ten feet, Carter spotted him and let go of Wendy's arm.

"How are we doing over here?"

"Mind your own business, house husband," Carter said.

"Let's all take it down a notch." David stopped when he was within four feet of them. A cloud of Scotch hit him so hard it almost made his eyes water.

"Walk away. This is between me and her."

"It's early," David told Wendy. "I'm sure you can still get a cab out front."

"Yeah. Okay." She turned, walking away fast, the stilettos echoing through the garage.

"Oh, now, come on," Carter shouted. "What the fuck?"

"You might want a cab, too," David suggested.

"You might want to fuck yourself straight up your own fuck hole."

David laughed.

Carter threw a sloppy punch, and David stepped in closer, blocking and catching Carter's wrist, pulling it down against his body. He put his other arm around Carter's shoulder, just as Wendy turned back to watch the scene, mouth gaping. The question on her face was almost comical.

"Carter's just had a bit too much to drink, that's all."
With David's other arm around Carter's shoulder, it
looked like he was holding the other man up. "Isn't that
right, old buddy?"

David dug his thumb into a nerve cluster at the base
of Carter's wrist.

Carter winced. "Yeah. Yeah . . . right. No problem."

"You have a good night," David called.

Wendy nodded, turned and left.

"You fucked up, man," Carter said. "I will sue your
fucking—"

Carter swallowed the words as David dug his thumb
in again, new pain lancing up Carter's arm.

"I wouldn't talk about suing," David said. "Maybe
there's plenty of litigation to go around. Maybe a young
law clerk named Wendy works in your office and now
has a sexual harassment suit on you."

He could tell by Carter's face he'd hit the nail on the
head.

"I'm just guessing," David said. "I'm no lawyer, so I
don't really know. But my wife's the new deputy district
attorney so maybe you could ask her about the rules."

He felt Carter wilt in his grasp, the fight going out of
him.

"Or maybe in between watching soap operas and
eating bonbons, I'll get bored and mention this to her,"
David said. "Or maybe I won't. I haven't decided yet."

"Hey, it's cool," Carter said. "You're right. Too much to
drink and I got out of hand. I can see that now. No worries. I owe the lady an apology, right? That should put an
end to it."

The lawyer had emerged. Plea bargaining.

"Right." He let go of Carter, stepped back. "I'll bet

your friends are still up at the party. Maybe one can give you a ride."

Carter nodded but didn't leave his spot. He looked like a two-year-old kid who had been scolded by someone else's mother.

"Okay, you have a good night." David turned and walked calmly back to the Escalade without looking back.

He got in behind the wheel, buckled his seat belt, and counted to five. He looked in the rearview mirror. No sign of Carter.

"Look, we'll figure it out Monday," Amy said into the phone. "It'll keep until then."

She closed the phone and looked at David. "Where did you go?"

"Oh, just checking something out. No big deal." He put the SUV into reverse, backed out of the space. "Let's go get the kids."

CHAPTER FOUR

It was way past the kids' bedtime, so they skipped reading.

Brent lurched zombie-like into the bathroom, brushed his teeth, and stumbled out again, shuffling into his room and falling into bed. Anna was out like a light. David carried her to bed, pulled the covers up to her shoulders, made sure her Dora night-light was on and left her.

Back in his own bedroom, he found Amy waiting for him, curled on the bed in a nest of pillows. She was naked except for black stockings.

David's heart beat faster.

She grinned at her husband. "Are they asleep?"

"Yep."

"How asleep?"

He tugged his tie loose and shrugged out of his jacket. "*Very* asleep."

She crooked a finger at him. "Come on then."

He took it slow this time, kissing a slow trail down

her body, luxuriating in her curves. Amy's skin was bright and clear, an exhilarating contrast to the black stockings. She was soft and warm, and they pressed hard against each other as they kissed, losing themselves to each other completely.

When neither of them could stand it any longer, he positioned himself over her. She guided him in, and he entered slowly, a little at a time. He rocked into her, picking up speed gradually. Her head went back, eyes closed tight, mouth open.

They were both getting close, and David picked up speed.

Amy wrapped her legs around him, crossing her ankles at the small of his back, squeezing him to her. She began to tremble, hands clawing his back, digging in and hanging on tight. Finally her whole body shook, and she groaned David's name into his ear. He grunted and went stiff and then slack and slid off of her. They lay panting together in bed.

A moment later, Amy trailed her fingers down David's back. "So. Ready to go again?"

David laughed.

David was predictably cheerful the rest of the weekend. He'd risen to the occasion and had given Amy the second round she'd asked for, and she'd even been receptive to a predawn quickie before he'd stumbled out of bed the next morning to start the coffeemaker. He'd gotten more action in an eight-hour span than he had in the previous three weeks.

Take it while you can get it, pal. He laughed to himself and whistled as he made pancakes for the family.

He dragged the Weber out that afternoon and grilled hamburgers. The kids chased each other on the lawn. Brent seemed not to miss the little blinking handheld game. Amy stretched in a lounge chair, shorts and bare feet, reading a trashy paperback. Life was good.

He burned the hamburgers. He couldn't seem to get the hang of charcoal. It didn't matter. To him it was a gourmet feast.

David tried not to wonder how long it would last. His wife had often been distant and David was acutely aware he was to blame. Since the Army had put him on indefinite leave to "recuperate" he hadn't done much with himself and he hadn't explained himself, not fully, not to Amy's satisfaction. He'd said he was home for a while because of fatigue. He'd been on an overseas deployment, managing the flow of personnel for a U.S. Army base in Germany.

At least, that was the story.

But there had been no sign of David returning to his duties, and when Amy had tried to ask him about it, he'd bristled and then had become evasive. She'd given him his space, but at a cost. She felt shut out, and the resentment bubbled up now and then. He thanked God Amy was a mature woman, but her patience wouldn't last forever.

Last night they'd been close in a way they hadn't been in months, and not just physically. David had felt . . . connected. He wanted that feeling to go on, but wasn't sure how to make that happen. Eventually the same old problems would circle back on him again.

Something had to change, but David didn't know what.

Tomorrow. He'd worry about it tomorrow.

A bright and lively day passed into evening. Baths then bed and story time for the kids.

Amy and David sat on the couch, sipping red wine. Amy neared the end of her paperback novel, her feet in David's lap. He absently massaged one of her feet while paging through a fishing magazine, another hobby he doubted he'd ever take up, but he did like the idea of boats. And rods and reels and lures. Anything with paraphernalia attracted his attention, although not often for long.

He turned to his wife. "This was a good weekend."

She smiled without looking up from her book. "Yes."

"I wish Monday was a holiday or something," David said. "So we could keep it going."

"So let's keep it going."

"Really? Can you skip work?"

Amy laughed and set the paperback aside. "No. Along with the promotion comes the high-profile, high-stress workload. I'm working on a *huge* case."

"Oh."

"But you can drive into the city tomorrow, and we can have lunch," she suggested.

David mulled that. "Can we get Thai food?"

"No."

"You *like* Thai food."

"I told you. I'm working on a big case," Amy said. "I'll have about ten seconds for lunch. If I'm lucky. There's a diner around the corner for my office. BLTs and chips and root beer."

"With this new promotion, I'm going to see even less of you now, aren't I?"

She tensed. "David."

He held up surrender hands. "Withdrawn, counselor."

Amy squeezed his thigh. "Look, we'll make it work."

"I know."

She squeezed again. "I'm serious."

"I know. I believe you," he said. "Tell me about this big case."

She grinned. Obviously, she'd been hoping he'd ask. "Naturally you've heard of Dante Payne."

"Nope."

Her mouth fell open. "Are you kidding? Don't you read the newspapers?"

His eyes fell to the fishing magazine, and she followed his gaze, rolling her eyes. David had to admit he'd kind of withdrawn from reality the last few months. His world had narrowed to PTA meetings, Little League, and peanut butter and jelly sandwiches.

"Okay, big-city crime one-oh-one," Amy explained. "Dante Payne is the biggest thing in organized crime since sliced murder. Your incredibly talented wife—"

"And beautiful."

"Your incredibly talented and beautiful wife is working to put a very bad man behind bars for a very long time."

"You're like a superhero," David said.

"I don't do capes," Amy replied. "But yes. Along with the promotion and a microscopic increase in my paycheck, I am now the proud owner of five big boxes of evidence that all need to be sorted."

"Sounds like you're up late tonight," David said.

Amy nodded. "Afraid so."

"Well, early to bed for me." He stood and kissed her on top of the head. "Coffee doesn't make itself in the morning."

David's eyes popped open to darkness. He listened, tried to understand why he was awake. He glanced at the glowing green numerals of the bedside clock: 2:51 A.M.

He turned over gently to look at Amy and Anna. Anna had been slipping into bed with them a lot lately. Sometimes a bad dream. Other times, she said she just didn't want to be by herself. Amy had come to bed around midnight after putting in some hours on her new case in the little office she kept downstairs. Both slept like logs.

Why am I awake?

He slipped out of bed quietly. He wore only pajama bottoms, bare feet moving silently on thick carpet. He paused down the hall to look in on Brent. The boy was sound asleep, one foot dangling over the side of the bed.

David stood perfectly still in the hall. He listened.

Maybe it was nothing. He was wide awake now, and the chances of his getting back to sleep anytime soon were—

There! A noise downstairs, the faint whisper of shuffling paper. David knew all the sounds the house made, the pipes clanking in winter, the hollow groan of the attic during a big storm. This was different. He padded downstairs quietly, knowing just where to step to avoid creaking floorboards. Sometime in the six years they'd lived in the house, David had made note of this, but he couldn't remember when. Instinct.

Downstairs. Down the hall, past the kitchen. At the end of the hall, light leaked from a cracked doorway, the little room Amy used as an office. A flicker of shadow. The rustling sound of somebody searching.

David exhaled slowly, controlled his heart rate.

He crept silently to the door, peeked inside. A man in black. A ski mask. All of Amy's desk drawers had been pulled open.

David mentally scrolled through his options. Back away, find a phone, call the cops. And how long would that take? What would this joker do in the meantime? Better to move in quick, take him out, then hand him to the cops all tied up with a ribbon on top.

Assess. Control the situation.

David watched for another second. The man plucked a padded manila envelope from one of the evidence boxes, read the front before ripping it open and dumping out its contents. David squinted and leaned forward trying to see. A flash drive.

Enough. Let's do this.

David swept the door open and charged into the room in the same motion. He had a fist cocked back ready to strike. With surprise on his side, it would be no problem to—

The intruder brought his fist up in a circular motion in front of him, blocking David's strike and then counterpunched to David's solo plexus. David blocked the jab easily, but the man had already dropped to the ground and connected with a leg sweep.

David stumbled back against Amy's desk chair and sent it rolling away, got tangled in his own feet, and went backward into a stack of cardboard file boxes that tumbled and sent reams of paper flying.

The intruder rushed forward to press his advantage, but David heaved himself to one knee, and kicked out hard with the other leg, catching the guy in the gut with his heel. He grunted and stepped back, giving David time to spring to his feet.

He didn't wait, pushed forward immediately, throwing a punch at the man's nose. He caught it under his arm in a martial arts trap, and when he counterpunched, David did the same thing. For a fraction of a second they were stalemated like that.

David reacted first, slamming his head forward for a head butt. He was hoping to flatten the man's nose. A broken nose takes the fight out of most guys pretty fast. But the intruder's reflexes were too good. He turned his head and took the hit on his cheek.

Skull on cheekbone made a loud *crack* even with the minimal padding of the ski mask. His arms windmilled, and he fell back into the desk, scattering pens and papers and a little plastic cup of paper clips. His hand closed on a large stapler, and he swung.

David rolled with it but still took a sharp hit to the side of his head. Little lights went off in front of his eyes. He brought his arms up to ward off whatever came next, stepped back, shaking his head and trying to clear the bells from his ears. He kept stumbling until he backed up against a set of shelves, knocking off framed photos, books, and ceramic knickknacks. David's hand closed around something heavy and stone, one of the Aztec bookends he and Amy had brought back from a vacation in Mexico. He threw it blind, without thinking, and was rewarded with a thud and a grunt.

David blinked his eyes clear just in time to see the man coming at him again.

"David, what the hell is the racket—oh, my God!" Amy's voice.

The intruder's eyes shifted to Amy, just for a split second. It was enough.

David barreled forward and tackled him. They both

flew backward into the desk, knocking off the computer and monitor. Amy screamed.

David and the intruder slid off the table, onto the floor, David on top. The intruder hit hard and grunted. Two hands came up fast and latched onto David's throat. He punched down hard across the intruder's face. The hands hung on to his throat. David felt his face turning red. He punched down again. Again.

The hands let go.

David rolled off the man, breathing hard.

"David?"

He lurched to his feet, rubbing his throat. "It's . . . it's fine."

"Oh, my God. David, are you okay?"

"Call the police," he said. "Use the phone in the kitchen."

"But—" She hesitated then nodded and left.

David ripped the electric cord from a clock and bound the intruder's hands behind his back. The cord from the printer went to bind his feet. He pulled off the man's mask.

There was nothing special about his looks. A little younger than David, a dark tight crew cut. But Davis knew there was more to the man. The fighting style was familiar, Special Forces maybe, some kind of professional.

In his house.

He grabbed a pen from the debris on the floor, snapped it in half, and poured the ink onto the intruder's fingers. He found a pad of paper.

"Okay," David said. "Let's see who you are, you son of a bitch."

He blotted the man's fingers on the pad then squinted

at it. The pinky finger smeared, but he had three good prints of the other fingers.

It was only then David realized he'd snapped in half the two-hundred-dollar pen Amy's boss had given her when she'd been promoted to deputy district attorney.

"Shit."

CHAPTER FIVE

David and Amy stood in their driveway, wearing bathrobes, awash in the blue of the police lights. They watched one of the officers shove the intruder into the back of the car. Some of the neighbors had come out to linger in doorways and gawk.

The point of living in such a neighborhood was that it was supposed to be quiet and safe. David felt an unreasonable pang of guilt. *Sorry, neighbors.*

Two more cops stood with David and Amy, one scribbling into a little notebook, nodding along as Amy and David explained what had happened. Someone had invaded David's home, but for the cops it was routine.

"It's just a good thing nobody was hurt," said the one with the notebook.

"We ran the douche bag through the computer," said the other cop. "Guy's got a rap sheet as long as your arm. Burglary, car theft, all kinds of stuff. He'll be going into stir a good, long time, I think."

"Glad to hear it," Amy said. "Officer, if you don't need me, I'd like to go look in on my kids."

"You go right ahead, miss."

When Amy was out of earshot, David said, "Officers, I think there's more to this guy than meets the eye."

The one with the notebook flipped it closed and stashed it in his pocket. "Oh, yeah?"

"He had pro moves. Training," David said. "And he was going through my wife's office stuff. It just doesn't seem like a standard burglary. More like he had something specific in mind. He didn't strike me as a common burglar."

The cop blinked at him. "You have a wide experience of burglars, do you, sir?"

David kept his face carefully blank. "Obviously, you'd know more about it than I would."

"Sir, the computer don't lie."

David smiled. It wasn't easy, but he did it. "I'm not casting aspersions on the computer. I'm just saying. He walked right past a new big-screen TV and Mac notebook to toss my wife's desk."

"You can't try to read the minds of these assholes, sir," the other cop chimed in. "Maybe he was looking for cash or something easier to carry. Maybe he was planning to grab the notebook on the way out. Who knows?"

"Do most burglars know a mix of jujitsu and krav maga?" David asked. "Because this guy wasn't playing."

"Well, then it's a good thing you're so skilled with your fists, eh, sir?" A hint of a smirk from the cop. "Otherwise, he might have gotten the better of you. Look, the important thing is we got the cuffs on him. The best thing now is to get to bed and try not to worry about it. I'm sure you've got to get to work early."

David rubbed his eyes. The fatigue was seeping in now. "I don't work. I stay home with the kids." As soon as the words were out of his mouth, he knew he'd messed up.

The cops exchanged glances. David had seen that expression on far too many faces the last few months. If there'd been any chance they were going to take him seriously, it was gone now. As far as these guys were concerned, he might as well put on a flowered housedress.

The cop with the notebook shook his head as he turned to leave. "Then you probably have a busy day of diaper changing or whatever. We've got this covered, Mr. Sparrow. You have yourself a good night, okay?"

"Yeah," muttered the other cop. "Don't trip over your apron."

There were both still laughing as they got in the squad car and then sped away.

David got the kids to school a little earlier the next morning so he could drive into the city. There was somebody he wanted to see, a person he'd known from the military. He drove to Amy's parking garage and left the Escalade. Trying to park in Charlie Finn's neighborhood wasn't a good idea.

He hopped on the subway and headed north. As he sat there listening to the click of the train along the tracks, he recalled what he knew about Charlie. A strange guy, but they liked each other.

Charlie had been David's handler his first year of solo ops. Eye in the sky, the voice in his ear through a satellite uplink. Charlie had guided David through a pretty hairy situation in Venezuela. David had taken a bullet in the side, but he'd gotten out. Barely. David had told Amy the scar was from a cycling accident.

After Venezuela, David had been sent back to the states, and when he was well enough, he tracked Charlie down and bought him a steak dinner at the best place in town. Charlie had saved David's ass. It was that simple. They'd hit it off. Charlie had been a little twitchy, which seemed standard with so many of those tech types, but he was amiable and sharp.

About a year later Charlie disappeared, and David was given a new handler. When David asked around, he heard a lot of rumors about Charlie going off the deep end with a bad drinking problem. David's perfunctory attempts to track down Charlie came up empty, and he eventually let it go. Sometimes people were hard to find because they didn't *want* to be found.

Then two years later, David got an e-mail from Charlie out of the blue. A name and address. *If you ever want to look me up, I'm here.* That sort of thing. David had moved on. Anna had just been born. So with a very mild stab of guilt, David filed away Charlie's e-mail and went on with his life.

Now David found himself on a subway headed for the Bronx, wondering if he was doing the right thing. He thought about calling ahead first, but somehow that felt like dipping a toe into a cold swimming pool. Better just to dive in and be done with it.

He got off the train at 161st Street and paused to look at Yankee Stadium. If he could get Brent more interested in sports, a day game would make for a nice afternoon. Hot dogs and cotton candy.

David headed up Gerard Street and then turned onto 164th, keeping track of the numbers on the sides of the buildings. A couple of the locals gave him the hard stare from their stoops as he passed. He wasn't worried, but he didn't let on like he noticed. The last thing he wanted was some confrontation that would delay him.

When he arrived at the building with Charlie's number, he double-checked to make sure. There was a burnt-out Toyota parked on the street in front of the building and a mountain of trash piled next to the building's entrance. David considered turning right around and going back the way he'd come. Charlie might not be in any position to grant favors. Nor in the mood for that matter. There was no reason to believe Charlie was the same man David had known six years ago.

Except you've ridden hell and gone out to the South Bronx to see him, so find your balls and ring the buzzer.

David thumbed the buzzer for 1-B, a basement apartment. He counted to ten. Slowly. He hit the buzzer again.

A moment later a voice crackled through the speaker. "I'm not expecting nobody, and I didn't order no pizza. So lay off that buzzer."

David grinned. A little more rust in the voice, but it was definitely Charlie Finn. David pressed the buzzer again.

"I said fuck off," squawked the speaker.

"Charlie, it's me. David."

"Well, pardon the shit out of me," Charlie growled. "Fuck off, *David*."

"It's David Sparrow, Charlie."

A pause. "Captain?"

It was Major now, but that wasn't important. "David is fine."

"Holy fucking shit. Hey, man, you want to come in? Shit, what a stupid question, like you just come all this way to stand on the fucking sidewalk. Hold on."

The door buzzed, and David entered the building.

He descended a dank stairwell with a flickering fluorescent light, gang graffiti on the walls, and at the bottom Charlie was already opening his apartment door and beckoning to David.

They grinned at each other and shook hands, and a second later hugged, slapping each other hard on the back.

Charlie's skin hung loose on his middle-aged frame as if he were a man who'd gotten fat over time and then lost it all quickly. He was half black and half Puerto Rican and all Bronx. He wore a Ramones T-shirt, sweatpants that had been cut off for shorts, and a battered Syracuse Orangeman ball cap. The full black beard was new. No reason to shave every day if the military isn't making you.

"Man, been awhile, Captain."

"David."

"Right. David. Sorry." He gestured him into the apartment. "Come on in, man."

Inside the apartment, David saw exactly what he was hoping to see. Where somebody else might have set up a big-screen TV and a stereo, Charlie had installed a circular desk. Multiple keyboards and monitors and printers and scanners and a big media setup. David would have bet dollars to navy beans there was a nice little satellite array on the roof of Charlie's building. If he asked Charlie to turn on the lights in Yankee Stadium, David had no doubt that his former handler could plop down at his computer and have them shining in five minutes.

"You want some orange juice? I'm off cola." Charlie shrugged. "And beer. Obviously. I could make some coffee."

"I'm good. Thanks."

"Have a seat."

David sat on the edge of the sofa, and Charlie sat in his desk chair, swiveled around to face David. "Kids are okay? Your wife?"

"All good," David said.

"Right. So. What are you doing here?"

David laughed. "Straight to it, huh?"

"You know I'm glad to see you," Charlie said. "But it's sudden, you know?"

"Charlie, I'm afraid I'm here to be a jerk," David said. "We haven't spoken in forever, and then suddenly I show up to ask you a favor. Not cool, right?"

Charlie scratched at his beard for a moment. "No, it's cool. I get it. I never had no kids, you know, but I can imagine. You had your hands full. You had your life happening."

"I wouldn't be bothering you if it wasn't important."

"You're not bothering me." He grinned. "Yet. Maybe I'd better hear what this favor is."

David told him the story. The man breaking into his house, how he nearly got his ass handed to him, the fact the intruder was poking around in Amy's desk. He even told him how the cops made fun of him for being a stay-at-home dad. He wrapped the story by reaching into his pocket and coming out with the sheet of paper with the intruder's fingerprints. He handed it to Charlie.

Charlie squinted at it. "You think there's more to this guy than the cops know?"

"I hope not," David said. "Frankly, if you could work your magic and confirm everything is just as the police claim then that would be just fine with me. I can forget all about it."

Charlie tugged at bits of his beard just under his bottom lip as he looked at the fingerprints again. "Okay, I think we can work with this. Sit tight and let me jam on these."

David sat back on the couch and watched him work.

Charlie scanned in the fingerprints and then started to bring up databases, stitching them together for cross-referencing purposes. His hands flew over two different keyboards, all the monitors coming alive with data.

Charlie glanced over his shoulder at David. "Back when I was your handler, I left behind lots of backdoors into the system. They purged some of them, but I can still get in, and the other systems will all spread their legs for any other system with higher clearance. Thank you, Patriot Act." He went back to work and then turned to David again a few seconds later. "Don't tell anybody that."

"Don't worry," David said.

Five minutes later, Charlie was nodding and pointing at the largest monitor. "Okay, here we go. Nolan Jakes. Got a police record here says everything you told me, robbery, burglary, petty larceny, the whole basic Whitman's Sampler of street crime."

"So it's the real deal?" David asked.

"Oh, sure."

David blew out a sigh of relief.

"But it's also bullshit."

"What?"

"I mean it's a real police record in that it's really in the system and official," Charlie said, "but I smell bullshit."

"What do you mean?"

"It's not messy."

"Talk me through this nice and slow," David said. "Because I'm not following you."

"If you've looked at police records before you know they're messy." Charlie pulled at his beard again, trying to figure how to explain. "You ever see a planned community?"

"I know what you mean."

"All the streets are laid out evenly," Charlie said. "A perfect grid. Planned and predictable. Then look at some old European city. The streets and alleys were made up as they went along. The place evolved over centuries. It's messy, but it's *real*. Has a completely different feel."

"You're saying the police report feels wrong?"

"Yeah. Because it's not messy," Charlie said. "With this kind of rap sheet, it all gets added on a little at a time. Reports come through the system from other precincts or from out of state. I should be getting search hits from all over the place on this guy, but instead it's all just right there. Boom."

"So . . ." David groped to follow what Charlie was saying. "It's like somebody wrote the whole thing at once."

"Exactly," Charlie said. "And look at the PDFs of the police reports. They're all typed perfectly. Not even one spelling error, nothing crossed out. Cops can't type for shit, trust me, I know. The file on this guy was put together and inserted into the system, so anyone looking him up would find *this* instead of his real record. And whoever did it wasn't figuring on somebody like me looking too closely at it."

David let that sink in. Ordinary beat cops like the ones he had spoken to last night wouldn't even blink.

They checked the record like they always did, and that was that.

He considered the flash drive the burglar had attempted to steal, thought about handing it over to Charlie to see what he could do with it. But he'd just connected again with the man and didn't want to push it so soon. Besides, David wanted to go over it himself first.

"Charlie, with those fingerprints is there any chance you can poke around and find out who this guy really is?"

A shrug. "Yeah. No guarantees, but it's worth a try. I'd have to run some really slow search programs, underneath radar encrypted type stuff. It'll take some time, but we can see what we see."

"Look, I know this computer stuff costs money," David said. "And you're spending time on this. You've got to let me toss you a few bucks."

Charlie waved him away, laughing. "Naw, man, this kind of thing is fun for me. Don't sweat it."

"Charlie, come on."

"Hey, you think I need the money? Don't worry about old Charlie. He's doing fine."

David glanced around the room. He hadn't bothered to notice when he'd come in but the interior of the apartment was far nicer than the exterior of Charlie's building would indicate. The furnishings and carpeting were every bit as good as what David had in his own house.

Maybe Charlie was reading his mind. "This is my neighborhood, you know? So I came back here. I could live anywhere, but I came home. These are my people. You pass that hot dog cart when you came out of the subway?"

David pictured the hot dog cart outside the station, the skinny old man standing next to it. "Yeah."

"That's Saul. I bought that cart for him and in return, he kicks back to me each month. I clear maybe thirty to forty bucks a month on Saul."

"Thirty to forty a month," David said deadpan. "So you probably hang out with Bill Gates and Donald Trump all the time is what you're saying."

"Yeah, yeah, you always were a funny guy," Charlie said. "But multiply that times a hundred and seventy-four carts and it adds up."

"Ah."

"And it's tax free in cash," added Charlie. "Don't tell anybody that."

David made a zipper closing gesture across his mouth.

"And with my setup"—he waved a hand at the computers—"I'm able to pick up an insider stock tip once in a while. Don't tell anybody *that*, either."

David held up his hands in surrender. "Okay. You can help me for the sheer fun of it. Hell, maybe you should lend me a few bucks."

Charlie laughed. "Look, Captain—David—it's good to see you again. Let me see what I can find out. Maybe nothing, but who knows? But if you've got motherfuckers breaking into your house, then hell yeah, of course I'll help."

"Thanks. It means a lot," David said. "Let me give you my cell number. It's unlisted."

"Don't bother." Charlie grinned. "Unlisted just means it'll take me an extra thirty seconds to find it."

CHAPTER SIX

Amy looked up at the knock on her office door. "Come in."

The door opened, and the district attorney walked in.

Amy stood. "Bert." She would have expected her assistant Jenny to announce him first, but this was one of Bert's favorite tricks, waltzing in and catching people off guard. Amy made a mental note to talk to Jenny about that.

"Please," Bert said. "Sit. Just a casual pop-in to see how my new right hand is getting along." Bert was a short, tidy man in his late fifties, neatly tailored gray suit, round glasses, and a tight haircut. Gleaming Stanford Law cuff links. He lowered himself into one of the chairs opposite Amy.

She sat, gestured to the ton of paperwork stretched across her desk. "Remember when I thanked you for the promotion? I take it back. This is all *one* case."

"But an important one," Bert said. "Dante Payne is the leading figure in the city's organized crime world, and hardly anyone knows it. He's done one heck of a job making himself look legitimate. He even won some kind of community award a few months ago for helping arrange a new hospital cancer wing. And there are three different politicians waiting to see how this turns out, so they can decide if they're going to take sizable campaign contributions from him or not. He needs to be put away, but if we botch it, we'll make some powerful enemies. I'd like for all of us to keep our jobs."

Amy nodded. She knew all of this already, and Bert knew that she knew. This was just his way of letting her know he was anxious, and that made *her* anxious. Bert's feathers didn't ruffle easily. He was nervous.

"I know," Amy said. "There's a lot hinging on a single witness. We've been trying to get others to corroborate his story and strengthen the case, but it's tough. People are afraid to come forward. And Payne butters too many people's bread."

Bert nodded, bit a thumbnail, jaw tight. "And where is our Mr. Preston now?"

Del Preston. The witness. The one man in the city prepared to sing his heart out and put Payne behind bars. Amy didn't know if he was brave or crazy, but the case hung on his testimony, which was the linchpin that allowed all of the circumstantial evidence to link up neatly. Without Preston the case fell apart.

"He's arriving soon. Any minute now actually," She said. "In police custody for his own protection."

"I'll feel better once he's inside the building," Bert said. "With all the metal detectors and bailiffs and security cameras, it's probably one of the most secure places in the city."

Amy would be glad when the entire affair was over. Since her promotion, her caseload had been reduced to one. Payne. For some reason, she found it more stressful to focus on this single case than it was juggling multiple assignments. As a rookie assistant DA, she'd been overloaded with so many cases she wondered every day why the whole system just didn't collapse. But somehow she woke up every morning and the cases were still there, the wheels of justice grinding slowly but still grinding.

It felt odd to look back on those days as relatively carefree. Now she felt like the eyes of the entire justice system were upon her. The mayor. The governor. Not for the first time, Amy suspected she wasn't really cut out for the limelight.

Amy knew that Bert was trying to kill multiple birds with one stone when he'd boosted her to deputy district attorney. There'd always been some vague pressure to promote more women, but it was more than that. Bert knew she could handle the job, was, in fact, counting on her. Amy would never have accepted the position just to serve as Bert's token female. She knew what she was doing. She was the right choice.

So why do I feel more stressed out than I ever have in my whole life?

She calmed herself. So. One case. For all the marbles. *Hey, it's just a career, right?*

Maybe it was all that pressure that had put a strain on things at home. David had always been stoic, but *stoic* had become *distant* these last few months. Normally, she'd give her husband space, let him work it out, but maybe she'd been too patient. The Army had put him on some kind of indefinite leave so he could rest. But rest from what? Maybe it was time she forced David to be more forthcoming about whatever it was that was eating him.

Still, they'd really connected the other night. Like old times. She'd felt a surge of optimism, which had sadly been undermined by the break-in. The incident with the burglar seemed to crank up David's stress level again. *Which is understandable. For God's sake, our children were right upstairs. Anything could have happened.*

Amy was about to cobble together some reassuring phrases for Bert when the phone rang. She answered. "Jenny? Yeah. Right. Tell them we'll be down in a few minutes."

She hung up and looked at Bert. "They're bringing him in now."

Amy and Bert stood between a brace of bailiffs as a squad of NYPD cleared the hall, motioning for the usual herd of lawyers and clerks who haunted the place to stand out of the way. At the far end of the hall, she saw them coming.

If Amy understood the procedure correctly, a team of police with bomb-sniffing dogs had arrived an hour ahead of time to sweep the level of the parking garage in which Preston had arrived. He then came up the elevator, surrounded by policemen in Kevlar vests. Preston wore one, too. The witness was now being escorted to a room where a stenographer waited to take his statement in front of Amy, Bert, and the witness's personal attorney. There was a lot riding on Preston's testimony, and they were making it all as official as possible. All of the stiff formalities and dire precautions rubbed Amy's nerves raw. She realized she was biting the inside of her lower lip—an old habit—and made herself stop.

Amy's eyes shifted to Bert standing next to her. He didn't seem worried, chin up and eyes bright as he watched the witness and his police escort approach. Not Bert's first rodeo, Amy realized. He'd been doing this a long time.

Her guess was that he was still nervous. Just better at hiding it.

She glanced the other direction at the bailiff standing on the other side of her. The man had his hand on his holster. She supposed everyone was tense, and maybe the bailiff was simply bracing himself for whatever might—

The bailiff unsnapped the holster. Amy blinked. Was *that* necessary?

The witness and his police escort had almost reached them now. Bert was already stepping forward, welcoming. He had a way of putting people at ease. Preston was looking straight at Bert, but the cops with him were looking off left and right as if expecting terrorists to come storming from a side hall at any minute. Bert was raising his hand to shake it. *That's it, Bert. Do your thing. Let's get this guy into the room, get his statement, and then we can all go to a champagne lunch to celebrate a job well—*

The bailiff had his hand on the butt of his revolver. He was drawing it. Amy opened her mouth, objections stuck in her throat. She wasn't sure what she was seeing. Her eyes blazed across the scene, taking it all in at once. The cops still scanned each nook and cranny, looking in every direction but hers.

The bailiff raised the pistol.

No!

Amy grabbed the man's arm, tried to pull his aim away from the approaching group of men.

He jerked his arm free and smashed Amy in the corner of her mouth with the pistol.

Pain exploded across her face, a white light flashing in her eyes. She stumbled back over her own high heels, skidded on the tile floor, and went down. She tasted blood in her mouth, spit, dizzy and nauseous.

A gunshot shook the hallway. Shouting.

Amy's ears rang. It seemed to take forever to blink the stars from her eyes and look up, but it was only a split-second. Bert lay on the ground.

The bailiff fired again, and almost simultaneously another smattering of gunfire smacked into the bailiff, three red blooms sprouting wet across his chest. He spun back, bounced off the wall and went down.

The hallway became a confused tumult, everyone shouting, police radios squawking. Somebody bumped into Amy and when she turned to see who it was, someone bumped her from behind.

She was still on the floor.

Amy crawled to Bert. He looked up at her, face ashen. His mouth worked to talk, but nothing came out. His jacket had fallen open, and Amy saw that his shirt stuck red to him low on his side. He reached for her with a trembling hand, blood dripping from the fingertips. His eyes pleaded.

"Take it easy, Bert." She scooted behind him, pulled his head into her lap. "I've got you. You're going to be fine. A little mess, that's all. Just keep still."

His eyes again. Afraid. She took his hand, squeezed.

She looked up. "Hey! Somebody call 9-1-1. We need a doctor. Over here."

A voice from the confusion acknowledged her.

Amy's gaze shifted to the other body sprawled a dozen feet away. Del Preston lay awkwardly on his side, eyes wide open and vacant. His life leaked red from the gaping wound in his head. A pool of blood spread under him in a slowly widening circle.

CHAPTER SEVEN

The first David heard of the shooting was when he'd tried to get into the building.

They'd turned him back as a matter of course, very edgy cops who were in no mood to hear excuses, and they didn't care whose wife was doing what where because the building was on lockdown and as far as they were concerned David could fuck straight off.

David wasn't one to give up easily, but it was obvious the direct approach wasn't going to work.

He alternated between calling Amy's office phone and her cell. He finally caught her in her office, and she sent down a bailiff—one she knew personally, she later explained—to escort him inside and up to Amy's floor.

He stood in Amy's office doorway, took her in at a glance. She held a hand towel full of crushed ice to the side of her mouth but otherwise looked fine.

He asked anyway. "You okay?"

She scowled at him around the towel. "I think he knocked a tooth loose."

"I'm sorry."

"It *hurts*."

"I'm *very* sorry." David stepped into the room, put his hands on the back of the chair in front of him. "Seriously, you need me to take you home?"

"Home?" She stood, slammed her hand down on the stack of papers on her desk. "When am I ever going to get home? I'm *in charge* of this circus now."

David hadn't considered that, but of course with Bert down, it all fell to Amy.

She hurled the towel of ice at the wall. It hit hard, cracking the glass in the frame of her law diploma and scattering ice. "Shit!"

David raised an eyebrow.

Amy's shoulder slumped immediately, the heat leaking out of her. She rubbed her eyes. "Oh, God. That's not fair. Poor Bert. I got word from the hospital a few minutes ago. He's stable. They say he'll be okay. It could have been me. I was standing right there."

She took a deep breath, let it out again raggedly. "It could have been me."

David circled the desk, lifted Amy's chin with a finger and examined the red blotch at the corner of her mouth. It would soon turn into an ugly green and purple bruise. "I'm glad you don't see the women at Anna's preschool drop-off. I'd hate to have to explain this."

Amy shook her head, stepped back. "Save the jokes. I'm in no mood."

"Okay, sorry. But you're being hard on yourself."

"I was promoted to do one thing and that was to put Dante Payne behind bars. Without that witness, I can just forget it. We've been holding Payne as long as we can without bail, but now we've got to cut him loose. I just gave the order ten minutes before you arrived. I don't even want to describe the rotten taste doing that left in my mouth. God, Bert is shot, and now I've let him down. This just sucks."

"What were you supposed to do?" David asked. "Jump in front of the witness and take the bullet for him? Look, this isn't your fault."

"But I should be able to figure something out, come up with an idea to stall or something," Amy said. "All I can do is sit here like some stupid . . ." She groped for the right word.

"Just stop. Okay? That's the problem with being one of the good guys. You have to play by the rules. It's not your fault."

She blew out a tired sigh.

"Do they know anything about the bailiff who did it?" David asked.

"Not yet," Amy said. "The police are looking into it. I mean if you can't trust—"

A blond woman of about twenty-five stuck her head in the door, pretty and bright, black-framed glasses just a little too hip, David thought.

"I'm sorry to interrupt," she said. "Mrs. Sparrow, you wanted to know when they were taking him out."

"Oh." Amy nodded. "Thank you, Jenny."

Jenny returned the nod and left.

"What was that about?"

Amy didn't answer. Instead she stared at a spot on the wall, unblinking. David had seen her do this many times before. She was on the razor's edge of some decision, probably something she knew was a bad idea but some stubborn part of her was insisting. Any minute she would—

Amy stormed past him out of the office.

"Amy!"

David ran after her.

She fast-walked past the elevators and banged open the door to the stairwell, David right behind her. The rapid click of her high heels echoed off cement as she descended.

David harbored no delusions that he'd be able to talk her out of whatever she was doing, but considering her mood, he gave it a try anyway.

"Amy, calm down and think about what you're doing," David called after her. "Whatever it is."

He kept chasing her but not too fast. Frankly, he wasn't sure what to do if he caught her. His wife didn't tolerate a lot of interference when she got up a head of steam like this. She was on the warpath and woe unto anyone who got in her way. The best he could hope for was to stay right behind her and try to mitigate any collateral damage.

She slammed through the door and out of the stairwell on the ground floor. She stopped, head turning as she rapidly searched for something. Her frown deepened as her eyes locked onto the object of her sudden obsession.

David followed her gaze to a group of men slowly making their way toward the main exit, escorted out by a pair of police officers.

"Hey!" Amy trotted after them.

They didn't turn. David sized them up. A bunch of dark suits, lawyers, all surrounding a man in a garish burgundy jacket.

"Hey!" Amy shouted again. "You hear me, Payne?"

Oh, shit. David hurried after her.

She tried to push through the lawyers, but they closed ranks around their client. The two police officers hesitated, not quite able to bring themselves to interfere with the deputy DA.

"How'd you get to the bailiff, huh?" There was a cold fury in Amy's voice. "You buy him off, Payne?"

One of the lawyers pushed her back. "This is *highly* inappropriate, Mrs. Sparrow."

Amy ignored the lawyer, pressed past him with a fresh surge of anger and latched on to one of Payne's burgundy sleeves, glaring hot daggers at him.

"Get her off him!" screeched the lawyer.

The police were moving in halfheartedly now to break it up, but Amy held on.

"You think you're untouchable?" Amy shouted. "You think you're safe?"

Payne moved fast, knocking her hand away and pushing her back. "Get your hands off me, woman." The hint of an accent.

Then David was there, slipping like a ghost in between the police and the lawyers. He slipped an arm around his wife's waist, intending to haul her away gently but firmly. "Easy. I got you. Forget it. Come on." She resisted, but not enough to stop him.

David felt a hard shove to his shoulder.

"Keep your bitch under control."

David spun, grabbed the burgundy jacket by the lapel. Maybe one good punch. He could do that much for his wife, couldn't he? Maybe he'd get a little satisfaction out of it himself.

David Sparrow and Dante Payne locked eyes.

"Are you truly so eager to die, little man?" Payne said

quietly only for David's ears. "Or do you want to watch your woman go first?"

Violence welled up within David, threatening to break through his control, and it would have if he hadn't felt many hands from behind, pulling him back.

CHAPTER EIGHT

David sat at his kitchen table, a bottle of Johnny Walker Blue in front of him. He was generally a beer-and-wine kind of guy, but on special occasions, he wanted something with a kick. He'd filled a Pokémon glass three fingers full and had been staring at it for about thirty minutes without drinking. The sounds of after school cartoons seeped in from the living room. He'd get to Brent's homework later.

It was impossible not to connect the break-in to Dante Payne. How could it be a coincidence? Answer: it wasn't.

He fished the flash drive out of his pocket and squinted at it. *Why did he want this?*

He picked up his drink and walked back to Amy's office, sat down at the computer. David had put the room back together the day after the break-in, sweeping up and throwing out anything broken beyond repair, salvaging what he could. The office still felt soiled, violated. Trying to access the information on the flash drive turned out to be a dead end. Password protected. He should have left the drive with Charlie. He was trying to figure his next move when he heard the front door open and close. Muffled voices, Amy greeting the kids. A second later, he heard her footsteps coming down the hall, the office door opening behind him.

David spun in the chair to greet her. "Hey."

"Some day, huh?" Amy's eyes drifted to the glass in his hand. "I don't blame you."

"Want one?"

"Do we have any wine?"

David nodded. "I'll open a bottle."

They ordered pizza and let the kids eat it in front of the TV. Anna thought they'd hit the jackpot, but Brent was just old enough to be a little suspicious. David assured him it was just a one-time treat. The truth was neither David nor Amy had it in them to cook a meal. A cheap pizza and garbage television one night wouldn't corrupt the kids forever.

They sat on the back deck, David with a second helping of Johnny Walker and Amy with a glass of pinot noir.

Amy slouched in a deck chair. She'd changed into yoga pants and a loose-fitting, faded Yale T-shirt. "So that was some display earlier, huh?"

David summoned a wan smile. "I should have just let you go after him. Might have solved everything right then and there."

"David, did you know him?" Amy asked. "There seemed to be a moment there. Like maybe you'd seen him before."

He sipped the Johnny Walker slowly, then said, "Just men like him. That type. I think I've heard that accent before. It just struck a chord."

It had been the threat against Amy that had riled David. If the police hadn't pulled David away . . .

She nodded, sipping wine, but David could see she wanted to ask more. Amy was a smart woman. Smart enough to know there *was* more. Smart enough not to press him about it. Some instinct told her it was a rabbit she couldn't chase.

The bulk of David's Army days had been spent going back and forth between assignments overseas and his home in the States. Each time David returned home, he told his wife a little less about what he'd been doing, or, more accurately, he repeated less of the cover story he'd rehearsed by order of the U.S. government. As far as the world was concerned, David used his keen organizational skills to set up supply chains at bases around the world. It was a good excuse to have him always traveling to different places. He hated lying to Amy, and she must have known on some level not to ask, some combination of his demeanor and facial expression or something, but her curiosity about David's work faded over time, and now she didn't ask at all anymore.

"Did you find anything out about the bailiff?" David asked.

"The police are still filling in the gaps," Amy said. "But apparently this guy had a bad gambling problem and was drowning in debt, like up to his eyeballs, about to lose everything, house, car, you name it. All of a sudden those debts were completely paid off. And"—she paused to sip wine—"he had a wife and two daughters."

"So Payne pays off the debts and leaves the daughters alone. Carrot-and-stick approach. In return, the bailiff pops the star witness. He probably knew he wasn't getting out of there in one piece."

"The trick is pinning it to Payne. The police are

bending over backward to make some kind of connection between him and the bailiff. I'm not optimistic."

"Give them time. Maybe they'll come up with something."

Amy shook her head. "My gut tells me we missed our chance. We could have put Payne away, but we blew it. Without Del Preston's statement we've got nothing, and Payne's as free as a bird."

They lapsed into silence, sipped drinks.

"Amy, how safe are we?"

She frowned. "What do you mean?"

"I mean, if this Payne guy can get a bailiff to murder a witness for him, what can he do to us?" David said.

"You're thinking about the break-in, aren't you?" Amy said.

He shrugged.

"It could be just a coincidence, you know," Amy told him. "The break-in probably doesn't have a thing to do with Payne. The police even said the burglar had a long list of priors. Maybe we were just being robbed, and that's all. It happens."

"Do you believe that?"

Instead of answering, she looked away and sipped wine, brow knit. David knew what this meant. It meant she *wanted* to believe it but knew better. Or maybe she simply didn't know what to believe at all.

Amy hoped Dante Payne would be satisfied with the witness's death, that he would feel safe now. But David's business had been knowing men like Payne. They were hard, cunning creatures with little forgiveness in them. It wasn't enough to defeat opponents. They wanted to *eliminate* them. A live enemy was still an enemy that could bite.

David didn't have all the answers yet. He didn't know what was on the flash drive, didn't know what Charlie might uncover on his covert safari into cyberspace. All he knew was that he didn't feel safe, and a gnawing gut feeling wouldn't let him forget about it.

So then. Decisions.

"We need to do something. We need to take precautions," David said. "And I don't mean just double-checking that the doors are locked each night."

Silence stretched between them for a moment.

David pretended not to notice Amy nibbling the inside of her bottom lip.

Amy tapped a fingernail against one of her front teeth, another nervous habit. "I might have an idea about that."

They stood in the driveway the next afternoon and watched a squad car pull up and park in front of the house. After yesterday's bloody events, nobody at Amy's office had objected to her request to take a personal day, although Amy found herself calling Jenny every twenty minutes, insisting on a status report.

"Are you sure about this?" whispered David from the side of his mouth.

"You wanted to feel safer," Amy whispered back. "It's just temporary until we think of something else."

"This is the guy who took you to prom, right?"

She shot him a look. "Roy is nice. It'll be fine."

Roy Bennett climbed out of his squad car and lumbered up the lawn toward them, flipping them a jaunty salute. His hairline was retreating fast and he was going soft in the middle although not as bad as some, but he had a friendly open face and alert blue eyes. The sergeant's stripes on his sleeve were the result of sixteen years on the force. That was some kind of accomplishment anyway.

Amy introduced David, and he shook hands with Roy.

"Roy, I can't thank you enough," Amy said. "This whole situation has just been so upsetting."

When Amy had called Roy, she'd kept the story simple. As deputy DA it was her job to put away bad people. Naturally some of the bad people didn't appreciate this, and Amy now had reason to believe that some of these people wanted to cause trouble for her and her family. The situation wasn't to the point that it was appropriate to fill out an official complaint, but some steps needed to be taken for Amy's peace of mind. Her old high school friend Roy had happily stepped up to the plate.

"I'm happy I can do this for you," Roy said. "I mean, it's the least I can do after—oh, here they are now."

About half a block away, a squad car slowed and parked across the street. A second squad car parked at the end of the street in the other direction.

"Just the sight of police vehicles will keep most of the assholes—er, sorry." Roy's eyes darted to Amy, embarrassed. "Jerks, I mean. Anyway, most of the bad guys will move along if they see a police presence."

"Thanks," Amy said. "I feel better already."

"I hope this isn't putting you out," David said.

Roy waved the idea away. "As long as the captain doesn't look too close at the duty roster, I'm fine. And I run a pretty tight ship, so he lets me run the precinct my way. Fact is I owe some of these boys some easy overtime, so that's for starters. But the fact is I owe your wife here a big one. Didn't see how I could refuse her a favor like this."

"Oh, really?" David raised an eyebrow at his wife. "I hadn't heard about this."

"David, don't pry into the man's business," scolded Amy.

"Wouldn't dream of it." David smiled and tried to look harmless.

"It's okay," Roy said. "When my kid sister graduated from NYU a few years ago, she celebrated pretty hard, drank a bit too much, and got into some trouble. I called up Amy and begged a favor. She didn't even hesitate. Fact is, Little Sis did need to learn a lesson, but maybe not to the point of having something on her record if you know what I mean. Your wife understood. She's good people, Mr. Sparrow."

David put a hand on Amy's shoulder, gave it a light squeeze. "I think so, too."

"But it's just for a few days." Roy looked apologetic. "That's about all I can swing."

"That's fine. I figure we'll have things sorted out by then. You don't have to rush off, do you?" Amy asked. "Come in for some coffee."

Roy smiled. "I'd like that."

CHAPTER NINE

The next two days crept by in seemingly normal fashion. Amy went to work in the city. David took the kids to school and tended house.

But underneath the facade of normalcy there was tension. David was the primary culprit. He knew what a criminal like Payne was capable of and kept thinking something bad was going to happen. His anxiety infected Amy, and even the kids seemed out of sorts, sensing there was something wrong in the house.

Maybe I'm wrong. Maybe Payne doesn't even care. With the witness dead, he's off the hook. Maybe he'll forget about us.

David knew he was kidding himself.

He picked the kids up from school and brought them home as usual. He forced himself to engage with them, helping with homework. He cooked dinner, did the dishes afterward. He felt like a fraud. The daddy robot going through the motions as the more active part of his brain thought about the perimeter of the house, how somebody might break in. He considered additional locks, entertained upgrading the alarm system. Sooner or later, Roy's overtime cops wouldn't be there anymore. What was the response time if he called the police? Could he count on them? And what, if anything, would keep Dante Payne at bay? Walls? Razor wire and land mines? How far was David willing to go?

When would David and his family get their lives back?

"Hey!"

David jumped. He hadn't even heard his wife come into the kitchen.

She pinned him with a hard look. "Stop it, okay?"

"Stop what?"

"You're stalking around like the grim reaper or something," she said. "Brent keeps asking if you're angry at him."

"What? No, of course not. Look I . . ." He exhaled. "You're right. I'm sorry."

"Ease up, okay? Don't be so nervous."

"Right. Easing up."

"I'm serious."

"I know."

"Good. Now take out the garbage."

David saluted. "Yes, ma'am."

He took the trash bag around the side of the house. He waved at the cop across the street, leaning against his vehicle, smoking a cigarette. The cop waved back halfheartedly. The police that Roy had put on watch duty had gone through a lot of cigarettes and a lot of cups of coffee. Roy had mentioned he'd owed some of his boys some easy duty.

Doesn't get any easier than this.

David dropped the trash into the can, snugged the lid back on. Amy was right. He was acting like an ass.

Yes, he needed to be alert and ready, but he could do it without freaking out his family.

Amy might understand the danger, but he owed it to his kids to act like the father they expected and depended on. It was unfair to make them feel anxious when they didn't even know why.

The sound of car doors slamming rapidly.

He turned to look as the squad car across the street cranked its engine. A split-second later the second squad car did the same. Both vehicles pulled away fast, squealing tires as they vanished around the corner at high speed.

David watched them go.

Okay. That's bad.

Maybe they'd been called away, some emergency around the corner. He stood with hands in pockets and waited for the sound of sirens.

A bird chirped.

Distantly, a little dog yapped.

A breeze rustled the leaves.

One of the cop's cigarette butts still smoldered in the street.

Okay, plan B. He'd go into the house and get Roy's number from Amy, give the guy a call. There was probably a simple explanation and—

A black sedan rounded the corner and glided almost silently down the street. It parked in the same spot the police car had just vacated. David turned his head, saw a black van coming just as slowly from the other direction.

He started walking back to the front door, forcing himself not to hurry.

He paused at the row of hedges under his house's

front windows and picked out some vines and dead leaves. While he did that, he watched the sedan and the van in the window's reflection. Nobody got out of either vehicle.

David knelt and pulled a few weeds before standing and stretching and going back into the house. He closed the door behind him, turned immediately to look at the vehicles through the peephole.

So far, they were just sitting there.

David made his decision in a split second.

He met Amy in the living room. "I need you to pack a bag for you and the kids and meet me in the garage in three minutes."

She frowned. "Is there something you'd like to explain—"

"Do it now, please."

Amy searched his face for a brief moment before turning and running up the stairs. "Brent! Anna! Get your shoes on. Now!"

David dashed down the hall and yanked open the door across from the kitchen, flew down the narrow stairs to their small basement. He went to his knees and pulled a footlocker from between the washer and the far wall. He quickly worked the combination and swung the lid open. There was a small, olive drab duffel bag within. He unzipped it and checked the contents.

David hadn't expected to need the guns when he'd locked them away upon returning home. They were tools he didn't need. The military had sidelined him. The duffel bag was filled with all the grim debris of a life that was slowly fading into memory.

A Navy Seal had put him onto the Sig Sauer P226 a couple of years ago, and he'd requisitioned a pair. They'd served him well in the field. He checked to make sure the pistols, shoulder holsters, ammo, extra magazines, knives, leather blackjack, and mace were all there. So was the little .380 automatic with the ankle holster. A light Windbreaker he could slip on to conceal the weapons. He zipped the bag and headed back up the stairs.

He closed the basement door behind him and heard the door leading into the garage open and close, the shuffle of feet and Amy's voice shushing the children who didn't understand what was happening.

David moved to join them, then froze, head cocked, listening. A low rattle. The back door. The knob turning.

David backed around the corner and waited. Whoever it was would have to come through the kitchen and past him. He debated briefly dashing for the garage, but even as he turned that idea over in his mind the back door opened, hinges he'd purposely never oiled creaking loudly. That decided it. David would have to deal with the intruder to cover his escape.

He tried to remember if he'd locked the front door. If they came from both directions at once—

A hand came slowly from the kitchen into the hall, holding a snub nose revolver.

David latched on to the wrist and dug his thumb into a cluster of nerve endings. A hoarse grunt and the man's hand opened, dropping the revolver. David kicked it away as he pulled hard on the wrist, yanking him out of the kitchen and into David's fist.

David cracked him hard on the nose, flattening it, blood and snot shooting from both nostrils. The guy howled. He was beefy and dark, black hair in a widow's peak, three days stubble on his jaw. He wore a blue suit without a tie, red shirt.

The guy recovered quickly, wiping his nose and bull rushing at David, head down.

An animal growl accompanied the charge.

David sidestepped and caught the man around the throat in a headlock under his arm, but the momentum still slammed him back into the wall behind him, plaster cracking. The guy tried to stand up, but David hung on, keeping him hunched over. The intruder couldn't get an angle to punch but tried anyway, flailing weakly at David's back. David pushed off the wall and slammed the guy's tailbone back into the kitchen doorframe with a sharp crack. He yelled in pain and doubled his efforts to twist out of the headlock.

David heard the garage door open.

He clamped down tighter on the headlock and pulled the man, back into the kitchen.

"You . . . mother . . . fucker," the guy grunted, voice a rough croak.

David smashed his face against the dishwasher to shut him up. He stuck his head around the corner and looked back down the hall at Brent approaching.

David forced his voice calm. "Don't come into the kitchen, okay, buddy? I spilled something." The guy struggled, and David squeezed tighter.

"We're all in the car," Brent said. "Mommy said to tell you to hurry up."

"Okay. Go back to the car."

"Well, come on," Brent insisted. "You know Mom doesn't like waiting."

"I know, buddy," David told him. "We're going on a fun trip, okay? I just need to fix something first."

Brent nodded, turned, and jogged back to the garage.

David let go of the guy suddenly and he staggered

back. He hadn't been expecting to be turned loose, stumbled. David didn't give him time to orient himself and kicked him in the balls. Hard. The guy went purple and fell to his knees.

David shifted to stand behind him, took his chin in one hand, the side of his head with the other. A sharp twist and a *crack* and the man went stiff a split second before going limp and collapsing dead to the tile floor.

David scooped up the duffel from the hallway floor and ran for the garage.

CHAPTER TEN

David climbed into the Escalade, handed the duffel to Amy, and buckled in.

"Please open that and load the guns."

Her eyes widened. "David, please tell me—"

"There are already rounds in the magazines. Just put the magazines in the pistols like I've shown you at the range."

Her hands shook as she unzipped the duffel. She reached in and brought out one of the 9 mm Sig Sauers, fumbled it to the floor at her feet.

"Calmly." David cranked the ignition. "Take a breath."

She did, picked up the gun, and smacked in the magazine with a decisive click. She handed the pistol to David.

David felt the weight, the cool metal in his hand. He held it a second longer than he need to before putting it in his lap.

David turned to look at Brent and Anna in the backseat. Anna was buckled into her car seat. There was a stack of books between them for the ride. Amy had packed them, obviously not sure how long they'd be wherever they were going. Brent was just starting the first Harry Potter.

David smiled at his son and daughter. They were smart kids and would see through a fake smile, which would only make them nervous, the opposite effect he was going for, so he did his best to make it sincere. "We're going to take a really fast car ride, so don't be scared, okay. Daddy's a very good driver."

"Cool!" Brent said.

"You can drive as fast as you want, Daddy," Anna said, "because I've been on a roller coaster before."

"Fair enough."

He thumbed the button to roll down the driver's side window. David touched the gun in his lap, feeling the cold metal again, mentally orienting himself, reminding himself of the weight and heft, what it would feel like when he squeezed the trigger.

Amy reached for the garage door opener in the cup holder between the seats.

"Don't," David said.

Amy jerked her hand back.

David shifted the SUV into gear.

And slammed his foot down on the gas pedal.

Amy screamed.

The Escalade slammed through the garage door, sending pieces flying in every direction. Two men coming up the driveway went bug-eyed for a split second before leaping out of the way. They looked to be cut from the same cloth as the guy David had killed in the kitchen, lethal and experienced thugs, but primitive bruisers, not like the slick professional David had fought in Amy's office.

In his peripheral vision, David saw a third man on the lawn raising a gun. There was the sharp crack of pistol fire and something tinged off the Escalade's hood.

David stuck the Sig Sauer out the window and squeezed off three quick shots. He wasn't trying to hit anything. He was just trying to keep them down while he got away.

He was still accelerating when he hit the street, jerking the wheel for a sharp left turn, tires screaming on asphalt. Another gunshot from behind, and David braced himself for the jarring clamor of broken glass but it never came.

"Kids, please duck your heads down. *Now.*"

They obeyed him instantly, eyes wild and childish, little faces shocked to silence.

David stuck his arm out the window again and emptied the pistol. He didn't bother to see if he hit anything, tossed the pistol into Amy's lap. "Reload."

She fumbled into the duffel for another magazine.

David slammed the SUV into reverse and stomped the gas. The Escalade flew back and smashed the front of the black sedan with a metallic crunch and the tinkle of broken head- and taillights.

Anna screamed.

David shifted into drive, pulled the SUV ahead forty feet, then shifted back to reverse and sped backward at full speed. When he struck the sedan this time he pushed it up over the curb and smashed it up against a tree. Steam shot out from under its hood.

"David!" Amy handed him the pistol.

He took it, turned just in time to see the man on the lawn leveling his weapon.

David held his breath, sighted, squeezed the trigger.

The shot caught the man high on the chest, and he spun away in a spray of blood. When he sprawled across the grass this time, he wouldn't be getting up.

The sound of car doors slamming jerked David's eyes to the rearview mirror. The van cranked its engine and pulled away from the curb, tires squealing.

David punched it, and the Escalade shot forward. The van flew up right on the SUV's bumper, engine roaring.

David ran the stop sign at the corner, turned hard right onto a cross street. The van followed.

The vibration of the Escalade's engine hummed from David's tailbone up through his spine as he pressed the accelerator flat.

Amy gripped the oh-shit handle over the window. "David!"

"Hang on!"

David took the next left. One of the Escalade's hubcaps popped off and rolled away.

"Daddy, you're going too fast!"

"It's okay, Anna. Just like the roller coaster, remember?"

"The roller coaster is on a track!" Anna yelled.

"Well, that's a good point, but—"

Another sedan veered in sharply from a cross street and side-slammed the Escalade on the passenger side. David felt the impact in his teeth. Amy screamed and flinched away as the window glass shattered and rained over her.

The two vehicles raced down the narrow residential street side by side, engines redlining.

Another glance in the rearview mirror showed the van coming up fast, its side door sliding open. A man leaned out with a small submachine gun, some sort of compact H&K maybe. David couldn't be sure from this distance.

David slammed one way into the adjacent sedan before yanking the wheel back the other way just as the man behind him opened fire. The little machine gun chugged and spat fire, digging up chunks of asphalt down the center of the road.

Picket fences cracked and splintered as David motored across lawns. David tried to look ahead and at all of the Escalade's mirrors at the same time. He wrestled the vehicle back toward the road, obliterating a mailbox along the way with a metallic *pop*. The SUV lurched and bounced back into the road, smacking into the sedan again with a loud crunch.

A car coming from a cross street slammed on the brakes just in time to let the battling vehicles pass by. It fishtailed around, slamming into the curb.

The machine gun behind them opened up again and the Escalade's back window evaporated in a glittering shower of glass.

Both kids screamed.

David glanced right, saw the sedan's rear passenger window lower and the shotgun barrel come out.

"Get down!"

Amy ducked.

David raised his pistol and fired over her through the open window. He kept pulling the trigger, filling the backseat of the sedan with lead, until the gun clicked empty. The shotgun barrel fell back into the car.

David looked ahead. They were nearing the edge of the residential neighborhood where the street emptied into a busy four-lane road.

David stomped on the brakes, and the SUV skidded and squealed to a halt. The smell of tire smoke drifted through the Escalade. The sedan flew past him and out into the intersection. The cross traffic vehicles blared horns and screeched tires, swerving to barely miss the sedan weaving between the cars.

The city bus didn't miss.

It plowed into the side of the sedan with a sickening crunch and swept it rapidly out of sight. David allowed himself some fleeting satisfaction.

The van hit the Escalade from behind.

David felt the impact in his neck.

The world became a blur in the windshield as the back of the Escalade fishtailed around, spinning a complete circle. David experienced a stab of panic as the passenger side tires slid into the curb and the Escalade started to flip. There was a harrowing pause before the SUV landed hard again on all four tires, and David allowed himself to breathe.

The roar of the van's engine focused David's attention. The van was coming hard.

He shifted into reverse and pushed the gas pedal flat. The van gained as the Escalade sped backward. David saw the man leaning out the van's side door raise the machine gun again.

"Everybody down!"

The gun belched blue fire, and David flinched as the windshield glass shattered inward, covering him and Amy.

"David." She shoved the pistol into his hand. Reloaded.

He pointed it out front, over the steering wheel and

squeezed off five rapid shots, the pistol bucking in his hand.

The slugs dotted a neat line across the van's windshield, spiderwebbing the glass. The van lurched one way then another and then turned sharply and slammed into a parked car with a racket of metal and glass.

David stood on the brakes and spun the Escalade around. He paused, looked back at the wrecked van for a long second. He gripped the Sig Sauer, ready. When the van didn't move and nobody emerged, he shifted the SUV into drive and headed away fast, merging swiftly into traffic and heading for the freeway.

In the backseat, the children sobbed loudly, sucking for air and hiccoughing.

"It's okay." David kept the Escalade steady, driving the speed limit. "We're okay now. Amy, call your sister. Tell her we're coming. Don't tell her anything else, not yet. Just that . . . something came up."

Amy dialed her phone.

"I want to go home," Anna wailed through her tears.

"Who wants to go to McDonalds?" David asked. "Who wants a Happy Meal?"

They cried harder.

"Disney World!" David said suddenly. "We're going to Disney World."

Anna's sobs dwindled to a trickle. "Really?"

Brent stopped crying altogether. "Can we stay in a hotel with a swimming pool?"

CHAPTER ELEVEN

David sat in the Escalade in his sister-in-law's driveway with his American Express Gold card on his lap and the phone to his ear. He was almost done making the arrangements, but kept getting distracted, his eyes sweeping the street.

How long would it take them? When would they figure out this was the next place to try?

He couldn't stop his brain from accumulating and categorizing information. Items that needed to be worried about immediately, concerns that would need attention in the very near future, and miscellany to be tabled until a more convenient time.

In the least pressing category were thoughts about the Escalade and the insurance deductible, the money he was currently putting on his gold card, the fact he'd need to call the school to tell them the kids wouldn't be there.

In the most urgent category was the knowledge he'd already sat in his sister-in-law's driveway too long. He needed to keep moving.

Just as he finished his phone call, he looked up to see Jeff emerge from the house. David got out of the car to meet him.

Jeff whistled and gawked at the Escalade. "Holy fucking shit, man. Amy sort of gave us the short version of what happened but . . . *damn*."

"It could have been worse," David said.

"Hell yeah, you could have been killed."

"Yes."

"Have you called the police?"

"Not yet," David said.

Jeff gave him the fish-eye. "Well . . . don't you think you'd better?"

David looked up and down the street. No cars coming. Nothing yet. David had neither the time nor the desire to get into a lengthy debate with Jeff. He needed to be as firm and as direct about this as possible. Jeff needed to understand and understand *now*.

"There were police guarding our house," David said. "They left only a few minutes before this started. It was a bailiff who shot Amy's boss at the courthouse. The line between good guys and bad guys is a bit fuzzy at the moment. So here's what we're going to do. We're going to make sure the people we care about are safe first, and then we'll talk to the appropriate authorities to get this straightened out."

"Damn, I mean . . ." Jeff scratched his head. "I mean, hell, you guys can hide out here of course. We're family. Or if you need to leave the kids—"

"I appreciate that, Jeff," David said. "But that's not good enough. I'm going to need you to pack up your family and mine and drive to Disney World. I've already made the reservations, and it won't cost you a dime."

"Disney World."

"Yes."

"That's in Florida."

"Yes," David said. "Far away."

Jeff shuffled his feet, rubbed the back of his neck. "Damn, David, I'm store manager. We do our schedules pretty far in advance and I can't just . . . you know . . . take off."

David sighed and nodded.

Jeff didn't understand that his whole world had just changed. It needed to sink in but wasn't happening fast enough.

David put a hand on Jeff's shoulder. Gently. He guided him around to the rear of the Escalade and gestured to the vehicle. "Those are bullet holes. From a nine millimeter submachine gun. These are people who wanted my wife dead and didn't care if there were children in the car when they started shooting. They are targeting her specifically, for something she knows or something they did, but they know all about her and came after her. That means they know who her sister is, too, and where you live. They haven't finished the job, and that means they'll come looking. They'll come right here to your house. If they think you might have useful information, they'll make you tell it. It won't matter if you don't know anything. They'll need to make sure. If they think hurting Elizabeth will make you talk, then that's what they'll do. And they won't leave any witnesses. It doesn't matter if they're children. They won't care."

The color drained from Jeff's face.

"It's not fair. You didn't do anything to make this happen, but that doesn't matter. It's happening anyway. Now here's what you're going to do." David spoke slowly, calmly. "You're going to call your assistant manager or whoever's next in line and tell him he's on the job. Do not tell him you're going to Florida. Make up a lie. Keep it simple. Then you're going to drive yourself and both of our families to Florida. If Brent or Anna asks where Daddy is you're going to tell them everything is fine and that I'm just taking care of some business. Then you're going to see Mickey or eat ice cream or whatever is fun and will keep them happy. I'll call Amy every day to update you guys. Understand?"

"I . . ." He seemed to have trouble finding breath. "I guess I can pack up and then first thing in the morning—"

"I need you on the road in ten minutes."

Jeff swallowed hard, nodded.

David squeezed his shoulder. "I'm trusting you with everything, Jeff. My wife and kids. You can do this."

Jeff nodded again. "Ten minutes."

David sat behind the wheel of the Escalade and watched Jeff toss the last piece of luggage into the back of his pickup. He'd already kissed Anna and Brent good-bye, and now he watched from his parking spot on the street to make sure they got off okay. He drummed his fingers on the steering wheel, willing his in-laws to move faster.

Amy walked toward him, the bag she'd brought from home slung over her shoulder. She climbed in the passenger side and shut the door. She looked straight ahead, specifically avoiding eye contact with her husband.

"What do you think you're doing?" David asked.

"Coming with you." Amy said. "Elizabeth can handle Anna and Brent."

"I don't think that's a good idea," David said.

She offered him a withering look. "You don't have the security codes to my building and office."

"You could give them to me."

"What's the senior administrative assistant's name at the DA's office?"

"I don't know."

"Who runs the bailiff's office and what are the watch captain's names?" Amy asked.

"I don't know."

"This is a DA problem on DA turf," Amy said. "This isn't happening without me. I'll admit being shot at was new. You can handle that part. But I'm going."

They looked at each other deadpan.

David broke eye contact first, turned his head to watch Jeff's truck back into the street. Jeff honked and waved out the window before pulling away.

Amy took her phone out of her bag. "First thing is to figure out who in my office to call. Somebody trustworthy."

"Put that on hold. Think about it," David said. "First thing we find a safe place and regroup."

"Okay then," Amy said. "So drive already."

David shifted the Escalade into gear, leaving the quiet neighborhood and finding his way back to the freeway. They were over the bridge and into the city when David's smartphone rang.

He didn't recognize the number but answered it anyway. "Hello?"

"You're making a lot of noise out there, man."

"Charlie."

"Are you near a TV?" he asked.

"No."

"Never mind," Charlie said. "I'll send the video to your e-mail."

"Not to mine," David said. "Send it to my wife's e-mail. Get a pencil. Write it down."

"It's okay. I already have it." Charlie hung up.

Of course.

They hit Midtown and crossed to the west side. The wind washed through the SUV. David felt conspicuous driving around in a vehicle with practically no windows, full of bullet holes, dents. Nobody much noticed. Welcome to New York City.

"Where are we going?" Amy asked.

"I know somebody."

Three blocks later, he turned into a hotel parking garage and backed the Escalade into the darkest most remote corner he could find. David grabbed his duffel and Amy her bag and they found the stairwell and took it up to the lobby.

They stood in line at the front desk, waiting behind a half-dozen people looking to check in. David exhaled, tried not to feel so impatient at how long the line was taking.

"Why here?" Amy asked in a low voice.

"A friend," David said. "I'm hoping for a favor."

When they finally made it to the front of the line, a cheerful young lady asked if they had a reservation.

"No, actually," David said.

She tsked. "That's a problem. We're filled to the max because of the convention. Even the overflow hotels are full." She fixed David with a *please go away* look.

David glanced quickly around the lobby. Roughly half the people wore little burgundy fezzes with gold tassels perched on their heads. Ties pulled loose, cheeks rosy, drinks in their hands. Shriners. David had been so occupied with his own thoughts, he'd failed to notice. He chastised himself. A lapse in awareness of his immediate surroundings could be exactly what got him or Amy killed.

"Is Larry Meadows here?" David asked.

"He's pretty busy," she said. "Again, the convention. If you need to speak to somebody, one of the assistant managers on duty would be happy to—"

"Thanks, but Larry and I are old friends and this is important. I'd appreciate it if you could get him for me. I understand he's busy, and I can wait in the bar until he's available."

"May I give him a name?"

"Tell him it's his old drinking buddy from Basrah."

She regarded him a moment before saying. "Okay . . . I'll try to get him."

"Thanks," David said. "We'll be in the bar."

It was made up like an old Irish pub, crowded, impossible to get a table, but a couple of Shriners stumbled away from a stretch of bar and David and Amy took their places. The harried bartender hurried over to take their orders.

"A club soda with lime," David.

"Club soda, huh?" Amy shook her head. "After our day so far I think I need something with a little more backbone. Double Scotch rocks. Whatever's in the well is fine."

The bartender knew his business, and the drinks arrived fast. Amy took half hers down in one go.

"Take it easy," David said.

She laughed. "Take it easy, he says. God, are you kidding? For Christ's sake."

"I know you," David said. "I married a strong, level-headed, smart woman. So you get thirty seconds to feel shock and awe, and then we have to focus."

"You know me," Amy repeated. "I thought I knew you, too."

"What's that supposed to mean?"

"Moving supplies around. Sitting behind a desk. That's not what you were doing in the Army, was it?" Amy sipped her drink again. "The guy driving our SUV today and shooting an automatic pistol out the window wasn't a pencil pusher."

David drank club soda to buy himself a few seconds.

He sat the glass back on the bar and turned to her. She was watching him, not with hostility. Just waiting. Her eyes gleamed with the same alert intelligence that had attracted him in the first place.

A formidable woman. God help me if I ever cross her.

"There are things I'm not allowed to talk about," David said. "Not to anyone."

"I'm your wife."

"Especially not to my wife."

She drained the Scotch and set her glass next to his.

"Do you want another one?"

She shook her head. "No."

They stood looking at their empty glasses a moment.

"Holy crap, Major." A voice behind them. "It *is* you."

In his peripheral vision, David had already caught Larry's reflection in the bar mirror. He stood, turned and extended his hand. "Sergeant."

Larry Meadows ignored the hand and swept David into a bear hug. They patted each other on the back, laughing. When they disengaged, David took a good look at his old friend.

Larry Meadows was a compact bulldog of a man with a bald head and very dark skin. He wore a sharply tailored double-breasted suit with a tasteful emblem of the hotel on the pocket, but whenever David thought about him it was in desert camo and a field rig.

The first time David met Larry Meadows, the master sergeant was saving his ass. He was part of a retrieval team meant to escort David back after one of his deep penetration solo missions. Larry and his squad were hunkered down a hundred yards from the Iran border, just inside Iraq. David was on the other side of the line, pressed flat against some boulders, pinned down by an Iranian patrol spraying AK-47 fire all over the place.

The sergeant's orders had been clear. He could *not* cross into Iran. It was Major David Sparrow's problem to drag his own ass back across the border into Iraq. The U.S. government would claim no knowledge of him if David got himself captured, but if he got himself back across the border under his own steam, Larry and his men would take him the rest of the way.

But David had sized up the situation, and it was obvious that if he ran for it they'd gun him down before he got twenty steps.

Without timely intervention, David was as good as dead.

Later, Larry would say that maps of the area were notoriously inaccurate and who could tell exactly where the border was anyway in that sunbaked hell. So he'd come in fast with his men and had driven the Iranian patrol back enough for David and the rest of them to hoof it out of there. Back in Basrah, David had spent a week's pay treating Larry and his men to drinks.

And Sergeant Larry Meadows could put away the beer.

Eventually Larry rotated back to the world and prospered in hotel management.

"So what brings you to my hotel, Major?" Larry asked with a big smile.

"You saved my bacon once," David said. "I thought you might enjoy the chance to do it again."

CHAPTER TWELVE

Dante Payne sat at his desk and stared at the phone. It should have rung hours ago, and when it hadn't he'd sent men to find out why.

Now he was waiting again for the phone to ring. He hated waiting. Not that anyone else *liked* to wait, but Dante Payne was hardly anyone else. Such mundane inconveniences were beneath him.

And yet here he was. Waiting.

A woman brought him a glass of red wine. Blond and tall. Short skirt. Her breasts were so large even Dante found them egregious.

"What is your name?" Dante asked.

"Michelle."

"You're new," Dante observed. "What kind of wine is this?"

"A cabernet sauvignon." Michelle told him the label and vintage but her words were forgotten even as they left her mouth.

Women. A wine cellar full of rare and expensive

bottles. A luxurious and obscenely expensive mansion. Various pricey automobiles. Wardrobe from the finest tailors in New York, Milan, and Paris. The desk at which he sat was a seventeenth-century antique.

None of it much excited him. There was a time when he thought it would.

Dante dismissed the woman, sipped the wine. It was excellent, and he didn't give a shit.

He stared at the phone.

Dante Payne had everything anyone could ever want and it wasn't enough. The more power and influence he accumulated, the more he wanted. The more he *needed*. It was every bit as much an addiction as cocaine or heroin.

That assistant DA bitch, Amy Sparrow, was a problem, one that—hopefully—would soon go away. Not because she was putting a case against him for racketeering and extortion—although, yes, there was that, too—but for the simple fact that she opposed him.

She opposed *him*.

Dante was an intelligent man and fully realized this childish flaw in his character, but that didn't stop his blood from boiling when he thought about her. That she—that *anyone*—would dare to stand in the way of even his slightest whim was not something that fit into Dante's world view. And if she'd seen what was on the flash drive, then all the more reason she had to die. And then he would recover the flash drive and they'd have nothing and Dante Payne could return unmolested to his endeavors.

The problem, of course, had started when the government man had turned on him. Dante should have realized, should have anticipated the possibility. Any man who could so easily be bought, could just as easily prove to be untrustworthy when the time came to—

The phone rang.

Dante picked it up and put it to his ear but said nothing. Another minor power play that Dante realized was petty, but he couldn't help himself.

The voice on the other end: "Boss?"

"Tell me."

"We lost some guys. And they didn't get her."

A pause. A sigh. This was disappointing news but not unforeseen. "The sister?"

"We checked her house. Nobody there."

Dante considered. "Check the rest of the places on the list and call me back."

He hung up.

Dante knew instinctively his men would come up empty, but leaving stones unturned was not his way.

The government man had been useful before he'd turned against Dante. His name was Calvin Pope. It had been Pope who had relocated Payne to America when he was no longer useful to the U.S. government in the Middle East. Dante learned that many like him were being relocated, men who traded their services and information for safety and a new chance on American soil. That's when Dante hatched his scheme. These men would be his soldiers, trained and dangerous men who would have similar ambitions to Dante's.

Like most Americans, Pope was pathetically susceptible to money and was soon in Dante's pocket. Dante would send the man a monthly cash payment, and Pope would relocate select candidates according to Dante's direction. Certain men Dante had known in his former life found their visas and clearances being expedited in record time and on transports to the States. In almost no time at all, Dante had a trained street force ready and willing to do his bidding.

It had all been so absurdly simple, and right under the nose of the American government.

And then a few months ago, a problem arose. The media uncovered the government program to relocate dangerous foreigners to live among law-abiding citizens. Congressmen scrambled quickly to protest and toss together oversight committees. Investigations followed. No politician of either party was eager to be seen as supporting any policy that put registered voters in harm's way, and there was fierce competition among those on the Hill to see who could protest mostly loudly.

Outrage was the fashion of the day, and midterm elections approached rapidly. Cable news pundits drew blood nightly.

That was when Dante decided Pope should be eliminated. His bosses would eventually be called in to testify before Congress, and as blame worked its way through the system in search of an appropriate sacrificial goat, there was too much risk that Pope's corruption would be uncovered and he would be made to tell what he knew. Pope himself would likely jump at the chance to testify in exchange for immunity.

Much simpler and safer for Dante to simply put a bullet in the back of the man's head and dump his body somewhere in Jersey.

It irritated Dante that he'd miscalculated.

Calvin Pope had been weak and corruptible but *not* stupid.

As an insurance policy, Pope had put the entire

record of all his transactions with Dante, including the names and addresses of all foreign nationals improperly relocated, onto a password-protected flash drive.

That Pope thought himself beyond Dante's reach infuriated the crime lord. The audacity!

The absolute, unmitigated audacity!

Dante struck fast, hoping to take Pope and also lay hands on the flash drive, but he hadn't moved fast enough. Pope had eluded him and sent the flash drive to the DA who had ambitions to put a case together against him.

The problem had become a mess, and the mess had become a disaster.

Pope would have to be found and killed. The flash drive recovered and destroyed. The Sparrow woman eliminated also on the chance she'd seen the information on the drive. The *burn everything to the ground* strategy was far from subtle, but in this case it was called for. This was a case in which nothing less than bold, decisive action would do. Find the Sparrow woman. Find Pope. Make sure no trace of them was left upon the Earth.

But to accomplish these things, Dante would need a better class of bloodhound.

He checked his list of likely candidates, all men he'd instructed Pope to relocate from overseas. Capable, hard men with very specific skills. He narrowed the list of a dozen men to six and then again to four.

He opened his laptop and composed an e-mail, using code language, but his intent clear. His e-mail address was also a code name, and his tech people assured him that what he was doing was untraceable. He cut and pasted the message into three other e-mails. All four men would get the same message. He attached a picture of Pope and also one of Amy Sparrow.

By some instinct or perhaps on a whim, he attached the picture of the husband. If it turned out to be important, he could find out the man's name later, but he'd been at the courthouse for the shooting, and one of Dante's men had snapped the photograph with a camera phone.

Dante didn't know which of the men would be available or if they would even reply, but they were all hunters. Money was no object. They knew Dante would pay top dollar, and they would only take the job if reasonably confident they could complete it.

Dante hit Send and felt better. It was good to do something besides sit and wait.

He lived in the fashionable section of Buckhead in Atlanta. He'd done well since coming to America, had spent an appropriate amount of time in Manhattan in service to his sponsor before striking out on his own.

Atlanta suited him. Not too big or too small. Not too cold. An airport to take him wherever business demanded.

He enjoyed, without reservation, the life of the infidel. Allah would most definitely not approve of the tumbler of twenty-year-old Scotch or the fifty-dollar cigar, but he'd never been religious, not really, and America had to be the most godless place on the face of the Earth. His Armani suits and his Mercedes coupe were more a religion to him than anything that had ever happened in a mosque.

He sat at his computer, pulled his tie loose, and sipped Scotch as he scanned his in-box. The message from Dante, even coded, caught his eye immediately. He opened it and read carefully.

If Dante had one fault it was that his temper often resulted in rash decisions. He'd made a bad situation worse and would pay handsomely for a remedy.

Providing remedies had paid for many Armani suits.

He was available for the job certainly, but he would need to mull this offer before responding to Dante. He was just coming off a job and was due for some downtime. It was a perk of his success that he could pick and choose his assignments. He clicked open the first picture.

The woman was one of those well-put-together professionals, attractive without trying, just short of glamorous. She was the sort that demanded to be taken seriously by her male counterparts, a tedious type all too common in America.

He clicked open the other picture. It was a shot snapped quickly, a photo of a man in profile, turning away, but the image was good enough to make out—

He blinked. Looked at the photograph again.

He enlarged it and sent it to the wireless printer, producing a glossy five-by-seven print. He studied it carefully, took in the face.

He filled the tumbler with three more fingers of expensive Scotch. He emptied the tumbler in two gulps and filled it again.

He grabbed the phone and dialed. Someone picked up on the other end, and when he heard no voice he knew who it was.

"It's me," he said.

A pause.

"I didn't expect to hear from you so quickly," Dante said. "I appreciate your swift attention. Do you feel you can handle this matter for me?"

"Yes. But I'll need more money. I don't think you understand who you're dealing with."

Another pause. "Explain."

"I know the man in the photograph," said Yousef Haddad. "And I can kill him for you."

CHAPTER THIRTEEN

"The penthouse suite takes up almost a third of the floor." Larry Meadows ushered them in, gesturing at the plush surroundings. "Sitting room here, game room through there with a bar and a foosball table and pinball machines. Three bedrooms and a full kitchen. Two bathrooms. It's the owner's place, but he's in Monaco, so you're all clear."

"Is there anyone else on this floor?" David asked.

Larry shook his head. "The rest of the floor is machinery, air-conditioning units, and stuff like that. And storage. This floor even has its own emergency backup generator if the power goes out during a storm or whatever. Nobody's going to bother you up here. The phone goes through the front desk, but I'll tell them to patch anything through to me if you need something."

"Perfect."

Larry handed David a copper key. "The elevator and the room use this. No key card. Nothing in the computer. Unless you order room service, not even the staff will know you're up here. You might as well be on Mars."

Amy came forward, shook Larry's hand, her other hand coming up to give his shoulder a warm squeeze. "Thank you so much for this, Mr. Meadows. You're helping us out more than you know."

Larry shrugged, sheepish. "Hey, you know, anything for the Major, right? We go back."

"Can I ask if this floor gets Wi-Fi?"

"All over the building, ma'am, but this floor, as you might guess, has its own separate Wi-Fi, too," Larry said. "Should be perfect reception."

"Thanks again," she said. "I'll set up my laptop on the desk. If I'm away for a minute, I get fifty e-mails."

"I know how it is, ma'am."

David walked Larry back to the elevator.

"Listen, Major," Larry said in a low voice, expression serious. "You want a place to lie low. I'm just glad I'm in a position to help. But you're obviously in some kind of fix. What else can I do for you?"

"You've already done enough. Seriously."

"Come on, Major."

"Maybe look in on her later," David said. "I might have to go out, and I don't want her to feel . . . well . . . abandoned."

"You got it."

The elevator arrived and Larry stepped aboard. David reached out suddenly and grabbed the door before it closed.

"Larry, you've got cameras all over the place, right? What's the setup like?"

"The security room is right next to my office," Larry said. "Three banks of monitors. Why? You want me to be on the lookout for something?"

"I'll let you know," David said.

Larry tossed him a two-finger salute, and the elevator door closed.

David returned to the suite.

Amy sat hunched over her laptop, pointing at the screen. "Is this the e-mail you were talking about?"

"Yes." He pulled up a chair next to hers. "Play it."

She clicked on the attachment and the computer's media player opened the file. Video footage. David instantly recognized the person with the microphone in her hand, an Asian woman named Patricia Choi, a field reporter for a local station David usually watched in the evening.

Amy gasped, her thin fingers going to her mouth. "David, that's our house."

Squad cars with flashing blue lights parked behind Choi, and there behind the police vehicles was David's house, an officer stretching yellow police tape across the open front door. Police swarmed the crime scene.

"Shit," Amy muttered.

"I'm surprised your office hasn't called," David said.

"They have. About fifty times." Amy's voice sounded strained. "I've been letting it go to voice mail."

The video switched to a two-shot of Choi interviewing a neighbor, and David rolled his eyes.

"Shit, that's Mark. Turn it up."

Amy thumbed the volume on the side of the laptop.

". . . a neighbor who witnessed the whole thing. Sir, can you tell us what you saw?"

"Man, I was just putting feed and seed on the side lawn and all hell broke loose," Mark said. "They were shooting all over the place, thought I was going to wet my pants, and then David comes crashing right through the damn garage door. Sounded like the world ending, let me tell you."

"And has he been your neighbor very long?" Choi asked. "Was there anything that might lead you to believe something like this could happen in your quiet neighborhood?"

Mark shook his head. "No way. I've known the guy for years. This is all straight out of the blue." Mark scratched his chin, thoughtful. "But he has been out of work for a while. Maybe the guy just snapped or something."

David groaned. *Damn it, Mark.*

The video switched to some shaky handheld footage with Choi's voice over the top of it. "This footage was taken by the eyewitness's camera phone and is a Channel Seven exclusive."

"Great," David said. "The exclusive Channel Seven Mark-Cam."

The video was jerky, probably as Mark tried to hide and tape the spectacle at the same time, but the Escalade was clearly visible as it backed into the black sedan, pulled forward, and smashed back into it again. Then David's arm emerged from the driver's side window, the pistol blasting back toward his lawn. Even in the laptop's tiny speakers the *pop* of the gunshots made Amy flinch.

"That doesn't look good, does it?" he said.

"No. It does not." She sounded pissed.

The video shifted back to a stand-up of Choi. "Again, that's New York City Chief Deputy District Attorney Amy Sparrow and her husband wanted for questioning for this startling eruption of violence in a quiet residential neighborhood. For Channel Seven News, I'm Patricia Choi."

Amy slammed the laptop closed. "Fuck!"

"Easy," David said. "We'll get it sorted out. We'll explain to them."

"Of course we will," Amy said. "I just don't want to be in handcuffs when that happens."

"Being in trouble with the police isn't the problem," David told her. "The man I shot probably has priors. The authorities will make the connection and put two and two together. The trick is staying alive until that happens. Dante Payne wants you dead."

"That's what I don't get," Amy said. "The witness was killed, and without the witness we've got zilch. There's no case. For crying out loud, killing me is just rubbing it in."

David scratched his chin, thinking. He went to his duffel, took out the flash drive. He turned it over in his hands, looking at it, considering. He felt Amy's eyes on him. This was going to sting.

He showed it to her. "Does this look familiar?"

She shrugged. "I don't know. Maybe. A flash drive is a flash drive."

"The night of the break-in," David said. "He was after this. It was with a big stack of evidence."

Amy gaped. "You *withheld* that?"

"That man who broke in was no ordinary burglar," he said. "I needed to follow up on it. I was worried about our safety. You and the kids."

"David, this is serious. That's evidence. You can't just put it in your pocket and walk off with it on a hunch. You *know* this."

"I know. And I'm sorry. But we're beyond proper procedure now. This is life and death."

"What's on the drive?"

"I don't know," David said. "It's coded. I know somebody who can break it. I need you to stay here while I take the drive to him and he can tell me what's on it."

"No." Amy stood, hand out, palm up. "Give it to me."

"Amy—"

"Give. It. To. Me."

David recognized that tone of voice. She was furious, right on the edge of losing it. He'd faced machine guns up close and sniper fire from afar, but he knew this was when he needed to tread most lightly.

"We have people who can look at the disk," Amy said. "For God's sake, I'm second in command for the DA's office of one of the biggest cities in the world, and I'm about to break the world record for making a complete mess of my first case. That flash drive is evidence. You should never have taken it. And you damn sure should have told me about it before now. Either I know my job and you respect what I do, or you don't."

"What are you going to do with it?"

Her eyes flared and for a split second, David thought he'd stepped over the line. She calmed herself.

"Bert," she said. "He's the only one I trust. I take it to him and we get it sorted out."

"I thought he was in the hospital."

"He is," Amy said. "But last I heard he was sitting up, talking. He'll know who to call, what to do."

"I have one condition."

Her eyes narrowed.

"If it's such important evidence, he'll want it," David said. "But I take it in. I'll hand deliver it. You're out of harm's way. That's nonnegotiable. I respect you. I know you can do your job. But this is husband's prerogative. This happens in a way that I know you're safe or forget it."

Amy stared at him flat and hard.

"You wanted to know what I did in the Army. You

were right. I wasn't a pencil pusher," David admitted. "My job was to . . . to handle tough situations, missions where I was all on my own. No help. Nobody to trust. My life was in danger every single time. I guess you could say we're in one of those situations now."

She thought about it. David could see the wheels turning. This wasn't just about her job now. It was about who he was, about their marriage and if she trusted him or not.

"Okay," she said finally.

He gave her the flash drive.

"Thank you," she said. "I'm calling the hospital. If Bert's awake, they'll patch me through."

"I want to listen in."

"Okay. Stand over here."

He stood next to her. She dialed and got the hospital switchboard. They connected her to the nurse's station on Bert's floor, and after checking to make sure he was awake and available for phone calls, patched her through to Bert's room. Amy tilted the phone so David could listen too.

"Hello?"

"Bert, it's me, Amy."

"My God, everyone's been looking for you. Are you okay?"

"You're the one who's been shot, Bert."

"You're all over the news," he said. "What the hell happened? Where are you?"

David shook his head.

"Somewhere safe," Amy said. "Bert, I need you to listen."

She briefly explained about Dante Payne and the break-in and the flash drive.

"I want to bring the flash drive into the office," Amy said. "But I need you to tell me which one of the other DAs would be best to approach. Who can I trust?"

"Don't bring it into the office," Bert said. "If you'd asked me a week ago, I would have sworn every one of my people was solid. That's before I was shot by a bailiff. I just don't know. Can you bring the drive to me at the hospital?"

David shook his head again, tapped his chest again with a finger.

Amy frowned but said, "I can have somebody bring it."

"Okay, then here's what we do," Bert said. "Give me a couple of hours. I'm going to hit up some people I trust at NYPD and arrange some security. We'll make this tight, okay. Come in the parking garage and take the elevator up from there in case somebody is watching the lobby."

"Okay."

"This is going to be okay, Amy," Bert said. "We're not going to let anything happen to you. Can you send somebody tonight?"

Amy grinned at her husband. "I'm sending my best man."

CHAPTER FOURTEEN

The subway stop was only half a block from the hospital, but David circled the block to enter through the parking garage.

He walked inside, eyes scanning the shadows, taking in his surroundings. Habit. So many old instincts had taken over since he'd retrieved his duffel bag from the basement. The weight of the guns felt right. Skills he'd worried had atrophied had all snapped razor sharp again as if he hadn't been sidelined these past several months.

It hadn't been his idea, being sidelined. His bosses told him he was close to burning out. Too close. And when he'd asked how long it would be before he could return to duty, he had been given a perfunctory wait-and-see speech. How far his requests might be getting up the chain of command he could only guess. David had waited and waited. Still, the military hadn't called him back to duty.

But fate had.

And David realized he was pleased with himself. He'd stepped up. His skills hadn't rusted, and he'd calmly and coolly gone about the business of taking matters in hand. The military had been wrong. David was solid. Ready.

A stab of guilt blunted his satisfaction. This wasn't an assignment. This was his family. His wife and children. And David suddenly wished the lie he'd told his wife for years could be the truth, that he was a simple pencil pusher for the Army, supplying military bases. So much simpler. It was what Amy deserved. And the kids.

David could make it the truth. When this was over, he'd forget waiting to be called back to active duty. He'd get a résumé together, send his suit to the cleaners. Other men did it; he could, too. He'd try it on his own at first, going to job interviews, pounding the pavement. If it didn't work out, his wife would pull strings. She had good contacts in the city, and it would make her feel good to help him. It would all be wonderfully, blissfully ordinary.

All David had to do was go upstairs, hand the flash drive to the district attorney of New York City, and then just wash his hands. Bert would have experts who could dig into the information on the zip drive, and then—

He was moving between two parked cars when he caught the blur of movement in the window glass of a Nissan.

David spun fast, a fist shooting out, striking hard, one knuckle out. He smashed the knuckle into the man's trachea, and he fell back sputtering, the knife falling from his hand, glinting metallic as it tumbled, and clattered on the cement.

The other two were already coming at him from the other side, crowding him between the parked cars. He ducked as the first swiped at him with a tire iron and smashed a car window, glass raining. David punched him in the groin, and the man folded, going to his knees. David vaulted over him and kicked out hard, catching the next attacker in the gut.

The guy grimaced but was already coming back at him with a short knife. David moved fast, trapping the man's knife arm between his own arm and his body. He twisted sharply, turning his body, and redirected the man's knife thrust into the other attacker who was getting to his feet behind him.

The guy grunted, slid off the bloody blade and hit the garage floor with a meaty slap.

David still had the other man's arm trapped and wrenched it hard. The guy yelled high-pitched like some agonized farm animal. Another sharp twist, and he was rewarded with a wet *snap*.

The guy screamed more high-pitched than David thought possible. "Fucking broke my arm!"

David grabbed a fistful of the man's hair and slammed his forehead against the hood of a car. He picked his head up, nose bloody, and slammed it down again. A third time for luck. David let go of the man, watched him slide down unconscious, blood trailing red down the hood.

He looked around the parking garage. Cocked his head, listened. He stood, muscles tensed, hands made into tight fists. Nobody else came at him.

He double-timed it into the parking garage elevator and thumbed the lobby button, all thoughts of suits and résumés and ordinary day jobs evaporating.

He moved through the lobby quickly, not drawing attention to himself, and found the exit to the stairs. He climbed until he reached Bert's floor, cracked the door and peered into the hallway. When he didn't see anyone, he stepped out of the stairwell and scooted down the hall, arrived at the corner, and peeked around it at the nurse's station.

A single nurse sat with her head down, scribbling something into a file folder. David had no idea if one nurse on duty was the usual thing at this hour or if the others were making the rounds, but he didn't want to dither. He needed to get past her to Bert's room unseen.

David backed down the hall, and when he thought he heard voices, he ducked into a random room. He turned, poised to apologize but cut himself short.

A full brass band wouldn't wake the old man in the bed. Some kind of coma patient, David guessed, hooked up to multiple tubes and machines. He looked shriveled and unreal yet at the same time peaceful.

He waited a moment, cracked the door and looked into the hall. Empty. He spied a closet across the hall. There would have been a security keypad if the closet had been for narcotics, but there was just a door. He darted across the hall, entered, and pulled the door shut behind him with a soft click.

Mundane supplies. Latex gloves, antiseptic wipes, paper towels, cotton swabs. He thought for a moment, improvising a plan. He rummaged the closet until he found the box he wanted. Thin-gauged hypodermic needles prepackaged in plastic. He grabbed a few and shoved them into the pocket of his Windbreaker.

After making sure the hall was clear, he darted across to the room with the coma patient again. David found the nurse call button, pressed it, then put it into the hands of the old man and ran from the room.

From the closet, he watched as the frantic nurse came running down the hall and entered the room of the coma patient. *That's right. He's not supposed to be calling for the nurse, is he? I bet that was a surprise.*

He wouldn't have long. David darted from the closet and jogged past the now-vacant nurse's station to Bert's room. He opened it, entered quickly, and closed it quietly behind him with a final look over his should to make sure the nurse hadn't spotted him.

Bert sat up in bed, paging through an issue of *Golf Digest*. He looked up when David entered, frowned. "Hello?"

It took Bert a moment to recognize him. "Oh. It's you." Bert's eyes shifted to the door then back to David. They'd only met a few times at office functions. David thought Bert seemed a little grayer than he'd remembered, but after all, the man had recently been shot. That would age anyone.

"You seem surprised to see me, Bert."

Bert cleared his throat. "No, of course not. It's just . . . you got here fast. Good."

"I was a little worried at first," David said. "The police you arranged didn't meet me in the parking garage."

"No? Well, I'll . . . I'll have to ask about that."

"But it's okay," David said. "I found my way up here just fine."

Bert was nodding now. "Good. That's good. Amy's okay?"

"She's fine. She trusts you. Thanks for helping us."

"Of course," Bert said. "We'll get this straightened out. I promise. You brought the flash drive?"

"Yes."

"Give it to me, and we'll make sure it's safe," Bert

said. "We have people who can break the codes, find out if there's anything useful on it."

"In a minute," David said. "I want to ask you a few questions."

Bert frowned. "Oh?"

David saw Bert's hand edging toward the nurse call button.

"I'd appreciate it if you didn't do that, Bert," David said. "I want this conversation to be private."

Bert blinked.

David's gaze shifted to a pole that held a bag of clear liquid, a tube down to Bert's arm. "What's that?"

Bert looked. "Just keeping me hydrated."

David went to it, leaned in, and squinted at the bag of fluid. "Too bad they can't put some Chivas in there for you."

Bert laughed nervously.

David took hold of the tube. Bert opened his mouth to object but shut it again.

David pointed at a plastic attachment halfway down the tube. "What's this?"

"That's where they give me injections," Bert said. "Sedatives and so on."

"I guess it saves poking another hole in your arm, right?"

"That's the thinking, I guess."

"So, like I said, I was a little disappointed the police weren't there in the parking garage. Made me think something had gone wrong."

"I'm sorry nobody was there to meet you," Bert said. "I can assure you, we're going to find out—"

"I didn't say nobody was there to meet me," David said. "Just not the police."

Like any seasoned attorney, Bert understood saying nothing was better than saying the wrong thing. He waited for whatever David said next.

"There were men waiting for me," David said. "Not nice men. The same sort that tried to get at me and my family at my home. And what I'm wondering, Bert, is how those men knew I would be here."

David and Bert locked eyes.

"Okay, I see where this is going," Bert said, his voice becoming firmer. "And you're chasing a rabbit down the wrong hole. I want you to listen to me because—"

"Don't do that, Bert."

"Do what?"

"That thing that men like you do when you think it's time to take charge of a conversation," David said. "Like you've been very patient with a small child, but now it's time for the adults to take charge. That's not going to work with me. I'm going to ask questions, and you're going to answer them."

The authority in Bert's voice kicked up a notch. "This is disappointing. I'd have thought a woman as smart as Amy would have picked better. Do you know who I am? I'm one of the most powerful men in this city."

"No, you're not, Bert," David said. "Right now, your entire world is you and me in this room. If I snatched you out of that bed right now, you'd only be the guy with his naked ass hanging out the back of a hospital gown."

David took one of the plastic wrapped syringes from his pocket. Bert's eyes focused on it immediately.

"You told Dante Payne I'd be in the parking garage, didn't you, Bert?"

Bert said nothing.

David peeled the syringe out of the plastic.

"We trusted you," David said. "You'd been shot, after all. I mean, you had to be on our team, right?"

David pulled the plunger halfway out of the syringe's cylinder, filling it with air. Bert looked straight ahead, as if he refused to acknowledge what was going on.

"I need to know what happened, Bert." David inserted the needle of the syringe into the IV. "I want you to imagine how much I love my wife and my children. Compare that with the fact I barely even know you, Bert. Do the math."

David's thumb hovered over the plunger. With almost no effort at all, he could push it down, and the air bubble would go right into Bert's bloodstream.

Bert didn't look at the syringe, didn't even look at David. His gaze shot straight ahead, unblinking. A long, heavy pause.

"I wasn't supposed to be shot," Bert said at last.

David didn't move, kept his thumb poised over the syringe. Let him talk.

Letting them talk is always better than making them talk.

"Nobody was supposed to be hurt. Nobody besides the witness, I mean," Bert said. "I want you to know, David, that I *never* intended anything to happen to Amy. You have to believe that. If I thought there was a chance of that . . ."

David didn't budge, syringe still firmly in his grip.

Bert cleared his throat. "Nothing ever goes quite as planned, I guess."

"What does Payne have on you?" David asked.

Bert sighed, deflated, but also David thought he

looked like a weight had been lifted, as if Bert felt some acute relief at what he was about to confess. Probably it had been gnawing at him a long time.

"I'd been stepping out on Marie," Bert said.

David fished around in his memory for an image. A woman just a few years younger than Bert with laugh lines and a welcoming disposition, streaks of white just beginning to appear in her hair. Marie, Bert's wife.

"It was nothing really," Bert said. "Stupid. And of course Dante Payne had pictures. Thinking back now, I sort of suspect it had been Payne who'd aimed the other woman at me in the first place."

"You allowed a man to be killed to hide your infidelity?"

Bert rubbed his eyes. "No. No, of course not. Small things at first. Little favors. And then I looked up one day, and I had a leash around my neck. There was money, too. I bought some nice things for Marie, trying to smooth over my guilt. A week in Saint Thomas."

"It got to the point where you couldn't say no to him even if you'd wanted to," David said.

"I could have. If I'd been strong enough to face the music. I wasn't."

"When my wife called and arranged for me to come here, you didn't call the police, did you?"

"No."

"You called Dante Payne."

"Yes."

"You knew he'd send men to kill me and take the flash drive."

Bert's eyes shot to the syringe in David's hand.

David asked, "If I give you the flash drive now, and you hand it over to Payne, will that end it?"

A long pause this time, long enough that David wondered if Bert hadn't heard him. Bert's gaze rose slowly, as if he were fighting gravity itself. His gaze met David's squarely at last.

"No," Bert said. "He'll kill you. He'll kill anyone who might have seen what's on that drive. He'll kill Amy."

Yeah. But I had to ask. Something cold began working its way up David's spine, but he immediately shook it off. Focus. Set personal feelings aside. Do the job.

"Are you in contact with Payne directly?" David asked.

Bert nodded slowly, his eyes never leaving the syringe. "I can get a hold of him if it's important."

"It's important, Bert," David told him. "It's your life."

David looked around, saw a pen and a small pad of paper near the phone. "Give me that pen and paper," he told Bert.

The district attorney did as he was told.

Keeping one hand on the syringe, David jotted notes onto the pad. He ripped off the top page and handed it to Bert. "That's a bullet point list of what I want you to say, but you can put it in your own words," he told him. "Just make it convincing."

Bert read the paper then looked up at David. The expression on David's face was stone.

Their eyes locked in cold silence.

Bert picked up the phone and dialed.

CHAPTER FIFTEEN

Dante's secretary transferred the call to his cell. He rode in the back of his limousine on the way to the airport, a dour bodyguard sitting across from him.

Dante frowned at his smartphone screen when he saw who was calling but answered it anyway. "Yes?"

"Your men didn't show," Bert said.

"Hold on."

Dante covered the phone and asked his bodyguard, "Who did we send to the hospital?"

"Carlo and his brother," the bodyguard said. "And that tagalong idiot that's always with them. Mustafa."

Dante sighed. "Have we heard from them?"

"No."

Dante put the phone back to his ear. "How do you mean?"

"He was just here," Bert said. "It was my understanding that wasn't supposed to happen."

Dante's mind raced. Could his men have gone to the wrong hospital? Idiots. Or maybe they'd been caught in a traffic jam.

"There's more," Bert said.

"Tell me."

"He left the flash drive. I have it right here."

Dante felt a palpable sense of relief. "That's one thing at least."

"I told you," Bert said. "I don't want to get caught with this thing. Can you send a man to get it?"

Dante covered the phone again. "Who's available to run a simple errand?"

"Send Fat Jon," the bodyguard said.

Fat Jon. Why in hell did he have somebody working for him named Fat Jon?

"I can send somebody right away," Dante said into the phone. "I'll send him up to your room."

"I don't think it's smart to be seen with one of your men," Bert said. "I'm going to wrap it up and leave it at the front desk in the lobby. Don't worry, it'll be safe. Tell me your man's name and I'll label it."

They concluded the phone call, and Dante hung up.

Good. He felt *much* better. The information on the flash drive in the wrong hands would have caused him no end of trouble. Slowly they were cleaning up the mess a bit at a time.

So. What business remained?

There was still the matter of the woman. If she'd seen what was on the flash drive, she'd have to be silenced. Her husband, too, and anyone they may have shown the flash drive to. Every little bit of clutter would have to be swept up. Only when the problem was erased from history as if it had never existed would Dante be able to relax again and return untroubled to his excellent life.

The limousine driver took the LaGuardia exit, and they spotted Yousef Haddad standing at the edge of a loading zone. He wore an olive suit with a muted red tie and carried an overnight bag. He stood straight and grim, and there was a small opening in the crowd around him as if some bleak aura kept others at bay. To Dante, Haddad looked every inch a cold and ruthless killer, but of course he knew the man and had seen his bloody work firsthand.

The limousine glided to a halt in front of Yousef Haddad, and Dante climbed out. The two men embraced briefly, patting each other on the back, then returned to the car and drove away.

Dante filled a tumbler with good Scotch from the limousine's bar, dropped in two ice cubes. "Do you want a drink? I'm having one."

"Thank you, no," Yousef said. "Do you have the items I asked for?"

Dante nodded at the bodyguard who slid a case across the floor to Yousef.

"If these aren't adequate we can find you something else," Dante assured Yousef.

Yousef put the case on his lap and opened it to inspect the contents.

The twin .40 caliber Glocks were a bit generic but wouldn't surprise him with any problems. Yousef had known Dante would provide him with adequate weaponry. Likely, the pistols were from Dante's own stash. Extra magazines. Shoulder holsters. A six-inch belt knife. Stun gun. He took off his jacket and began strapping on the gear.

"These will do," Yousef said.

"There have been developments," Dante said.

Yousef's eyes met Dante's. "Oh?"

"Three others answered my call to arms just as you did."

Yousef frowned. "You didn't think I could manage it?"

Dante held up a placating hand. "I thought you could use some seasoned soldiers. They understand you're in charge. Use them as you will."

Yousef thought about this for a moment, then nodded. "Anything else?"

"Part of your work has already been done." Dante briefly explained.

"I told you to wait for me," Yousef said.

"The opportunity arose while you were en route," Dante said. "It doesn't matter. One of my men is on the way to get the flash drive."

"And you sent men after Sparrow?"

Dante shrugged, a half apology. "It seemed an opportunity."

"Have you heard from them?" Yousef asked.

"Not yet."

Yousef shook his head. "They're dead."

Dante's eyes widened slightly. He gathered himself, forced himself to calmly refill his tumbler with Scotch. "You're guessing. You can't know that."

"I know this Sparrow—the husband—and men like him. I know his type." Yousef sighed. "Your men are dead."

CHAPTER SIXTEEN

David sat in the hospital lobby, head down, pretending to play a game on his smartphone. He'd picked a good spot and could see both entrances, the front desk, and the little gift shop off to the side selling mugs and magazines and flowers and get-well cards. His eyes snapped up to scan the area every ten seconds or so.

After Bert had finished his phone call, David had jerked loose the cords for the telephone and nurse call button and had tied Bert's wrists to the railings of his hospital bed. The urge to push down the syringe plunger and inject an air bubble into Bert's bloodstream was almost too instinctual to resist. Not because of any hostility he might have felt toward the man—although there was that, too—but simply because his training screamed at him not to leave a live enemy in his wake who might cause more mischief.

Bert was a loose end, and people in David's line of work had a low tolerance for loose ends.

But the thought of what Amy would say was all it took to stop him from pushing the plunger down. She'd worked with the man for years, and it might be a shock to her system to learn so starkly the sort of things David considered a routine part of his job.

David had also sent Amy a text message:

Don't answer calls from the office. Not even
Bert. I'll explain later. STAY PUT.

Ten minutes later, a guy came to the front desk and asked for the package. David had told the teenager behind the counter in the gift shop to gift wrap it in bright red, so it would be easier to see. He also made sure the box was too big to shove into a pocket.

The guy turned it over in his hands like he wasn't sure what he was looking at. He had a fat sweaty face and a broad stomach and didn't fit well into his dark wrinkled suit. Tie pulled loose, his entire appearance was vaguely disheveled. A bristly black mustache curled down over his upper lip. Soup strainer.

The guy shrugged, tucked the package under his arm, and headed for the exit. He didn't appear to think there could possibly be anything tricky about picking up and delivering a package.

David gave him a few seconds, then rose and followed.

The pedestrian traffic out on the sidewalk was light, but at night, one man in a dark suit looked pretty much like another, from behind anyway. David congratulated himself for thinking of the bright wrapping on the package. He kept his eye on it and stayed about twenty yards back. He pretended to window-shop when the man stopped briefly to buy coffee and a Danish from a cart although there didn't seem to be anything especially sharp or alert about the guy.

He eventually took a set of steps down into the subway. David followed. He'd prepared for this eventuality, too, and fished the subway pass out of his pocket. David stood on the platform with a half-dozen people between himself and the man with the package. He thought about pretending to look at his smartphone again, but the man he was following was oblivious, licking the remains of the Danish from each thumb and finger in turn.

The train arrived, and David shuffled along with the crowd. He boarded the same car as the man with the package but at the opposite end. There were plenty of seats, and he took one that allowed him to keep an eye on his target.

The guy pulled a folded magazine out of his jacket pocket, opened it up and began to read, his lips moving as his eyes moved down the page. David took this as a sign the man had settled in for more than a few stops. Maybe.

David took out his smartphone and thumbed the text icon. He scrolled down to Charlie Finn's number and began composing a new text message. He hit Send at the next stop when he had service again:

Can you look something up for me? The home residence of Dante Payne.

Men like Payne had unlisted telephone numbers and generally didn't advertise where they lived. Payne might even be feeling a false sense of security, thinking himself safely hidden at home. If David could move fast, strike before his opponent was set—

The phone vibrated in his hand just as the train

pulled out of the station, and he looked down at Charlie's reply.

> He owns a building on the Upper West Side, so you're heading in the right direction.

At the next stop, they exchanged texts again.

> How do you know which direction I'm heading?

Charlie's reply:

> Most smartphones are easy to track. I called up your location on Google maps and just put a subway map over it. You're northbound on the C, right?

David typed:

> Oh, yeah? What color underwear do I have on?

Charlie:

> I just hope they're clean. But if you're trying to find Payne, this might not be the best way.

David paused as the train began moving again. Charlie wasn't stupid. That much had always been obvious. But David had forgotten the man could be intuitive also. Charlie sensed what David was contemplating.

At the next stop, David typed:

> I'm thinking it's time to go on the offensive.

Charlie:

I figured. Just like old times, right?

David managed a smile.

Why is going to Payne's not the best way?

David didn't get the reply until the next station.

Charlie:

He's required by law to list a specific domicile as his primary residence, but he owns properties all over the city and in Jersey and Connecticut. A lot of them are businesses he uses for money laundering but plenty of the others are residences. I have a list of sixty-eight properties if you'd like to see it.

David:

Don't have time to sort through all that. Besides, I've got a fish on a hook, and I'm giving him plenty of line.

Charlie:

That's different then. You need support?

David thought about it while waiting to get to the next stop on the line. He considered the flash drive in his pocket then typed:

Can you meet me downtown later?

Charlie:

I only come into the city for Chinese food.

David:

My treat.

David saw the man with the package fold his magazine and stash it back into his jacket as the train slowed for the next stop.

Stay tuned. Fish is swimming.

He followed the man onto the platform and up to the street. A good neighborhood on the Upper West Side just as Charlie had described. He rechecked the address Charlie had given him and confirmed he was headed in the right direction.

David followed him down the quiet residential street, closing the gap a little at a time. He timed it perfectly, and was right behind the guy when he turned up the steps to Dante's building. The guy reached for the buzzer, and David stopped him cold by putting the barrel of his pistol in the small of his back.

The guy must have known what he was feeling because he didn't budge, didn't even turn around.

David asked, "This is Dante's building?"

"I don't know who that is."

David goosed him again with the pistol.

"Okay, yeah," he said. "It's Dante's building. What now? You going in there to get yourself killed? If you know who Dante Payne is, then you should know better."

"What do they call you, friend?"

"Fat Jon."

"Are you strapped, Fat Jon?"

"In my jacket pocket." Jon wagged his elbow to indicate which side.

David reached in and fished out a .38 caliber Airweight. The revolver told him almost everything he needed to know about the man. It was the gun of somebody who wasn't really expecting to be shooting at anyone anytime soon but didn't want to be caught naked out in the dark. David dumped it in the pocket of his Windbreaker. Maybe it would come in handy later.

"This all?" David asked, meaning the revolver.

"That's it."

"What's the layout on the other side of the door?"

"Elevator. Lobby. Front desk."

"How many?"

"A man behind the desk at least," Fat Jon told him. "More if the boss is home. I don't know."

David wished he'd had better intel, but there was no help for it. He had too much momentum to stall now. Better to bully his way in and keep going. Dante wouldn't expect David to come at him like this. If he could just get upstairs, he could catch them flat-footed. There was a good chance Payne still didn't know the men he'd sent to the hospital parking garage were dead, didn't know his plan had gone south.

"Okay," David said. "Get ready to hit the buzzer. We're going in."

"You're making a mistake," Fat Jon said. "Turn around and go. I won't say anything."

David caught the faintest hint of an accent. Most people probably wouldn't even notice.

"Are you Turkish by any chance, Jon?"

Jon's shoulders flinched like he wanted to turn around and then thought better of it. Being recognized as a foreigner had surprised him in some way a gun in the back hadn't.

"Here's what you're going to do," David said. "When we get inside, go to the man behind the desk and give him the pretty red package. Say it's something for the boss and reach out and hand it to him. You understand?"

Fat Jon nodded.

"Say the words."

"I'll hand him the package," Fat Jon said.

"Don't try to signal him or do anything unfortunate," David said. "I want you to know—and this is a scientific fact—that there is no scenario in which I'm dead and you're still alive. You want to get through this, then you help me do what I'm trying to do. Right?"

"Right."

"Then hit the buzzer."

Fat Jon pushed the button, and a second later they were buzzed in.

They walked into the lobby, David a half step behind Fat John. He stuck his pistol in his belt at the small of his back. The Windbreaker hung down over it. He reached into his pants pocket and pulled out the leather sap, cupping it in his hand and keeping in low.

The lobby had been decked out expensive and modern, white gleaming marble and mirrors and a big desk with a guy behind it almost as big. He wore a dark suit. No-nonsense haircut. He stood as David and Fat Jon approached.

His eyes shifted to David. "Who's that?"

"Forget him." Jon held out the gift-wrapped package

as instructed. "I'm supposed to drop this off for the boss. Important stuff."

It almost never fails. When someone is handed something, they reach out to take it. Reflex.

So when the guy behind the desk reached for the package, David stepped forward quickly and brought the sap down hard on the man's wrist. There was a muted *snap*, and the man hissed breath into his lungs for a scream.

But David didn't let that happen. A backhand swipe with the sap caught the guy just under his eye. Bone cracked and the guy folded, dropping into a heap behind the desk.

David drew his pistol again and pointed it at Fat Jon. The Turk's eyes were wide. He hadn't made any move to flee or fight and had gone pale.

David kept the gun on him as he circled behind the desk to examine his handiwork. The man was on the floor, but trying to push himself up, head twitching and wobbly. David brought the sap down hard on the base of his skull and that shut him down for good.

"Do you need a key or anything to take the elevator up?"

"The call button is behind the desk."

David found it and pushed it. A moment later it dinged and the doors slid open. David handed the red wrapped package back to Fat Jon who took it like he was being handed a rattlesnake.

David paused a moment when he felt his phone vibrate in his pocket. He took it out and read the text from Amy.

Where are you???

He ignored the message and returned the phone to his pocket. *She's going to be pissed.*

With his pistol, David motioned Fat Jon toward the elevator. They boarded.

Then up.

"He said to wait, so we wait."

The Chechen shrugged, went to the sideboard, and poured himself three fingers of bourbon. The name he'd taken since being relocated to America was Reagan Washington, a choice he now regretted, but it was too late to change his driver's license, passport, and other forged documents. He sipped the bourbon. At least Dante Payne's booze was good. Dante had expensive tastes. Reagan glanced around the room in which they'd chosen to wait. Billiard table. A long, richly polished wooden bar, leather chairs and tables. There were three doors leading out to plush bedrooms, a full kitchen, and a wide veranda with an excellent view. It looked like a London club for MPs and the nobility had been transported to Payne's building. Dante Payne was worth millions.

Which is why Reagan supposed Payne had hired five men to do a job Reagan could easily have accomplished solo. He supposed men with copious amounts of wealth cared little for how they wasted money.

"If I'm told to wait then I will," Reagan said. "But I'm not going to pretend to like it. My time's as valuable as anyone else's."

"Drink bourbon or kill a man," said the Arab behind him. "You're paid the same, so why rush? Why worry?"

Reagan shrugged again without turning. He didn't need to see the Arab or the other two. He'd memorized the room in an eye blink before turning away to pour his drink. The Arab sat at the bar drinking a cup of strong black coffee. Whereas Reagan was a lean, wiry man with angular features, the Arab was thick like a wrestler, light skinned, head bald and gleaming, a jaw so square it made him look like a cartoon character, dark blue stubble like icing.

The other two sat on opposite ends of the leather sofa. The one who looked a little too old to be here was also an Arab, gray at the temple and a salt-and-pepper mustache. He wore the most expensive suit in the room and seemed more like a prosperous merchant than a hired killer. He spent most of his time glaring down at his smartphone. The man on the other end of the couch paged through the style section of yesterday's newspaper. Reagan guessed he might be a Serb. He had a dour expression and sunken cheeks and smoked a harsh foreign brand of cigarettes.

Reagan hadn't been informed yet if they were working as a team or individually, so he'd put off learning their names.

He filled the glass with more bourbon, no ice.

"Go easy on that."

Now Reagan did turn around. Slowly. It had been the other Arab who'd spoken, the one on the couch. "Is that advice?" Reagan asked. "Or are you telling me what to do?"

"I'm telling you that if we have business tonight, I don't want a drunk watching my back."

Reagan drew breath to spit an insult, but the other Arab chimed in first.

"He's right. I never touch liquor. It addles the brain. Let me call the serving girl back. She can fetch you a coffee."

Two against one now. Reagan elected to change tactics. "What about you?" he asked the Serb. "You don't talk?"

The Serb's gaze flicked up from the newspaper. His eyes were like two polished, black river stones. "I talk," he said softly. "When I have something to say." He went back to reading.

Reagan turned abruptly back to the sideboard and filled the glass with bourbon, loudly clinking the bottle against the glass and spilling some over his fingers. He turned back and scowled at the others, tossed back the bourbon in one go. It burned going down, and Reagan liked it.

It occurred to him that he should summon up some kind of clever insult, for the Arab on the couch at least. Something subtle to show he would not endure a slight, but nothing harsh enough to provoke—

A ding.

Four heads turned toward the elevator door.

It slid open and two men walked out, a fat one with a slow face and a Christmas present in his hands, and behind him some tall American. The way he was standing behind the fat one . . .

Reagan's mind shifted into a different gear, everything going into slow motion. His brain processed and ordered a thousand bits of information in the split second it took his hand to flash inside his jacket and draw his pistol.

He recalled the file Dante had sent him and the picture of the woman he wanted eliminated, the lawyer from the district attorney's office. He could also vividly picture the third photograph in his mind.

The husband.

Reagan lifted his pistol to shoot, but before he could squeeze the trigger, the room shook with gunfire.

He saw the Serb shooting in his peripheral vision. Reagan was fast. It was impossible the Serb could be faster, but Reagan put it together in a fraction of a second. The Serb's pistol had been in his lap the whole time, hidden underneath the newspaper.

Everyone in the room was in motion.

The fat man with the Christmas gift died first.

When the Serb opened fire, the husband grabbed the fat one and dragged him along as a shield as he moved rapidly to the side. Bloody red flowers bloomed across the fat man's chest, and the husband's pistol came around him to return fire, bucking in his hands and spitting lead.

That's when the coffee-drinking Arab at the bar went down, a shot ripping through his throat. Blood sprayed, and the Arab's hands went up uselessly to staunch the hot flow as he tilted from the barstool and hit the floor with a thud.

The two on the couch had already rolled over the back of it, ducking behind as the husband blazed away, stuffing flying up in white puffy clouds.

Reagan squeezed the trigger three times fast, but the husband shifted his shield and the shots smacked meaty and wet into the fat man's gut.

In the slow-motion scene that unfolded before him, Reagan saw what the husband was doing. He was trying to keep the shield on his feet long enough to make it to the door on the other side of the billiard table. But the fat man was full of holes and bleeding. His legs had turned to noodles, and the only thing keeping him up was the husband's grip on his collar. What had started as a shield was now a liability, the dead weight slowing him down.

The husband dropped the body as he darted for the hallway beyond the billiard table. That's what Reagan had been waiting for. He lifted his pistol to fire just as the husband leaped for the open doorway. He fired twice, missing his target by a fraction of an inch.

"Shit!"

He looked back at the second Arab and the Serb who were emerging from behind the couch. They were both slapping fresh magazines into their pistols.

Reagan waved his gun at them. "Come on! He's getting away!"

Reagan headed for the doorway, sensing the others behind him. He rounded the corner cautiously, gun up and ready. In this sort of situation, the prey had the advantage over the predator, especially if the prey had teeth. The husband could flee as fast as he pleased, but Reagan had to round each corner carefully, gun raised in anticipation of a possible ambush.

He moved down the hall to an intersection where another hall led out to a wide veranda. He waved the other two down the hall toward the veranda and followed the main hall himself. He came to a narrow stairwell and spiraled down.

And down.

On the ground floor, he paused at an outside door and looked at a row of eight hooks screwed into the wall.

Car keys hung from seven of the eight hooks. He kicked open the door into the ground-floor garage, went into a crouch, and brought his pistol up to the ready.

Nothing.

He stood, looked around. The garage door to the street was open. Eight parking spaces and only seven vehicles. The space between a mint condition 1965 Corvette Stingray and a brand-new Land Rover was empty.

Fuck. Fuck. Fuck.

Reagan sighed heavily and returned to the billiards lounge upstairs where he found the Arab and the Serb waiting for him.

The Serb held the red gift-wrapped package in his hands. "This is what Mr. Payne was waiting for."

"Don't open it," Reagan said.

The Serb's face remained blank. "I wasn't."

All of their cell phones rang at once.

Reagan looked at his phone. No name but a number he recognized. "It's him."

CHAPTER SEVENTEEN

David dropped the fat man and dove through the open doorway as the pistol shots whizzed over him. He tucked, rolled, and came up running. Down the hallway and then down the stairs.

That didn't go like I'd hoped.

David's plan had been to catch Dante Payne and his cronies flat-footed. If there was a chance to end all of this quickly, David wanted to seize it. Instead, he'd walked into a shooting gallery. He'd wanted to go on the offense, but now found himself running. Whatever advantage of surprise he might have had before was blown now.

He paused at a line of hooks on the wall with the car keys and examined his options. One of the key chains said Audi. He grabbed it and rushed into the garage.

Dante apparently enjoyed spending a chunk of his wealth on expensive automobiles. The Audi was a silver R8 Spyder convertible. The top was already down, and David hopped in and cranked the ignition. The garage door opener was clipped to the sun visor. David mashed the button. The garage door went up, and he pulled out onto the quiet residential street. He drove to the end of the block, and when he didn't see any pursuit in his rearview mirror, he flipped on the headlights and pointed the Audi toward Midtown.

David fished his phone out of his pocket and composed a text to Charlie.

Two hours. You pick the Chinese restaurant. Prefer midtown.

A moment later:

Imperial Garden on 55th.

David confirmed the meeting and headed for the hotel as fast as he could without drawing attention. He'd ignored three more of Amy's texts and was entering dangerous marital territory. Facing a room full of gunmen was something David was used to. God help him if Amy felt ignored.

He arrived at the hotel and eschewed the ramp down into the parking garage, choosing instead to park out front, uniformed parking valets scurrying out of his way as David brought the Audi to an abrupt halt.

One of the college-age valets stepped forward to open the driver's side door for David. He was pretending the smudge on his upper lip was a mustache. "Valet-park it for you, sir?"

David pulled a roll of cash out of his pants pocket, peeled off a twenty, and handed it to the valet. "Can we keep it close? I might have to leave in a hurry."

The kid sheepishly looked from David to the

twenty-dollar bill in his hand and back to David. "Honestly, sir, I'm supposed to keep this lane clear. Lots of taxis. Lots of pickups and drop-offs. Just policy, you understand."

"How about doing me a favor? Just this once."

The kid looked pained. "I'm really not supposed to."

David gave the kid three more twenties.

"This car won't budge from this spot, sir," the valet said. "Count on it."

"Thanks," David said. "Leave the keys in, okay? I might not have time to look for you."

"Understood, sir," the valet assured him.

David headed into the hotel lobby at a brisk walk, eyes darting into every shadow. His instinct was to hunt down Larry and find out if anything had changed. It was difficult to disregard his training. Secure the perimeter. Reinforce the defenses, plug the holes. But he had to see Amy. His wife was alone. It wasn't fair to leave her sweating it out up there, not knowing what was happening. So he headed toward the main bank of elevators. He'd see Amy and let her know that—

He saw the bellhop on an intercept course for him.

At first glance, the kid didn't seem like much, skinny and young. David scanned his clothing for pistol bulges but didn't think the bellhop was packing. He tensed as the kid continued toward him, a basic instinct telling him to draw his weapon.

A more sophisticated instinct told him not to.

The bellhop dodged drunken Shriners and doggedly beelined for David. He clutched the rolled-up newspaper with purpose. *Gun,* thought David. It would be simplicity itself to hide a pistol in the newspaper. Again, he itched to draw his pistol on the approaching bellhop but restrained himself. David's eyes pinballed around the lobby again in case the bellhop was a decoy, but didn't see anything obvious.

The kid stopped abruptly in front of David, bowed crisply, smiled, and offered the newspaper. "Mr. Sparrow, here's the newspaper you asked for."

A pause. Then David reached out and took the newspaper. "I almost killed you."

The smile dropped from the bellhop's face. "What?"

"Never mind," David said. "Thank you for the newspaper."

The bellhop nodded curtly, turned on his heel, and sped away.

David stepped to the side, out of the ebb and flow of the Shriners who milled about the hotel lobby. He unfolded the newspaper and found a handwritten note on hotel stationery.

Cops in the hotel. They found the Escalade in the parking garage.

L

Good of Larry to give him the heads-up. David folded the note and shoved it into the pocket of his Windbreaker. His eyes flicked to the hotel's main entrance. Two uniformed police officers were talking to the doorman, showing him a photograph.

Shit.

David had no doubt they were showing around a picture of him. He wondered briefly if it was his driver's license photo or his service photo. Or something else.

He turned away before they could look up and spot him. He ducked into an alcove, a couple of potted plants on either side of him. He took out his phone and punched in a number.

She picked up after the second ring. "Where the hell have you been?"

"I'm in the lobby," he said quietly. "But I can't come up."

A pause. "Why not? What's going on? Why are you whispering?"

"Police," David said. "I'm sorry. I've got to get out of here."

"What are you going to do?" she asked.

"I'm already doing it," David said. "I've got to take care of this now. Tonight. Or we'll never be safe."

"What about Bert?"

David thought a moment before saying, "He sold us out."

Amy's breath caught. A few seconds later, she said, "What are our options?"

"I finish it," David said. "It's the only choice."

Long seconds passed and for a moment David thought she'd hung up on her end. At last she asked, "What do you need me to do?"

"Nothing," David said. "Stay where you are. Stay safe. I'll come for you when it's done."

Another long pause. Finally she said, "I love you."

He cleared his throat. "I love you, too."

"Call me later."

"I will."

They hung up.

David glanced back. The two cops were crossing the lobby, coming toward him, not urgently but not casually, either. No way to get back to the Audi out front without walking straight past them.

He turned and headed deeper into the hotel.

"Sir?"

David ignored the voice behind him, kept walking but at the same pace. *Just act like you don't hear. Go about your business. You're not doing anything wrong. No problems.*

"Sir!" More vehemently this time.

David kept walking until he got around the corner and out of their line of sight, and then he broke into a run.

He found himself in the convention center part of the hotel, and the wide hall was packed with rosy-cheeked Shriners, drinks in hands, sports jackets, little fez hats perched at jaunty angles on balding heads. David dove into the crowd, hoping to lose himself completely before the police caught up with him. He allowed himself a glance back and saw two blue police hats bobbing along across the fez sea.

David paused at a table on which a fruit platter and an assortment of cheese and crackers had been mauled over by the crowd. Someone had absently set his fez on the corner of the table. David snatched it up and put it on, slumped his shoulders and bent to conceal his height. He continued weaving his way through the crowd into a large ballroom.

There was some kind of big party under way, a raised stage against the far wall with a podium and microphone, all the trappings of an awards ceremony or some similar event. David looked up and saw the netting covering the ceiling. It sagged with balloons, poised for a drop. The Shriners were ready to celebrate something big.

Looks fun. Wish I could join you.

David headed for a door off to the side of the stage.

If it went back to the kitchens, maybe David could cut through and circle back to the front where he'd left the Audi parked. Or if that was too risky he could head out on foot. He just needed to get out of the hotel. The closer he got to the stage, the thicker and rowdier the crowd became. Somewhere somebody had flipped on a stereo system and the Hollies' "Long Cool Woman" jazzed the crowd into a party frenzy.

He pushed through the mass of people until he reached the door next to the stage. He glanced back. The cops were gently but insistently easing people out of the way as they kept walking directly toward him.

Losing them in the crowd hadn't worked. He'd have to bolt.

He was about to dive through the door when he noticed the rope hanging down near the stage. He followed it up to the netting, thought about it for a fraction of a second, then gave the rope a yank.

The netting split and released the balloons, and along with it confetti glittered down like cheap starlight. The display had the desired effect. The crowd let out a big cheer, and partygoers hugged one another, slapped one another on the back, and the two cops suddenly found themselves in a logjam of revelers.

David went through the door and closed it again, muting the party behind him. He was in a service corridor. Less crowded, easier to move.

A waiter approached him with a tray of dirty glasses. "Sir, guests aren't allowed back—"

"This is a medical emergency," David said quickly. "Larry Meadows said I could get to the bar from here. There's no fast way to get past that party crowd."

"Oh, of course." The waiter gestured back down the

corridor. "Turn the corner and keep going until you come to the T intersection. Right takes you back to the kitchens, but turning left takes you up to the lounge."

"Thanks." David headed the way he'd been directed at a fast walk.

"Sir," came the voice from behind. "Sir, we'd like a word if you please."

David broke into a run. No point pretending anymore.

"Stop!" yelled the officer.

Their footfalls echoed loudly as they gave chase.

David scrolled through his options as he ran. Two New York street cops. Probably good tough men, but with David's training he could put them out of action quickly. But what if he hurt them too badly? He had to believe that he and Amy would come through on the other side of this mess okay, and when that happened he didn't want to have to explain injuring or killing two of NYPD's finest. There was too much to explain already.

No, he couldn't engage them on that level. The only choice was to evade and escape.

He rounded the corner and spotted a cart filled with dirty dishes and empty wine bottles. He grabbed it as he ran past, pulled it into the center of the corridor behind him and kept running.

A second later, David heard the crash and clatter behind him followed by some inventive curses from the cops, but he didn't bother to turn and see the result. He turned left at the T intersection and found himself in the hotel bar two seconds later.

The bartender cast him a curious glance as David emerged from the kitchen but was too busy and uninterested to say anything. David kept walking until he was out of the bar, through the lobby, and back at the hotel's front entrance again.

To his great relief, the Audi was still where he'd left it. It comforted David in some strange way to know he could still count on a New York City parking valet to take a bribe seriously.

He hopped in, cranked the ignition, and pulled into traffic. A glance in the rearview mirror showed him two pissed cops bursting out of the hotel room. They watched him drive away, one already bringing a radio to his face to report what had happened.

David gave himself exactly five minutes to ditch the Audi. It was an exquisite vehicle but far too conspicuous.

He zigged and zagged until he found himself on a quiet street. At the very least he could park the car and walk away. The subway could take him to meet Charlie, but David didn't like the idea of waiting around on subway platforms the rest of the night. He had too much work to do. He needed a vehicle.

A second later, he spotted a likely suspect. He pulled the Audi alongside a guy who was just getting out of his car with a bag of takeout. David wished the guy didn't look so honest, but beggars couldn't be choosers.

And what does a dishonest guy look like anyway? An eye patch and a tattoo of a skull on his neck?

"Hey," David called. "That your car?"

The guy paused, frowned. "Yeah."

David took the keys out of the Audi's ignition, held them up for the guy to see. "Trade you."

"Fuck off."

"I'm serious," David said. "I've got to get out of here, and I can't take this."

The guy's eyes went from the Audi to his twelve-year-old Toyota. It had minor body damage along the front fender. David could tell he was thinking it over.

"I don't know, man," he said. "Seems like some kind of setup."

"You probably know somebody who can make this work," David said. "A cousin or a friend with the right connections." David's father was fond of a saying. *In every heart there is a little larceny.* Even chopped for parts, the Audi was worth twenty times the guy's junker.

But he'd paused too long to think about it.

"I'll trade you." A voice from the shadows.

David's gaze shifted to the next stoop, a man sitting in the dark, grubby, drinking a can of something from a little paper bag.

Damn, I didn't even see him. I'm rustier than I thought.

The guy with the takeout looked relieved and walked away.

The guy on the stoop heaved to his feet with a grunt and took a set of keys out of his pocket. He gestured with his chin at something across the street.

David looked. And was not impressed. "What is that?"

"A 1977 Dodge Aspen."

"That's more rust than I've ever seen on a single car before."

"I work on the engine myself," the guy said. "Changed the oil last week. New spark plugs. That V8 hums, man."

David sighed. "Right."

They traded keys.

"Just let me get one thing out of the trunk," he said.

He watched as the man opened the trunk, the hinges complaining with a rusty squeal that made David wince.

The guy took out a stained and ratty canvas tarp and tossed it over the Audi.

He looked at David. "You'd better get moving."

David nodded. "Good doing business with you."

David climbed in behind the wheel of the Dodge. The interior smelled like cigarettes and stale beer. A cardboard air freshener in the shape of a pine tree hung from the rearview mirror. *Nice try.* He rolled down the window.

He cranked the engine and was relieved when it turned over on the first try. He revved the engine experimentally. It ran just as smooth as the guy had claimed it would.

Good enough.

He hit the headlights, pulled away from the curb, and went to find the Imperial Gardens Chinese restaurant.

Dante Payne stood fuming in his billiard parlor, surveying the damage and dead bodies. The carpets would have to come up. So much blood. A stupid and idle thought, but there it was.

"He dares." Payne's voice trembled with barely controlled rage. "In my own home, he dares."

Yousef stood behind the bar and found a bottle of good Pinot Noir already opened. He poured himself a glass, sniffed it, and sipped. Not bad. "If you knew this man the way I do, you would not be surprised. He will not wait passively while you go after him."

"Yes, thank you for your assessment, Yousef," Payne said sharply. "I realize I should have waited for you to handle things. You've made that abundantly clear, so give it a rest."

Yousef shrugged and appraised the other three gun-men in the room—the living ones. Upon first blush all of them seemed competent and dangerous, but there was something about the Chechen that gave him pause. Arro-gant hostility boiled just below the surface, some fester-ing resentment that threatened to erupt. If that happened at the wrong moment, it could be bad. They all carried scars inside and out, harbored grudges, nursed vendettas. Yousef himself had been lured to the city for just such a chance at payback. But a man waited until the right time, kept control of himself, remained professional.

The young Chechen—Reagan was his name, Yousef recalled—seemed on a hair trigger. He would bear watching.

Payne cursed and paced the room. He paused over one of the corpses, the fat one. He kicked it, hard. "Use-less bastard!"

The body shifted, and something that had been half hidden underneath the body caught Payne's eye, he bent and picked it up, showed it triumphantly to Yousef. A small package wrapped brightly in red. The relief upon seeing the package erased all thoughts of the ruined carpet.

"You see, Yousef, my methods are not entirely with-out merit after all," Payne said smugly. "Here we've won half the battle already."

Payne unwrapped the package slowly, savoring the moment. He tossed the wrapping aside. He opened the box, looked into it, and the smiled dropped abruptly from his face.

He slowly withdrew the ceramic mug, turned it over in his hands like he was examining some obscure alien artifact. There was a crude illustration of a curvaceous woman in a skimpy nurse's uniform followed by the words *Get Well Soon. There are better things to do in bed.*

"Son of a bitch!"

Payne hurled the mug against the wall where it shattered into dozens of pieces.

Yousef turned his back to hide his grin and topped off his glass of wine.

CHAPTER EIGHTEEN

"Noodles. Pork. Duck. Ribs. Pot stickers. Egg rolls." Charlie Finn scanned the table, frowning at the spread. "No, no, something's missing."

"There's enough here to feed Hong Kong," David said.

"There is a delicate balance of flavors at stake here," Charlie explained. "I need just a little bit of every—" He snapped his fingers suddenly. "Dumplings!"

Charlie flagged down the waitress and reminded her to bring pork dumplings.

David anxiously pushed rice around on his plate with a fork. He wasn't hungry and didn't have time for this. But Charlie Finn was doing him a favor. *Another* one.

"You're not hungry?" Charlie shoveled noodles into his mouth with chopsticks.

"I'm worried," David said. "I'm not getting the job done."

He'd already related to Charlie his failure at Payne's building, how he'd almost gotten himself shot. And the police had chased him away when he'd tried to get in to see Amy. Getting back inside, onto the elevator and up to the top floor to see her would be too risky until matters were finished. Getting arrested wasn't an option. He wouldn't be able to fix this situation from a jail cell.

"I don't mean to spoil your meal, Charlie. But I've got a lot on my mind."

"You're not spoiling it," Charlie said. "This is the *best* kind of Chinese food."

"What kind is that?"

"Free. You're still paying, right?"

David allowed himself a tired smile. "I thought you were the hot dog cart czar of New York. Surely, you can afford your own noodles."

"I never pay for Chinese food."

"Explain."

"Because it's my favorite."

"Explain better."

"I started eating it all the time." Charlie paused to bite off half an egg roll. "It became less special. It got old. It was my favorite, but it got old and dull, and your favorite's not supposed to do that. So I decided I'd never buy it again. It could only be a gift. And now it's special again. Like Christmas."

"You're a philosopher, Charlie."

"Philosophy is just tricks you play on yourself to get through the week."

The dumplings arrived, and Charlie snatched one with his chopsticks almost before the dish hit the table. He popped it into his mouth. The look on his face might have indicated the dumpling had been flown straight from China just for him.

David put his napkin on the table. "Charlie, I gotta go. It's not that I don't want to hang around eating noodles . . ."

Charlie's face turned serious. "Yeah. It was just, you know, good eating with you. Let me see the flash drive."

"Here?"

"Might as well."

Charlie's leather satchel hung from the back of his chair. He pulled it around onto his lap, opened it, and took out a laptop and some little black piece of hardware David didn't recognize. It was connected to the computer by a USB cord.

Charlie reached out. "Let's have it."

David looked around then took the flash drive out of his pocket and handed it over. Charlie plugged it into the black box then started typing at the laptop with one hand. He used the other to grab another egg roll.

Charlie chewed and typed. David waited.

"It's going to take me awhile to get at these files," Charlie said. "Better than average security on here. But half the time, they secure the files but not the directory, ya know? I mean, security, yeah, but not the same."

"You're talking over my head, Charlie."

"Like a bank," Charlie said. "They might lock up all the money, but nobody covers up the sign out front. They hide the money, not the bank. You can't get inside, but at least you know which bank you can't get inside of, right? If this guy used his own personal computer to save these files, the . . ." Charlie blinked at the computer screen. "Whoa."

"What?"

"Pope," Charlie said.

"I'm having trouble believing this conspiracy goes as far as the Pope."

"Not *the* Pope," Charlie said. "Calvin Pope."

A flicker of a spark deep in David's brain. "Why do I know that name?"

"You've met him. The debrief hangar when you'd bring somebody back," Charlie reminded him.

The debrief hangar. Any number of hangars on any number of American military bases in the world actually. When David had been an active solo operative, his mission could have been almost anything. Take a message to somebody deep undercover or bring a message back home. Blow something up. Bring somebody out or make sure somebody stayed lost. He'd been nearly killed a score of times, the worst being getting out of Iran with pictures of a uranium enrichment facility.

On those occasions when he brought somebody out, they'd usually all end up in the debrief hangar, David taken to one end for his debriefing and whomever he'd rescued getting similar treatment on the other side. The hangar was simply the most immediate and convenient place to set up shop. After debriefings, they'd be escorted to separate aircraft and away they'd go never to cross paths again. David would be rotated back to a base in Italy or Germany for R&R before starting the brief for his next mission. The target would be turned over to some handler, usually a CIA spook or maybe somebody for Military Intelligence depending on the situation. More often than not, the guy was . . .

David closed his eyes, using the memory recall exercise from training and remembered . . . the debrief hangar—

—Men in uniforms—

—Spooks in darks suits and—

—The face of—

Calvin Pope.

David's eyes popped open again, and he looked at Charlie. "What does it mean?"

"I don't know," Charlie said. "But these are his files, or at least, somebody used his computer."

"How long to break the security?"

Charlie waved at the laptop. "I'll need to use a setup with a little more horsepower than this. But, yeah. I'll get in there. Maybe a few hours. What about you? You still hoping to take the battle to Dante Payne up close and personal?"

"I was hoping . . . but I blew any chance of surprise."

"Maybe that could work for us. If he knows you're coming at him, he'll hole up, circle the wagons."

"So he holes up somewhere, but I don't know where. You're the one who told me how many properties he owned," David said. "And even if I did find them, I'd be facing Payne's entire goon squad, all of his guns against me alone."

"And how's that different than what we did together for almost four years?" Charlie said. "Pakistan. Iran. Syria. You were *trained* to be surrounded and outnumbered. You run into the places where everyone else is running out."

Charlie grinned. "Remember what they used to say? What's the good thing about being surrounded?"

"You get to shoot in every direction," David said.

"Right." Charlie speared another dumpling.

David sighed. *He's right. I've already given up before*

*I've even started. This is why, isn't it? The Army saw some-
thing in me I couldn't see in myself until now. This is
why they sidelined me. I've lost my edge.*

"And one more thing," Charlie said. "You're not alone.
You've got me. Just like old times. You running once
more into the breach, and me as your eye in the sky."

Charlie reached into his shirt pocket and came out
with a folded piece of paper. He unfolded the paper and
slid it across the table toward David between the
dish of dumplings and a pot of green tea. A computer
printout. Five street addresses.

David took the paper, squinted at it. "What's this?"

"You're right about Payne having too many properties," Charlie said. "So I narrowed them down. Anything purely commercial, I crossed off the list. There
were plenty of residential properties but filled with
tenants. It was easy to check. So I ended up with a
list of five places where he might hide. It's a place to
start."

David nodded. "A place to start." *Running into places
where everyone else is running out.*

"How long for you to get back to the Bronx and get
set up?" David asked.

"I don't need to go back." Charlie pointed out the
window.

David looked out the window at a hot dog cart parked
next to a Con Ed step van. "One of yours?"

Charlie glanced out the window. "The hot dog cart?
No. Well, yes actually now that I get a look at it. I meant
the Con Ed van. I have a complete setup in there, satel-
lite dish on top with an uplink." He handed David a
Bluetooth. "And I'll be in your ear every step of the way.
There's just one last thing."

David looked at him, waited.

"My payment," Charlie said.

"Payment?"

"If you ever get back inside," Charlie said. "You take me with you."

David didn't need to ask what he meant.

"Charlie, the Army put me on indefinite leave. I gave up waiting for them to activate me again. I'm a washout."

"I know." Charlie frowned. "I can see the give-up in your face. I know what it looks like because I've been there. So believe me, man, the first step back is just to say, hell yeah, I'll grab the chance if it comes along. It might never come, but you'll be ready if it does. Sounds simple, but it's a very necessary attitude adjustment."

David thought about it, tried to think if that meant anything. It was important to Charlie, and that was enough.

"Okay," David said. "If they ever call me back, I'll speak up for you. And be proud to do it."

They shook hands.

"But first, I finish the dumplings," Charlie said. "And you go on the hunt."

CHAPTER NINETEEN

David drove the Dodge Aspen through the park to the East Side, and affixed the Bluetooth to his right ear. "I'm online, eye in the sky."

"I've got you," Charlie's voice buzzed in his ear. The reception was strong and clear. Charlie only used the best equipment. "GPS has you heading east on the Sixty-fifth Street Transverse. Which one you trying first?"

"You put these places in order of likelihood?" David asked.

"Yeah. I ran a program that sorted according to proximity, square footage, defensibility—"

"I trust you," David said. "Let's not sweat the details. Number two on the list is closest."

"That's East Sixty-ninth Street. Hold on." Charlie came back a moment later and said, "No police activity in the area. I think you're clear."

"Good. Tell me about this place."

"A bar called Jerry's," Charlie said. "One of the first buildings Dante Payne bought when he was an up-and-comer. I'm pulling up the financials now. Looks like he took over payments from the old owner. Probably some kind of strong arm situation there."

"Why did this place make the list?"

"I'm looking at construction permits," Charlie said. "The entire upstairs was done over residential two years ago. Payne could be hunkered down there with his boys, no problem."

"Charlie, how do we know he didn't check into a hotel suite or hop a plane to Hawaii?"

"He hasn't used his credit card."

"You know that?"

"I know everything."

"How's it coming with the flash drive?" David asked.

"I have a code breaker program running now, wrote the software myself. Just a matter of time."

"Let me know."

On the other side of the park, David turned the Dodge north on Madison and then hung a right on Sixty-ninth. A few blocks later he spotted the old neon sign flickering the word JERRY's in dingy red. He parked on the street.

"I'm offline for a bit, Charlie."

"Understood. Good hunting."

David took off the Bluetooth and slipped it into his pants pocket. He checked his pistols. He used one of the calming techniques to prepare. He took in a deep breath. He was an instrument of cold metal. His veins flowed with ice. He imagined himself in a world of cool blue colors. He let the breath out slowly.

David got out of the Dodge and entered through the bar's open door, pausing just inside.

The interior was dim, lighting from behind the bar and over the pool table and an old glowing jukebox in the corner. David's eyes raked the place. Head count: bartender behind the bar. Two guys playing cards at a table to the right. Two more shooting pool to the left.

Exits: Two doors for restrooms near the bar. On the far side of the room beyond the pool table another door with a sign on it saying *private*.

He mentally flagged that door for later.

All heads turned to David, hard men with grim eyes. This wasn't a drinking establishment. It was a weigh station disguised as a bar. These troops probably reported to some lieutenant instead of to Payne directly, low-level bagmen and leg breakers, running numbers, keeping the streetwalkers in line, and making sure the dime bag pushers were supplied. Payne likely had places such as this all over the city, the cash flowing up through the food chain, laundered along the way before finding its way into various safe deposit boxes.

Payne was rich now. He didn't need the pittance of tribute a place like this would produce. For a man like Payne, it was the network that was more valuable to him, ground troops to do his bidding, his eyes and ears.

"We're closed," the bartender said.

David ignored him and walked toward the bar, keeping an eye on the men playing cards and pool in the mirror behind the bartender. They were clumsy bruisers, and David almost dismissed the need to keep track of them in the reflection.

But he did anyway. Instinct. Training.

"I guess you didn't hear me, friend. We're closed."

David leaned on the bar. His smile didn't touch his eyes. "You look open to me."

"Fuck how it looks to you. Turn around and start walking."

"Is Dante Payne upstairs?"

The name made the bartender's eye twitch.

In the mirror, David watched one of the card players push away from his table and rise. He went to the front of the bar, pulled the door closed, and turned the lock.

David's eyes shifted to watch one of the pool players coming toward him, gripping a cue like a club. He moved with quiet confidence like a man about to calmly and routinely take out the trash.

"You made a mistake," said the bartender.

The guy behind David swung the pool cue at his head.

David spun and caught the fat part of the cue in his palm with a loud *smack*. His other hand shot out to strike his attacker in the solar plexus. The guy staggered back, mouth working for air.

David spun back to the bar, bringing the pool cue around fast. The bartender had produced a double barrel shotgun and leveled it at David's face.

David knocked the shotgun upward with the stick, and both barrels discharged into a rack of glasses over the bar, glass spraying over the scene.

David jabbed the end of the cue hard into the bartender's eye. He screamed and dropped the shotgun, turning away to paw at his face.

The others closed on David.

He broke the cue over the other pool player's head with a crack, and the guy went down. David kicked him in the face for good measure, felt his jaw crunch and go loose on impact.

A glint of metal caught David's eye.

One of the card players thrust a wicked little stiletto straight at David's gut.

David sidestepped and grabbed the attacker's wrist and twisted until he heard a sickening snap. The man screamed and dropped the knife, and David kicked him back into the last man and both went over into a heap on the floor.

The man with the broken wrist writhed and moaned.

The other one was still game and began scrambling to his feet. David closed on him in a split second, slamming a fist into the cheekbone under his left eye. His head spun around, and he went down and stayed there.

"Shit, you broke my wrist," said the other one. "Fucking broke it."

David kicked him hard in the head, and the complaining stopped.

He circled behind the bar and saw the bartender curled on the floor, both hands clapped tightly over one eye, bright red blood oozing through the fingers. He was struggling to decide if he should climb back to his feet again or just lie there, and the result was a pathetic squirming that wasn't accomplishing anything.

"You blinded me."

"Stay down there," David told him.

He picked up the shotgun and broke the breach, removed the spent shells and tossed them aside. He searched behind the bar and found a cubby with a box of twelve-gauge double aught. He reloaded and shoved a handful of loose shells into his pocket. He pointed the shotgun down at the trembling man. The bartender's one good eye went wide.

"Dante Payne."

"I don't know," the bartender said.

"Try again."

"I'm telling you, I don't know," said the bartender.

"I've never even met him. I've never seen him in here. You think he comes slumming around here? He doesn't have to do that. Why should he?"

"This is his place," David said. "He owns it."

"Sure. He's got lots of places. He has other people run them. We never see him."

"Who do you answer to?"

"Marco Jakes."

"Is he upstairs?"

"No."

"Who's up there?"

"Just Gina."

David slammed the butt of the shotgun into the bartender's gut. The man yelled and gagged, coughed up a mouthful of bile that dripped over his lips and made a little puddle on the floor next to his head. He sucked ragged for breath, spit more bile onto the floor.

"Jesus," he croaked.

"Who else?" David asked.

"Nobody. I'm telling you, just Gina. That's all."

"What does she do?"

"Like a hostess," the bartender explained. "But there's no party tonight."

"You tell me who else is up there or you get both barrels," David told him.

"Christ, just Gina. I swear."

David stuffed a rag in the bartender's mouth. Then he ripped an apron in half and bound his wrist and ankles.

He grabbed the shotgun again and went back around to the front of the bar. He gave the others a kick as he passed them, but they were all still out cold.

He went to the door marked PRIVATE, paused and listened, gripping the twelve gauge tightly. He didn't hear anything, but anyone upstairs would have heard the racket when the bartender had cut loose with the shotgun earlier. David wasn't going to catch anyone by surprise, but it couldn't be helped. He had to go up there. He hadn't come all this way and knocked the hell out of five men *not* to have a look.

He pushed open the door. Narrow stairs leading up, dimly lit by a single bulb hanging from a wire. It cast fuzzy yellow light. David climbed. The stairs creaked. There was a similar unremarkable door at the top, and again he paused to listen.

Nothing.

He took hold of the knob, turned it slowly and quietly. Inhale, hold it a second, exhale.

David swung the door open and rushed inside. He swept the shotgun in a wide arc, searching for a target, but nothing moved.

Upstairs was a different world from downstairs. David moved cautiously across thick white carpeting. The foyer was spacious, modern, and mirrored. The place smelled good, clean with a hint of vanilla. It looked like the same decorator from the lobby of Payne's building on the Upper West Side had taken a hand here.

Maybe Payne liked entrances bright with clean lines, like some kind of architectural sorbet to cleanse the palate before going into the rest of the living area. A hallway led right. The left side opened into a mirrored living room. Low white leather couches. A modern-art glass chandelier hung down from the ceiling casting glittering clean light over the room.

There were two more doors leading in different directions from the living room. David moved slowly keeping the shotgun in front of—

Movement.

He turned and fired at the movement, but it was a reflection in one of the wall mirrors. The shotgun blasted the mirror. Instinct kicked in, and David dove for the floor as the *pop pop pop* of a small automatic pistol echoed in the room. He rolled, fired blindly with the other barrel of the shotgun. The chandelier exploded in glass and sparks.

You're shooting at shadows, idiot. Identify the target. Don't fire wildly. Come on, man, you know how to do this.

He came up to one knee, one of his automatics in his hand like magic. He took a bead, but only glimpsed a wisp of thin cloth disappearing through the doorway across the room like an errant carnival banner in the wind.

David leaped up and chased after her.

She turned on him just as he caught up with her in the hallway. She tried to bring her gun around to have at him again, a little silver automatic, a .22 or .25 caliber, David thought.

If she'd fired from the hip, she might have had him, but she stretched her arm out, trying to shove the pistol in his face, and David's hand closed over hers, pushing the gun away and squeezing hard.

A sharp crack and another *pop* of gunfire that gouged the wall plaster. She yelped pain and dropped the pistol.

David grabbed her by the wrist, and she tried to twist away.

He shoved his pistol under her chin. "Stop it. Hold still."

She obeyed but stabbed at him with her eyes. David took a good look at her now. Tall and lean, body graceful and athletic. The silky thing she wore was long and laced up the middle. The fabric was light and clung to her. Muscles toned. Pilates maybe. Dark hair glossy and mussed. Lips so red and full that even her sneer looked good.

"You must be Gina."

She said nothing. Glared.

"I'm going to let you go," David said. "Don't do anything rash or I'll lay my pistol across your nose. You understand?"

Her glare didn't waver, but she nodded curtly.

"Step back."

She obeyed.

He bent, keeping his eyes on her, and retrieved the little silver pistol. He started to put it in the pocket of his Windbreaker and realized the Turk's Airweight revolver was still in there, so he switched sides and put it in the other pocket. He'd have a nice little collection by the end of the night.

If he made it that far.

Gina cradled one arm against her chest.

David said, "You're hurt."

"You broke my pinkie finger."

"I'm sorry."

She smiled contempt. "I'm sure you feel terrible."

"You were shooting at me."

"You shot at me first."

David considered that. There was a big difference between having an edge and being *on edge*. "Fair enough. If it matters, I wasn't looking for you. I was looking for Dante Payne. He owns the place, right?" *First you make them answer a question you know the answer to. That starts them talking.*

Gina crossed her arms and went stone-faced.

David returned the hard stare. "You've got nine more fingers."

"You'd enjoy it, I suppose."

"No, but I need answers to questions," David told her. "And I'm in a hurry."

"It's Dante's place. He lets me stay here. Part of my compensation. But he doesn't come here. I never see him."

"Then what's the place for?"

"People he wants me to entertain," Gina said. "Men."

"What kind of men?"

"Important men," she said. "Men Dante wants to impress or influence. They come here for . . . entertainment."

"You handle that yourself?"

"Occasionally," Gina said. "Mostly I coordinate. Find out what the men like, bring in the girls, supervise everything."

"Which men specifically?"

"We don't have to stand in the hall like this," she said. "We can have a seat. I can fix you a drink or—"

"Which men?" he repeated firmly.

"All kinds. Councilmen. Zoning commissioners. A congressman from upstate. Too many to remember all the names."

"And you organize everything?"

"Yes."

"There must be a list," David said. "A log of the men who come and go."

She hesitated, her mouth going tight.

"That's what I thought." David took her by the elbow,

not too gently but not hard enough to bruise, and guided her down the hallway. "Show me."

She jerked her arm away. "Fine."

She led him past a couple of bedrooms to a spacious office at the end of the hall. Bookshelves, chairs, a desk with a computer on top. A sideboard with a crystal decanter of random booze and a few tumblers. Bland modern art on the walls.

Gina went to one of the paintings and pried at the corner of the frame. The painting swung out revealing a small wall safe. Her thin fingers danced over the dial, working the combination. When finished, she turned the lever. There was a muted metallic *clunk*, and the safe door swung open. She started to reach inside.

David lifted his pistol. "Don't."

She backed away from the safe.

David glanced inside. No gun. He pulled out a leather-bound ledger. Underneath were other documents and a few bundles of cash. He left them.

He motioned Gina to one of the chairs with his pistol. She sat.

David circled behind the desk and sat on the other side. He opened the ledger and began scanning the pages. The entries were carefully written in a woman's neat penmanship. Names. The time and date of their visits. Contact information. Margin notes such as *plays rough* or *foot fetish*. In the wrong hands, the ledger could ruin hundreds of lives.

"Why don't you keep these records on the computer?"

Gina shrugged. "They told me to keep track. This is how I did it."

"What about the footage? Digital?"

Gina said nothing.

David's eye came up from the ledger to hers.

"Somebody else handles that," Gina said. "The cameras are hidden in the bedrooms. They record to a server somewhere. I don't have any sort of tech skills. I don't mess with it."

On a whim, David scanned the pages, searching. He found Bert's name, two entries about a week ago. Another entry three weeks before that.

This was taking too long. He stood, tucked the book under his arm. "I'm taking this."

A nervous smile flickered across Gina's face. She was trying now. No angry glare. "Well, that's bad news for me then. Marco won't like that."

"I'm thirsty," David told her. "Fix me a drink."

The smile faded before it really got started. She turned her head to look at the sideboard then looked back at David. "Sure."

She stood, went to the sideboard, her back to David. She reached for the decanter, uncorked it. She was a smart girl and moved slowly, some instinct telling her what was coming.

David raised the pistol and pointed it at the back of her head.

"I suppose I can just tell Marco that I refused to open the safe, and that's when you broke my finger." She tried to force a laugh, but her breath caught and it came out like a croak. She poured the drink, the lip of the decanter rattling against the rim of the tumbler as her hand shook. "You know, I wouldn't say anything. I wouldn't tell them about you."

Training. Protocols. He knew what to do with a loose end, knew that leaving her alive would just make trouble for him down the line. If David left without taking care of her, Gina's courage would come back, and she'd be on the phone in two minutes.

He lowered the pistol.

Gina waited, the tumbler in her hand, back muscles tight with anticipation.

"There's a lot of money in that safe," David said.

She turned slowly to face him, confusion on her face but a glimmer of hope, too.

"You could get far away with that much money."

"Yeah." A sigh rushed out of her, and she wiped her eyes. "Right. I could do that, sure. I won't even pack. I'll just go." She looked down at the tumbler in her hands, came forward and held it out for him.

"You drink it," David said. "You need it."

He turned and left her there. He glanced at the unconscious men on the way out. More loose ends. He left them, too.

He went outside and climbed back into the Dodge.

The Army had been correct in its assessment. David had lost his edge.

And he couldn't quite feel sorry about it.

CHAPTER TWENTY

Yousef stood in the luxurious kitchen and watched the coffeemaker drip. He found the rich aroma of the outrageously expensive Kopi Luwak coffee tantalizing and yet also slightly disappointing. At three hundred and fifty dollars a pound, Yousef had been expecting . . . what? An orgasm?

It occurred to him that perhaps Dante Payne had so much money that he had to constantly think of new and inventive ways to spend it.

Yousef still thought it wasteful, and considered the coffee again with vague disapproval.

Payne stood behind him, cursing and glaring into a gleaming steel refrigerator the size of a bank vault.

"I wish I'd known we were coming here," Payne lamented. "I would have alerted the staff. I can't remember the last time I prepared my own meal."

"A bad idea," Yousef said. "Servants talk. The fewer who know you're here, the better."

"Yes, of course."

Payne had ordered men in to clean up the blood and

bodies in his west side building and had retreated to a penthouse apartment on the Upper East Side. His men were in the lobby. More men in the stairwells. Still more men in the hallway by the elevator. If Sparrow tried to get at Payne here, it would get very noisy very quickly.

But first Sparrow would have to know Payne was here, a fact they weren't advertising.

Yousef watched the coffee drip.

Payne took a jar of Greek olives from the refrigerator and frowned at it. "Shouldn't you be out killing people? It's why I'm paying you."

"I'm waiting."

"For what?"

"For him to show himself."

"He killed two men the last time he showed himself," Payne said.

"I could roam the streets of Manhattan shouting his name if you prefer."

Payne slammed the refrigerator door closed. "This is ridiculous. All of my money, my power and influence. And I can't step foot out of this penthouse because of *one man*. He should be afraid of *me*. Not the other way around. I feel like a prisoner in a cell."

"A very *nice* cell. You should relax," Yousef said. "I will take care of everything. Trust me. Have patience."

"Have patience, he says. Relax."

The coffeemaker hissed and puffed. "The coffee is finished. Do you want a cup?" Yousef asked.

"No, I do not want a fucking cup of—"

"Sorry to interrupt, boss." One of Payne's flunkies had walked into the kitchen. "But Marco called. He heard from Gina. There's been trouble at Jerry's."

"Who the fuck is Gina?"

"That cooze that runs the love nest over the bar," the flunky reported. "Says some guy came in and kicked the shit out of the boys downstairs and forced her to open the safe. Got away with the book."

"Son of a bitch! What the fuck was he doing at Jerry's?"

The flunky shrugged.

"It's your building," Yousef said. "He was looking for you."

"It's not common knowledge I own that building."

"No," Yousef said. "But it is uncommon knowledge, and it is an uncommon man who hunts you. He was with the government. Maybe still is. Someone is helping him. He knows your haunts."

"Then he knows about this penthouse."

"Without a doubt."

"He could come here next."

"A distinct possibility."

Payne grimaced. "Well, then, that's *bad*, isn't it?"

"No," Yousef corrected. "That's good." He took a mug from the cupboard above the coffeemaker and filled it. "Now we can take control of the situation."

"I'd like to hear exactly how you're going to do that," Payne said.

"Only too happy to explain," Yousef said. "First, I'm going to need one of your credit cards."

After stopping to use the restroom and to buy an energy drink, David was back behind the wheel of the Dodge, on his way to the next place on Charlie's list, a penthouse on the Upper East Side.

"Major, you there?" Charlie buzzed in his ear.

"You don't have to call me Major, Charlie."

"I like it," Charlie said. "Like old times."

Yeah. Old times.

"I hope you're calling with good news," David said. "Did you break through the security on the flash drive?"

"Not yet. But I got a hit on the Net. A place not on the list I gave you."

"Let's hear it."

"Payne owns a luxury yacht," Charlie said. "A hundred sixty feet, all the amenities. You got a pen? I'll tell you the marina and the best way to get there."

"Just tell me. I'll remember."

Charlie told him.

"And we think this is a good bet?"

"Dante Payne just used his American Express card at the marina to buy an amount of diesel fuel that more or less matches the tank capacity of his yacht," Charlie explained. "Twenty-two minutes before that, he used the same card to purchase three hundred and fifty-eight bucks worth of groceries at a market two blocks from the marina entrance."

"Sounds like somebody is going on holiday."

"With that much food and fuel he can make circles around Ellis Island for a week and we'd never find him," Charlie said.

"But you *did* find him."

"Yeah," Charlie said. "But you better get there before they shove off."

"On it. Back at you later."

David turned the Dodge around and headed downtown.

Something buzzed in his pocket, and he checked his smartphone. A text from Amy.

You okay?

David felt a strong urge to apologize. She shouldn't be stuck there all alone. He shouldn't have had to send his kids away. Why hadn't he fixed everything yet? He wanted to say that he loved her and that he'd do better. He texted:

I'm good. More later.

He put the phone back in his pocket.

David passed Chinatown and Gilbert Park then made a right turn toward the water. The marina was a little north of the piers with the big commercial ships. He drove through the gates and along the dock to pier nine, which was the last one. A mix of motor yachts and sailing vessels docked here, various pleasure craft the idle rich could not only afford to buy but also to maintain and park here at the marina. David's father had been fond of repeating a saying he'd heard about boats. *A boat is a hole in the water you throw money into.*

If that were true, then Dante Payne's motor yacht *Avenger* was the biggest hole in this part of the water, although David didn't doubt Payne had enough money to fill it. The *Avenger* was docked along the left side of the pier, taking up most of the available space, her stern facing toward him. He parked across from the pier and killed the lights.

It was getting late, and the marina was mostly deserted, but the *Avenger*'s lights were on and a trio of men carried boxes and bags up a short gangplank. Charlie's assessment of the situation looked solid.

David considered it from Payne's point of view. Sooner or later the police would find David. Eventually Amy would have to surface. Payne could hide out in comfort on his yacht in the middle of Hudson Bay until everything blew over. The clock was working for Payne and against David.

Payne would have men with him. How many? How good? David could only make lousy guesses based on incomplete information.

So yeah, business as usual. Just like Charlie said.

The men who'd carried aboard the provisions came back down the gangplank and began casting off ropes. David needed to make his move, and he needed to time it just right. There was a swimming platform at the stern, one of those flat landings for zero entry into the water. That would be his best access point.

They were pulling up the gangplank now. The engines turned over, and water churned behind the yacht.

They were leaving.

David took the Airweight and Gina's little automatic out of his Windbreaker pockets and dropped them on the car floor. They weren't the sort of weapons he found particularly useful, and he didn't want them clanking around his pockets if he had to move fast.

He checked the magazines in his automatic pistols and the load in the shotgun. He scanned the dock, and when he didn't see anyone, he got out of the Dodge.

The yacht picked up speed, and David jogged down the pier after it. It would have to make a sharp left-hand turn when it reached the end of the pier, and that would be his best shot. If he didn't time the jump exactly right, the result would be very embarrassing and very wet.

The yacht started its turn, and David ran faster.

He hit the end of the pier and launched himself, just as the stern of the ship passed below him. He easily flew the distance, holding the shotgun close to his chest, and hit the swimming deck, tucked and rolled. He came up with his back against the large transom. He paused to listen, but couldn't hear anything over the engines.

He touched the Bluetooth, made sure it was still in place. "Charlie."

"I'm here."

"I'm aboard. I'm going to keep the channel open, so you can follow along."

"Understood. I'm not going anywhere."

So, you're Dante Payne on a luxury yacht. Where do you go? Up on deck to get some air? Down below to get a drink? Do you retire to your stateroom with some floozy to blow off steam?

It was a big boat, but it could get really small really fast if they all came at him at once. He stood and peered over the transom. He didn't see anyone, but he discovered that the transom lowered to allow the launch of inflatable dinghies with small outboard motors. There were also a couple of Jet Skis.

Payne would surround himself with his hired muscle. Maybe there was a way David could get rid of a few. Even the odds a bit.

"Charlie, can you pull up the specs on this yacht?"

Yousef stood next to the *Avenger*'s captain on the bridge. "You're on course? All is well?"

"Up the East River as you directed," the captain said. "You still want to go to North Brother Island? Nothing is there but abandoned buildings and birds."

"Good," Yousef said. "I want someplace secluded."

Yousef had assured Dante Payne that David Sparrow would be captured alive and interrogated. He would be made to tell the whereabouts of the flash drive, if anyone else had seen the contents of the flash drive, and where his wife could be located. Afterward, he would be cut into many pieces and the teeth would be pulled from his head to prevent identification via dental records. His remains would be scattered, never to be found. Yousef would gleefully attend to these matters personally.

Yousef knew Sparrow wouldn't give up any information about his wife. His certainty stemmed from the fact that in this respect Sparrow was a man like Yousef. No amount of pain would make him betray the woman he loved although Yousef would still make the best effort possible to force Sparrow to talk. One still needed to go through the steps after all.

Yousef would have given anything, endured any torment, to have saved his wife and daughters. Sparrow had taken this opportunity from him, had assured him his family was safe. Lies. Through his connections, Yousef had learned the fate of his family, raped and humiliated before finally being butchered. Sparrow would suffer, and before he died, he would be made to understand that his wife would suffer the same fate as Yousef's family.

If there were time and opportunity perhaps he would also hunt down the man's children.

But . . .

Best not to think too far ahead.

For now it sufficed that his man back at the marina

had seen Sparrow arrive, park and board the *Avenger*. Even now Sparrow crouched behind the transom, preparing to make some move, unaware that preemptive actions had already been taken. Reagan and a half-dozen of Payne's guns for hire waited hidden where they could easily capture Sparrow if he showed himself. If Sparrow resisted, they would likely suffer losses, but the men had been given explicit instructions to take their target alive.

And if some of Payne's men were killed, then so be it. That's what fodder was for after all.

A red light blazed angrily on the control panel next to the ship's wheel, accompanied by a harsh alarm buzz. The captain immediately throttled back, and Yousef felt the ship slow.

"What are you doing?"

"Somebody's lowered the transom," the captain said. "We've got to stop, or we'll take on water."

He knows. Somehow Sparrow knows we're setting a trap for him.

Reagan burst onto the bridge. His pistol was drawn. "He's getting away!"

Reagan turned and ran, and Yousef followed, drawing one of his own Glocks. They ran down the portside all the way to the stern where four of Payne's gunmen looked out across the water. Yousef followed their gaze and saw one of the inflatable dinghies motoring away fast, skipping along the waves.

"Shit," Yousef spat.

With the transom down, the water was ankle deep in the launch area at the stern of the ship. Yousef jerked the anchor straps loose from one of the Jet Skis and floated it out in front of him. He threw a leg over like he was mounting a horse and cranked the engine.

"Take charge here," Yousef told Reagan. He pointed at one of Payne's men. "Get on the other Jet Ski. You other two launch the other dinghy and follow as fast as you can."

Yousef didn't wait to see if they obeyed. He cranked the accelerator and shot from the stern of the *Avenger* after Sparrow. He had a good lead, but the Jet Ski was slowly gaining. Water sprayed his face. He glanced back and saw the other Jet Ski following. It was too dark to make out the second dinghy, but the *Avenger*'s running lights glowed brightly across the black water.

He faced forward again, raised his pistol as he steered the Jet Ski one-handed. On dry land, he would have been within range, but bobbing on the East River made the shot difficult. He forced himself to be patient, and a minute later he pulled alongside.

Yousef lifted the pistol, aimed at the broadest part of Sparrow's back. It would be easy, and maybe the smart thing. Kill him now. Finish it. But Yousef was too in love with his plan for Sparrow, too eager to inflict long, drawn-out revenge upon the man he'd hated for so long. For his wife and for his daughters, it would go hard and slow for David Sparrow.

He shifted his aim from Sparrow's back to the sputtering little outboard that propelled the dinghy. He fired once and sparks flew, a ricochet. He squeezed off two more shots, and the outboard coughed and belched smoke and died.

Yousef noticed Sparrow hadn't flinched at all at the sound of gunfire.

Without the motor, the dinghy eased to a stop, the current spinning it around. Yousef blinked at Sparrow's hunched figure.

Only it wasn't Sparrow.

A Windbreaker had been draped over a pile of life jackets, something stuffed in the sleeves for arms, a small round dive buoy with a watch cap stretched over it.

"Son of a bitch!"

The other Jet Ski pulled up behind him.

Yousef pointed at the dinghy and the pile of life jackets. "Bring that back with you."

He turned his own Jet Ski around and sped back toward the *Avenger*.

CHAPTER TWENTY-ONE

Charlie had been spot on when he'd pulled up the specs for this make and model of luxury yacht, and he'd been able to talk David through exactly what he'd wanted to do. Lowering the transom had indeed sent an alarm to the bridge, which resulted in bringing the ship to a full stop.

David had hastily built the dummy out of life jackets and his Windbreaker, a buoy and a watch cap, yanked the cord on the little outboard and sent it across the water. He'd barely had time to fold himself into the storage locker where he'd found the life jackets when Payne's goons came stomping around the elevated lounge area, splashing and yelling. He couldn't see them, but they'd obviously spotted the departing dinghy.

There was a brief noisy frenzy during which David deduced they were preparing the Jet Skis and the other dinghy for a hasty pursuit. Engines cranked, and somebody yelled instructions. Soon the Jet Ski engines faded. He heard a man say something to another, then shallow splashes as one of them moved away.

David held still, listened, clutching the shotgun to his chest. He was pretty sure one of them was still out there. He hoped there weren't two because unless they were standing together, the situation could rapidly get awkward.

He waited twenty more seconds but didn't hear anything helpful.

David cracked the locker door, which allowed him to see back toward the elevated lounge but didn't see anyone there. He opened the door and slipped out of the locker, pivoting toward the stern, the shotgun raised and ready.

A man stood smoking a cigarette. He was looking out over the water, but turned to look at David as he approached. For a long second, the man seemed not to understand what was happening, puffing the cigarette. A moment later his eyes went wide as he realized David wasn't somebody he recognized, and his hand went into his jacket for a gun.

But David was already moving forward fast. He brought the butt of the shotgun down hard, smashing it across the guy's mouth. Blood and teeth flew, and the guy spun back into the water. David watched him float a second, satisfied he wasn't coming back.

He hit the button to raise the transom, and an electric motor hummed to life, the transom moving slowly back into position with a clank. He paused to toss a coil of yellow rope used for dive buoys over his shoulder.

David headed up the stairs to the elevated lounge, stepping lightly. He wanted to stay quiet as long as possible, but he gripped the shotgun, ready to cut loose. It would have to get bloody eventually.

He moved along the starboard side and climbed a short set of stairs to the bridge, entering quickly.

The captain saw him, eyes popping. He opened his mouth to say something, but David shut him up by raising the shotgun.

"Start the engines," David told him. "Get us underway."

The captain hesitated, but a glance down the gaping barrels of the twelve gauge convinced him. He took the ship's wheel in one hand and the throttle in the other. "What course?"

"Upriver."

The captain turned the wheel slightly and pushed the throttle forward to half speed.

David looked ahead of them at the river, saw something low and lumpy ahead on the water. "What's that ahead of us?"

"A garbage barge," the captain said. "Don't worry. It's in a slow lane. I can go around it easy enough."

"Head for it," David said.

"*Head* for it?"

David jammed the shotgun into the captain's ribs.

"Jesus." The captain brought the ship in line right behind the barge. It was still some distance away, but the *Avenger* closed slowly.

"How long to catch up to the barge at this speed?"

The captain considered. "Seven or eight minutes."

David grabbed the throttle and shoved it forward from half speed to full. He felt the vibration of the engines grow more pronounced beneath his feet as the ship plowed the waves forward.

"Are you trying to kill us?"

David motioned with the shotgun for the captain to step back and sit in his chair. The captain obeyed, and David tied him securely with the rope.

"You've got to listen to me," the captain said. "We have three minutes. Maybe a little more before we hit. I'm not sure what you want to happen, but at this speed it's not going to be pretty."

"Whatever happens, you'll have a good view of it," David said. "Charlie."

"Here," Charlie said in David's ear.

"Give me a countdown from three minutes. Let me know every thirty seconds."

"You got it."

David left the bridge, taking an interior spiral staircase to the deck below, the shotgun up and ready to blast anything that moved. His heart beat hard and fast like it was trying to get out of his chest.

Calm down. Breathe in and out. Take care of business.

He was in a cabin with a small table, charts, a coffeemaker . . . maybe some kind of office for the captain. He moved aft, as quickly as he could, sighting down the shotgun barrel, ready for anything that might pop out at him. He exited though a hatch, moved through a breezeway and into another hatch. A big room with an open-floor plan, low couches and a bar and an air hockey table. Pinball machines. Some kind of party area.

"Two minutes and thirty seconds," Charlie said in his ear.

Shit.

The *Avenger* was a big boat. David regretted pushing the throttle to full speed. He sped up his search in spite of the risk. Down another staircase to the deck below, a hall with doors on either side, presumably sleeping cabins.

He kicked open the doors to the first three, the sinking feeling creeping into his gut that he'd made a mistake.

"Two minutes and counting," Charlie said.

The corridor on this deck spanned the length of the ship, and David was already approaching the stairway at the other end. He'd come up empty. There was no doubt now. Payne wasn't here. Sure, there were still a few places on the yacht he hadn't checked, but his gut instinct told him something had gone wrong.

"One minute, thirty seconds and counting."

He paused at the stairs leading back to the deck above. Time to get off this overgrown sardine can before—

The pressure of cold metal at the base of David's skull. He froze. David knew what a pistol felt like.

"Don't move," said the voice behind him. "Don't blink. Don't even fart."

David caught the accent. "Chechen?"

"Smart," he said. "But maybe not so fucking smart, eh? I was told you were a real fucking badass. You move, I blast a hole through your fucking skull, badass. You get me?"

"You're the boss," David said.

"Damn right. Toss down that scattergun."

David did as he'd been told.

The cold pressure against the base of his skull vanished, and the Chechen said, "Turn around."

David turned. The man was younger than he'd thought, but there was still a cold experience in his eyes. He was close enough to shoot David point-blank but had stepped back just far enough to make going for his gun a bad idea.

"Take out the pistols," he said. "Very slowly. Forefinger and thumb. One at a time."

David plucked each pistol from each shoulder holster one at a time and dropped them on the deck as instructed. The Chechen kicked them back skittering down the corridor.

"One minute and counting," Charlie said in the Bluetooth.

"Pull the pant legs up," the Chechen told him.

David did it, exposing the ankle holster and the .380.

"Get rid of it."

David unstrapped the holster and tossed it aside.

"You're a lucky man." The Chechen had his pistol pointed straight at David's face. "They want you alive. Me? I don't much care. They told me to be careful of you. Because you're a bad man. I guess you're clever. Maybe. I'm not impressed."

"I'm out of practice," David said. "But I can load a dishwasher better than anyone you know."

"I don't get that joke, bad man," the Chechen said. "But points for trying with a gun in your face."

"What's Payne paying you?" David asked. "Maybe I can do better."

The Chechen laughed. "This is Payne's boat. That should give you an idea how big his wallet is."

Good point.

"Thirty seconds and counting," Charlie said.

"So what happens now?" David asked.

He motioned up the stairs with his pistol. "Not up to me. We go topside and the boss can decide. You stay well ahead of me out of arm's reach, you understand?"

David counted down in his head. *Twelve . . . eleven . . . ten . . .*

"Let's just talk about this a minute," David said.

"There's nothing to talk about. You can go up those stairs on your own two feet, or I can shoot your knee-caps and have you carried up."

. . . three . . . two . . . one . . .

David braced himself.

Nothing happened.

"Go." The Chechen shook the pistol at him for emphasis.

David turned slowly, still waiting. Obviously the estimation could have been off by a few seconds. He just needed to stall. He put his foot on the first step, froze. *Come on!*

"Whatever you're thinking of doing, forget it," the Chechen warned. "You think you're fast. Or good enough. Put that out of your mind. You lost."

David began to climb the stairs slowly, feet leaden, mind racing for a plan. Someone could have found and freed the captain, altered the *Avenger's* course. Or the garbage barge could have seen the yacht coming up fast and—

The impact was so sharp and sudden, David felt it from his feet up through his spine. The scream of metal and fiberglass. The ship tilted sharply, and David had to grab the banister to keep from being thrown off the stairs.

The Chechen lost his footing, fell back against the bulkhead, arms flailing for something to latch on to.

David leaped at him.

He crashed into him hard, smashing him against the bulkhead. Air wheezed out of the Chechen, and David grabbed his wrist, smashing his gun hand against the bulkhead until the Chechen gave up the pistol.

David turned to reach for it, but the man recovered faster than predicted and brought a knee up into David's gut.

David grunted and pushed away from the Chechen who was already pressing forward with a martial arts chop at David's throat. David blocked it, punched with his other hand, but the Chechen dodged his head and caught David's arm, trying to trap it in a quick arm lock.

Instead of trying to pull out of it, David heaved himself forward going in for a head butt. Smashing a man across the bridge of his nose with one's forehead usually took the fight out of him quickly. He hadn't had a lot of recent luck with head butts. Maybe this time.

The Chechen saw it coming and lowered his head to protect his face, and David drove his forehead into the top of the man's skull with a loud crack.

David stumbled back, lights flashing in his eyes, half blinded by pain. Probably the Chechen's bell had been rung just as badly, but David couldn't assume anything, didn't know which of them had the upper hand. He swung a wild backhand.

And got lucky.

His fist hit the Chechen's jaw, hard. A grunt through clenched teeth.

David kicked, hoping to find the man's balls. He missed his target but struck hard with his heel into the man's thigh muscle. The Chechen went down to one knee, and that put him level with David's own balls, but David knew what was coming and turned away, taking the punch on the hip. He kicked out again and connected with the Chechen's teeth. The man went down face-first into the water, which was now ankle deep.

David blinked his eyes clear, vision finally snapping back into focus.

Get out of here. Move!

He turned and rushed for the stairs, fighting against the tilt of the listing vessel, pulling himself up by the banister. He made it up to the next level and heard the sharp report of a pistol shot behind him.

The Chechen was at the bottom of the stairs, raising his pistol to fire again.

But David was already moving when the next shot came, racing up the stairway to the next deck. He sprinted along the gangway to the first hatch he saw and exploded through it to the starboard side rail, stepped on the lowest rung, and launched himself over it just as three more shots sounded behind him. Flying lead missed his ear by half an inch.

The world blurred as he plummeted toward the dark water below, but in his peripheral vision he glimpsed the *Avenger* smashed up against the stern of the garbage barge. On the deck of the barge, men ran around like ants who'd had their hill kicked over. Spotlights shone on the point of impact and—

The surface world vanished as David plunged into wet darkness, sound and vision cut off abruptly. He kicked for the blur of light above him, surfaced just long enough to gulp air and hear another gunshot.

David dove back under the water, swimming hard. His lungs strained and burned.

But he didn't come up for air again soon.

CHAPTER TWENTY-TWO

"I had him," Reagan said. "If the ship hadn't wrecked—"

"Be silent." Yousef's voice was calm in that way which was somehow worse than if he'd shouted. "You let him get away. Details at this point do not matter."

Reagan's jaw muscles worked in frustration. Yousef could sense the anger ready to boil over. The young man had skills, but his attitude made him a liability. Payne had picked him. Yousef would not have.

"Maybe he drowned," Reagan said.

Yousef shot him a look that said, *Yes and maybe he rode away on a unicorn.*

Reagan at least had the good grace to look away, embarrassed.

Yousef and the others had returned just in time to take Reagan off the sinking vessel. They'd found a dock and had tied up the dinghies and Jet Skis and were attempting to assess the situation and regroup.

The acute sensation of an opportunity lost nagged at Yousef. The ploy had worked to draw Sparrow into the open, but the government man had still managed to outwit them. It had been a close thing, and Yousef now regretted the order to take their prey alive. Reagan could have put a bullet in the man's head and it would have been finished.

One of Payne's goons returned from the end of the dock with a Windbreaker in his fist. "This was all there was." He handed it to Yousef.

Yousef turned it over in his hand, examining and frowning. He searched the pockets and came out with a wet, folded piece of paper. He unfolded the sheet of paper, slowly, careful not to rip it. He read it:

> Cops in the hotel. They found the Escalade in the parking garage.
>
> L

Yousef's eyes shifted to the top of the letterhead. *Royal Empire Hotel.*

That was information Yousef filed away for later. He asked, "Who's the man we left back at the marina?"

"Ramirez."

Yousef took out his cell phone. "Give me his number."

David was sopping wet.

He staggered up the bank, gasping for air and taking stock. Guns lost on the yacht. Phone and Bluetooth at the bottom of the East River. Without a doubt, his endeavors aboard the *Avenger* had resulted in an all-around net loss.

He wasn't even sure if he'd swum ashore at the right

spot. But he stumbled between the pilings until he found himself in the light, looked up, and saw he was back at the marina.

So at least I'm not lost.

He patted his pocket quickly and was relieved to feel the car keys still there.

He slunk into the shadows again and circled back to the Dodge Aspen. Thirty feet from the automobile, he squatted behind some trash cans and watched. A man leaned against the Dodge, just waiting. He lit a cigarette, puffed, glanced at his wristwatch.

I could just leave, David thought. But the logbook he'd taken from Jerry's was in the vehicle. Too valuable to leave behind. He stayed there a moment, thinking about rushing the guy but wishing he had some kind of advantage. He reached into his pocket and found he still had the leather blackjack. That was something at least. He needed to pick his moment, catch the guy unaware and put him down fast.

He scanned the rest of the marina, but didn't see anyone else. He wondered if Amy had tried to text him again and felt a pang of anxiety. It was probably at least some comfort to her when he texted back proving he was still alive, but with the phone lost in the river—

A sharp bleeping sound drew his attention back to the man next to the Dodge.

He took a phone out of his pocket and answered it.

This is probably the best diversion I'm going to get.

David came in low, beelining directly for the man on the phone. In this situation, David elected for speed over stealth and the crunch of gravel under his shoes gave him away. Just as he raised the blackjack to strike the man at the base of the skull, the guy turned, confusion in his eyes at seeing David suddenly upon him.

David brought the blackjack down hard across his face, bone and teeth cracking. The guy spun around and slammed against the side of the Dodge, the phone flying out of his hand.

The guy didn't quite go down, braced himself against the car, trying to push himself up, head flopping around and spitting blood. David took more care this time, placed the next slap of the blackjack at the base of the man's skull like he'd tried to do the first time. This time the guy went down and stayed there.

David scanned the ground until he saw the man's cell phone. He picked it up and put it to his ear.

"—you there or not?" An accented voice. "Ramirez, I said to get back to the penthouse if he doesn't show up within the hour. Do you hear me?"

David ended the call and put the cell phone in his pocket.

"Hey!"

David's head jerked around to a man coming toward him down one of the docks. Flashlight beam swinging in front of him. He caught sight of a khaki shirt, the glint of metal over one pocket. Security guard.

David didn't have time to get tangled up with a rent-a-cop. He already knew his next destination. He turned back to the Dodge, taking the keys out of his pocket, moving deliberately but not rushing as he climbed in behind the wheel.

"Hold up, buddy! What are you doing over there?"

David ignored him, started the car, and drove away.

The voice on the phone had mentioned a penthouse,

and a penthouse was exactly where David had been heading when he'd changed course to investigate the *Avenger*. In David's world, it was an annoying truth that two plus two did not *always* equal four, but in this case, he figured it was a safe bet.

He ran the next two red lights getting there.

Yousef frowned at his cell phone.

"What's the matter?" Reagan said behind him. "Didn't he—"

"Quiet," Yousef said. "I'm thinking."

He thought for two more seconds before rapidly dialing another number.

Dante Payne answered. "Did you get him?"

"Get out of the penthouse," Yousef said. "Now."

CHAPTER TWENTY-THREE

Charlie Finn had heard the whole thing through the Bluetooth, the conversation with the Chechen, the fight, gunshots, and then the sudden burst of white noise filling the speakers in the back of his Con Ed van.

The entire time, Charlie had tried to think fast and figure some way to help David, but the last thing he wanted to do was fill David's ear with distraction in the middle of a hairy situation.

The instant he'd lost communication with the Bluetooth, Charlie's hands flew over the keyboard, calling up the marine channels including the secure Coat Guard frequency. It wasn't difficult to put together a picture of the situation, the collision of the two vessels and the ensuing chaos.

He was positive David had gone into the water, but if accidently or on purpose, Charlie couldn't be sure. He monitored the radio channels, alert to reports of survivors either being picked up in the river or on shore. But nothing led him to believe any of them were David.

He tried texting and calling David's smartphone.

Nothing.

This shit just got FUBAR real fast.

He sat back, reaching for the carton of leftover chow mein. The noodles had gone cold, but he didn't care, shoveled them into his mouth with a pair of chopsticks, racking his brain for what to do next. Chew. Swallow. Think. Repeat.

In this situation, doing nothing was preferable to doing the wrong thing, but sitting and waiting didn't make him feel very helpful.

Maybe the major had simply been in over his head this time. If the Army had sidelined him then there had to be reasons.

Yeah, because the Army never makes a mistake, right?

Still, it didn't take long to get rusty in this business, especially for the guys out in the field. High stress. The Army could expect to get a few good years out of men like David before an operative started to unravel. It showed in the eyes first, a sort of haunted stare. When a man was constantly surrounded by enemies it hardened him and kept hardening him until he cracked. There had been operatives who'd gone back to the real world not quite able to function, not the same men they'd been when they'd started out. The Army did their best to pull an operative from duty before it got that far.

When Charlie Finn looked at David Sparrow, he did not see a man who'd cracked.

But he did see . . . something.

He could imagine the toll it would take for a man to lose his wife and his children, what he'd risk to protect them. A family had to be the biggest investment a man could make. All that love and responsibility for a lifetime.

Not that it always lasted a lifetime.

When Charlie had been very young, just out of high school, he'd met a girl. *The* girl, so he'd thought. She was the hottest thing he'd ever seen and so damn funny and they both liked heavy metal and that was enough for them. They'd gotten married after knowing each other for six weeks.

It lasted just over a year. Nothing dramatic. They'd simply grown bored with each other.

Charlie ate cold noodles and wondered what his life had been like if he'd done it right, waited for the right woman, had kids, the whole American dream thing.

He couldn't quite picture it.

But David Sparrow fit into that picture perfectly, or at least, that's how it seemed to Charlie. And the idea that it might all be taken away could be what finally cracked the man.

Charlie hoped not. He hoped David wasn't at the bottom of the river.

He finished the noodles.

Charlie tried calling again but knew it was useless. David would have called by now if he'd been able. At some point the only choice would be to shut everything down, start up the Con Ed van, and drive back to the Bronx.

But not yet.

He reached for a cold egg roll.

One of the other computers chimed for his attention, and Charlie swiveled in his chair, instantly alert.

The code breaker program Charlie had turned loose on the flash drive David had given him had finally done its work. Charlie excitedly scrolled through the files. This is what they'd been waiting for.

It wasn't clear at first exactly what he was looking at, and Charlie forced himself to read more slowly. It took him a few seconds to realize what he was reading.

Another few seconds to realize what it meant.

"Well." Charlie sighed. "Shit."

David parked around the corner from the apartment building's main entrance.

If he made a long list of weapons he'd be willing to take into action, the Airweight revolver and the little silver automatic he'd taken from Gina would rank almost at the end of the list, maybe edging out boomerang and slingshot. The Airweight still had a full five rounds. He checked the little automatic's clip. Two bullets left.

He got out of the car, slipping the automatic into his pants pocket on the left side. He kept the Airweight cupped in his hand down low next to his leg on the right. He was still wet, clothes clinging uncomfortably to his body, but he'd gone into battle in worse conditions.

He circled the building to the main entrance.

The uniformed doorman saw him coming up the steps and gave him the fish-eye, raised a hand to fend him off. "No panhandlers here, buddy. Move it along."

David climbed the last two steps and stuck the Airweight into his ribs.

The doorman looked down at it. "Fuck."

"You know who lives at the top?" David asked.

A pause, then the doorman said, "I know."

They stood like that a moment, revolver firm in the man's ribs, David dripping on the doorman's shoes.

"You need a coffee break," David told him.

The doorman didn't hesitate, walked down the steps, turned the corner, and kept going. He didn't look back even once.

David went into the lobby.

Four of them draped over plush chairs and sofas, flipping through magazines or heads down staring at smartphones. This had to be fast. If any of them got off a call upstairs then the trip would be for nothing. The range on the Airweight was crap, and with only five rounds he couldn't waste them. He'd have to cross the lobby fast and get close. With the Airweight's snub nose, his best bet was to shove the gun right up against whomever it was he wanted dead before pulling the trigger.

David was almost to the first one when the guy looked up from his magazine. "Hey, what are—oh, shit!"

David stuck the revolver against his forehead and squeezed the trigger.

A thunderclap shook the lobby. Brains and blood and pieces of skull exploded out the back of the guy's head.

David was already swinging the revolver toward another one who sat in a plush leather chair three feet away. At that range, he thought it was *still* too far but he pulled the trigger anyway.

A red, wet hole bloomed in the guy's chest. He fell back in the chair, legs going straight and arms flopping out to the sides.

But David hadn't been as fast as he'd hoped. The other two had drawn pistols and had drawn a bead on him.

David leaped on the corpse in the chair, the momentum sending him, the chair and the corpse tumbling over as gunfire erupted, lead whizzing past overhead. He dropped the Airweight and reached into the dead man's jacket, pulled out a Beretta M9.

He thumbed off the safety and rose to one knee and fired from behind the chair four times, a tight grouping across the goon's chest. The man shivered and folded on top of himself into a dead heap.

David stood, watched as the final man turned and ran. David lifted the Beretta, held his breath and let it out slowly as he sighted and popped off a single round.

The fleeing gunman took the shot between the shoulder blades. It knocked him forward, and he skidded along the glossy tile and came to rest against a big potted plant.

David made a slow circle, gun up and ready for whatever might come, but nobody else in the lobby remained alive. Cordite and the copper smell of blood hung in the air.

He went to the elevator and pushed the call button. When the elevator arrived he looked at the button for the penthouse, and as he suspected he needed a key card to gain access to that level.

He found it in the jacket pocket of the man whose head he'd blown apart with the Airweight. He also took the man's pistol, another 9 mm but a Browning. There were two extra magazines, and David took those also.

This is taking too long. If the doorman takes the hint to stay away then good. But if he decided to call the police . . .

In every operation, luck played a part. David was using up his allowance for the next ten.

He stepped back onto the elevator, inserted the key card, and pressed the button for the penthouse. It was on the thirtieth floor.

David had killed the gunman in the lobby before they

could warn anyone in the penthouse. He should have the element of surprise.

I hope. But that sort of assumption had been wrong before.

Dead wrong.

The Chechen—Reagan—had gone to support Yousef's efforts aboard the yacht, but Dante Payne had been correct to heed his instinct and retain the other two specialists he'd hired. He needed them for protection. Yousef had shown him how pedestrian his usual muscle was, an oversight Payne would remedy as soon as the current situation had been concluded. They were men suited well enough for running errands and shooing away flies, but he needed professionals for more dire situations.

For now, he addressed the five gunmen he still had at his disposal—men originally in his employ before he'd sent for Yousef and the other three specialists.

"I want you to go to the outer hallway and wait for the elevator," Payne told them. "Get your weapons out. Point them at the elevator and wait. When the elevator door opens, start shooting. Don't wait to see who it is. Our men aren't coming back here, so just shoot. You understand?"

They nodded, drawing weapons.

Payne gestured to the Arab with the gray at his temples and the Serb who was lighting yet another of his toxic cigarettes. They were not especially good company, but they were the men who would keep him alive. "Follow me."

They followed him back though the penthouse to a

door behind the kitchen, and then through that to a maintenance entrance where there was a small service elevator. When originally shopping for a penthouse, some instinct told him an escape route was a good idea.

"This goes all the way down to the parking levels," Payne told his protectors. "It's a back way out and not generally known."

They traveled down and got off on the first parking level. Payne started for his limousine, but the Arab put a gentle hand on his shoulder to stop him.

"Wait."

Payne waited.

"What is the driver's name?"

"Emile," Payne told him. "He has bad teeth."

The Arab nodded. "Just a moment."

He crossed the garage to the parked limousine and rapped on the driver's side window with a knuckle. The window came down. Payne couldn't hear the exchange, but the Arab turned back to him and waved them over. "It's okay!"

Payne felt the Serb at his back as they crossed to the limousine. The men were taking their task seriously.

Good.

Once inside and buckled up, the limousine circled to the exit and twenty seconds later, they were on the streets of Manhattan.

Payne didn't like this. He wasn't bound for one of his other properties because Yousef had said Sparrow might find him at any of his usual haunts. Payne felt like a bit player in the story of his own life, set adrift in a luxury life raft waiting to be contacted and told the coast was clear.

He fixed himself a Scotch on the rocks from the limousine bar and guzzled half in one go.

Dante Payne despised waiting, hated depending on somebody else. He glanced at his wristwatch. What next?

Back at his penthouse, the elevator arrived, and the doors slid open. His men opened fire at once, emptying their pistols in an apocalypse of fire and lead.

After David hit the elevator button for the thirtieth-floor penthouse and the doors closed, he hit the button for the twenty-ninth as well.

He exited on the twenty-ninth floor, heard the elevator chime and the doors close behind him as he jogged across the lobby toward a door marked EXIT.

The stairs. As predicted, the key card unlocked the stairwell doors, too. He was halfway up to the penthouse floor when he heard the storm of gunfire.

Instead of hesitating, he ran faster.

David reached the top, exploded through the door, and into the thirtieth-floor lobby, the Beretta in one fist and the Browning in the other.

Smoke hung in the air. A gaggle of Payne's goons stood staring slack-jawed into the empty elevator. David felt no inclination to offer them a sporting chance.

He walked toward them, deliberate, swinging the pistols in a slow arc, firing steadily. The slugs hit hard, blood spraying on the walls and across the carpet. Men twitched and staggered and fell.

A few attempted to return fire without result. Their pistols were empty from blazing away at the empty elevator.

A couple were game for the fight and ejected spent magazines, trying to reload fast, but it was hopeless. David kept shooting until they were all down. One quivered, and David shot him again. A groan from another one, and David blasted him.

David stood a long silent moment, guns pointed at the corpses as if he expected one to rise up and come after him. The only sound was the bump of the elevator doors trying to close on one of the bodies that had fallen halfway into the elevator.

He tossed away the Beretta. It was empty, and he didn't have spare magazines for it. He reloaded the Browning. He searched the bodies quickly and opted for a Glock and three extra magazines.

A pistol in each hand, he entered the penthouse.

Room to room. Eyes sharp. Ears open.

Nothing. David was too late.

Or maybe Payne had never been here at all.

No. That's not right. The welcoming committee at the elevator. They knew I might be coming. They were covering Payne's escape.

Every time David thought he was ahead, he found out he was a step behind.

It was starting to piss him off.

In the kitchen he paused at the refrigerator, opened it, and took out a bottle of water. He didn't realize how thirsty he was until he started drinking. He tilted it back and kept drinking until it was gone. It was good to get the taste of the East River out of his mouth.

He was acutely aware of his cold, wet clothes sticking to him. He knew he'd been in the penthouse too long. Dawdling invited ten different flavors of trouble, but suddenly, irrationally, the most important thing in the world was to be dry again.

He ripped off his wet shirt and tossed it aside, shimmied out of his pants, kicked off the shoes. He gathered his wallet, car keys, blackjack, cell phone, the guns, and extra magazines and went in search of a bedroom. He found it, found Dante Payne's closets and dresser drawers. Silk suits, tennis outfits. It took some searching but David found jeans, a green V-neck pullover, socks, and deck shoes. The fit was close enough.

Upon feeling dry again, sanity returned, and he considered his next move. He couldn't hang around here. He found the same service elevator Payne must have used and took it down to the street level, then left the building via a loading dock.

He circled the building back to the Dodge and got in, pulled away from the curb slowly as if everything were normal. He passed the building's front entrance. Quiet. No sign at all that anything was amiss. The doorman hadn't called the police and hadn't returned. He probably knew that when one of your tenants was Dante Payne, there were just bound to be nights like this.

David kept driving until he found a dark quiet spot, parked, and dialed Charlie Finn.

CHAPTER TWENTY-FOUR

Reagan and Payne's men waited for Yousef on the sidewalk outside of Jerry's. Yousef had insisted on going in alone, and they'd indulged him. Reagan was the only one who chafed at Yousef's orders, pestering him with insistent questions. Every minute he spent with the brash Chechen, Yousef liked him less and less.

"You talked to her?" Reagan asked.

Yousef nodded.

"Why?" Reagan demanded. "What can she tell us about Sparrow we don't already know?"

"I wasn't looking for information. I didn't ask her anything about Sparrow," Yousef said.

"Then why?"

"Sparrow let her live. Would you have?"

Reagan shook his head. "No."

"Now, how would you use this information to your advantage?"

Reagan thought about it. "I don't know."

"That's why I give the orders," Yousef said. "And you take them."

David sat in the parked Dodge in a spot next to Central Park. He'd dialed Charlie, and it rang five times before going to voice mail. He switched to text messaging instead.

Charlie, it's me. David. New phone.

Ten seconds later the phone rang, and David answered.

"Holy fucking shit," Charlie said. "I thought you were dead at the bottom of the fucking river. It's all over the marine bands. I've been scanning in case they found a body."

"Good thing I'm a strong swimmer," David said. "Thanks for hanging in there."

"Well, it was a close thing. I was about to pack up my van and my leftover Chinese food and haul ass back to the Bronx."

"I still need you," David said.

"Bring me up to speed."

"Payne wasn't on his yacht," David said. "I thought if I moved fast, I could catch him at the penthouse. I came up short. I've been crapping out all over town, Charlie."

"Then maybe you could use a little good news," Charlie said.

"Tell me."

"I cracked Calvin Pope's flash drive."

David sat up in his seat behind the Dodge's steering wheel. "Start talking and don't leave anything out."

"We all know what Pope did," Charlie reminded him. "Once you or other solo operatives got a guy out of the danger zone, Pope took charge of him. It would be embarrassing for these guys to fall into enemy hands, right?

They could talk about everything our government is doing, incursions, all kinds of stuff."

David knew this already. It wouldn't look good for America to talk big about respecting another nation's sovereignty under the bright lights of the world stage only to find out America was pulling strings behind the scenes to undermine that very same sovereignty. But Charlie was building up to something, so David let him talk.

"So when those guys were no longer useful, when their cover was blown or whatever, guys like you would get them out," Charlie said, "and guys like Pope would hide them someplace. Relocate them to the States. The information on the flash drive is a detailed log of every man Pope relocated—name, country of origin, where he was relocated to, all of his personal data and everything."

"I'm not getting it," David said. "That was his job, wasn't it?"

"No, you've got to listen to me, man," Charlie insisted. "This information has been compiled in a very specific way to communicate a very specific message. Pope's job was to hide these guys in out-of-the-way places. You stick a guy in Boise, then the next one in Baton Rouge, then another in Little Rock. Spread them around and they blend in, and then everyone can forget about them."

"And you're saying that's not what happened."

"That is most definitely *not* what happened," Charlie said. "A bunch of these guys are clustered around New Jersey and New York. If you're paying attention, it's pretty easy to see that a guy like Payne could bring over all his old cronies and reassemble his network right here in Manhattan. A bunch of loyal and experienced foot soldiers all ready to go. There's also a column with a dollar amount next to each name."

"Bribes?" David asked.

"That's what it looks like," Charlie said. "If Pope was on the take, then that's one thing, but I think it's even worse. Consider this from a citizen's point of view. Remember that badass terrorist dude they took from Guantanamo and gave him a trial in the States?"

"Of course."

"Everyone went ape shit. Nobody wanted a dangerous guy like that on American soil, not in their own backyard. Well, that was just *one* guy. Now imagine people find out terrorists are being relocated by the fucking planeload right in your neighborhood, maybe down the street from your kid's school or near your church. All because Calvin Pope wanted to line his pockets. How do you think that would sit with people?"

"I think," David said slowly, "it might well be seen as a massive policy failure on the part of the federal government."

"Benghazi on steroids," Charlie said. "With every politician in Washington rushing to point fingers or get out of the way."

David let that sink in. Subverting a government official was serious. It would be enough to put Dante Payne away for a few years, something Amy had hoped to do before her star witness had been murdered. But in the process, information would be revealed that would set the State Department on its ear. David could imagine the *Washington Post* headline: "Government Relocates Terrorists and Murderers to Your Neighborhood."

"The stuff on this flash drive isn't just random information that got out," Charlie said. "It's a *confession*. Calvin Pope wanted people to know. For whatever reason, he wanted your wife to know."

A long silent moment. It stretched into another.

"You there, Major?"

"Charlie, I don't know what to do."

This time it was Charlie's turn to pause. "Maybe we need to call somebody. This is bigger than we thought at first. There are people besides Payne who won't want this flash drive making it to the public. We're getting into some deep water here. Deep water with sharks."

David thought about it. The information on the flash drive could put Payne behind bars. But that wasn't a guarantee. There were never guarantees. Only one course of action would guarantee that Dante Payne would leave him and his family alone, and that was to make Dante Payne go away forever. Knowing what was on the flash drive didn't change that plan of action.

"I've got to think about this," David said. "Call you back in a few."

"I'll be here."

They hung up.

David felt a strong urge to call Amy, but the urge to wait until he had better news was stronger. He was failing. He'd spent the night killing men, and yet he was still failing. The strongest feeling of all was shame. He was ashamed of himself for his attitude these past weeks. He'd felt sorry for himself. Pathetic. A sad selfish man, wondering if the Army would call him back to work. To do what? Strap on a gun? To do *this*?

David would give anything to return to his drab life of a few days ago, to make Amy coffee in the morning, to drive the kids to school and clean the house and trade banal pleasantries with the moms in front of Anna's school.

He'd give anything to go back to a time when his wife and kids were safe and happy.

And if he ever started feeling sorry for himself again, he would remember this moment right now. Sitting in a rusty Dodge Aspen with no idea if he'd be able to save his family or not. If he made it through this, he would get out the goddamn charcoal grill and make goddamn hamburgers on a Saturday afternoon. He'd talk to his neighbor over the fence. He'd go to the PTA meetings.

All he needed was the chance.

David let out a long, tired sigh.

He turned his head, and his eyes fell upon the logbook he'd taken from Jerry's. He pulled it into his lap and opened it, began scanning the pages, name after name in Gina's tight, neat penmanship. He paused and raised an eyebrow a few times at prominent names. Dante Payne's reach went even further than David had guessed, but at the moment none of those names suited his purpose.

David had to go back nearly six months before he found the name he'd been looking for. He wondered absently if Gina had seen to Calvin Pope's needs personally, or if she'd simply supervised, bringing in a redhead or a blonde or a black girl, whatever it had taken for Payne to cement his hold on the man.

Except he hadn't cemented it at all, had he? Calvin Pope had betrayed his government when he'd taken Payne's money. And then he'd betrayed Payne. Considering the situation, David thought Pope was currently short on friends.

Maybe he could use one.

He scanned across the page, taking in what little

information there was that Gina had seen fit to include in the log. No notations about any deviant sexual proclivities, no other personal information. Under contact information, Gina had listed a single phone number. David didn't recognize the area code, probably a cell.

He pulled the cell phone he'd appropriated from his pocket, dialed the number. His thumb hovered over the Send button.

Pope won't answer, just like Charlie didn't when he didn't recognize the number.

David erased the number and switched to text messaging.

I want to talk. This is David Sparrow.

He remembered the text would show up as somebody else and followed up with:

I took this phone from one of Payne's men.

He couldn't think of anything else to say that might convince Pope to reply, so he simply waited. Five minutes turned into ten. At the twenty-minute mark, David figured it was time to come up with plan B. Maybe he could call Charlie back and find out if—

The cell phone vibrated in his hand.

He looked at the phone, eagerly read the incoming text.

Prove it.

Prove it. How was David supposed to prove who he was?

He sat back in the car seat and closed his eyes, trying to recall the memory techniques from training. David had met Pope on only a few occasions, and he tried to recall the last time. An Air Force hangar in Frankfurt, Germany. He tried to place the faces, reconstruct the scene.

Calvin Pope came into focus. David saw him clearly in his mind. A heavyset man, but more thick than fat. He wore a dark, rumpled suit, tie pulled loose. Pope needed a haircut, brown hair down over his neck. Glasses. He shook a cigarette loose from a crumpled pack.

David texted:

You smoke unfiltered Camels.

The return text:

Quit two years ago.

David:

Air Force Hangar in Germany. Bringing back the runaway Al Qaeda prisoner. You were still smoking then.

Pope:

Okay. What else you got?

David closed his eyes, picturing the scene again and zoomed in on Pope. The tie pulled loose. It was U.S. Naval Academy tie.

You went to the Naval Academy.

Pope replied:

Not true. You lose.

Fuck. Fuck. Fuck. David worked the keypad frantically.

I only said that because of your tie. In Germany, you were wearing an Academy tie.

Nothing.
Come on, come on.
David stared at the phone, willed Pope to text him back. The man was in hiding, likely paranoid as hell. He'd see traps around every corner. What would David do in his position?
I wouldn't believe some stranger sending me texts out of the blue, either. That's for damn sure.
But if the man's desperate . . .
The phone rang and startled him.
"Hello," he answered.
"Remember this address." The voice was barely above a whisper and told David an address and an apartment number. "Thirty minutes."
He hung up.
David cranked the Dodge and was already calling Charlie as he pulled into traffic and headed for his next stop.

CHAPTER TWENTY-FIVE

David parked across from the old building on the edge of Chinatown, the neighborhood gray and shabby and quiet. Nobody on the street this time of night. He watched the walk-up for signs of life as he called Charlie back.

"It's me."

"You look up that address?" David asked.

"Yeah," Charlie said. "It's a put-up job all right. The apartment is leased to somebody named Sean Doolittle, social security number, paystubs, everything you need. But Doolittle didn't exist before two months ago. It's a pretty sloppy job by certain standards, but good enough if you're looking for a crap apartment to hide out in."

"Okay," David said. "I'm going in. Call you later if I don't get killed."

David left the Dodge behind and crossed the street to the walk-up. He wore his new shirt untucked to cover the Browning stuck in the front of his pants and the Glock in the back. He hoped this wasn't a shooting trip. He needed Pope to talk.

He needed answers.

David climbed the stairs to the second level and went down the hall to number three, paused and listened. Somebody upstairs played a television too loudly, so he had to press his ear flat against the door. When he didn't hear anything coming from within the apartment, he knocked on the door.

No answer. He knocked again. Waited.

David put his hand on the knob and turned it slowly. The door wasn't locked. He eased the door open two inches and peeked inside. Not a fancy place to live, bare floor and walls. A scratched, wooden table with a single chair. An open throughway led off somewhere David couldn't see. Maybe a kitchen.

David cleared his throat. "Pope?"

Pope wasn't a behind-the-lines solo operative like David, but he was plenty dangerous in his own way. If he didn't respect the man's abilities, the results could be lethal. David raised his voice and tried again. "Pope."

He pushed the door open. It creaked on old hinges.

David entered, shut the door behind him.

He drew the Browning and slowly moved into the apartment. There was an issue of *Sports Illustrated* and a half-full ashtray on the table.

Quit, huh?

The whole place had a musty closed-in smell, like the windows hadn't been open in a year.

He moved into the kitchen. Scratched linoleum and appliances from the Carter administration. A Chinese takeout menu stuck to the front of the refrigerator with a NY Mets magnet. David opened the refrigerator and looked inside. Takeout cartons, a jar of pickles, and half a six-pack of Heineken.

He passed back through the living room, took a quick look in the bathroom. A faded green towel hanging on the rack. No shower curtain.

The bedroom was the last room. A single bed with rumpled covers. Nothing in the closet. No suitcase. Not a stitch of clothing.

"Shit."

Calvin Pope had reconsidered. Whatever part of him had wanted to talk to David Sparrow, a stronger part of him had overruled the idea. Maybe the part that was afraid. Whatever light Pope could have shed on this mess was gone now. David didn't really even know Pope's background. CIA? Military intelligence? He was a smart and devious man and could be anywhere by now.

David left the apartment and returned to the Dodge.

Back to square one. He couldn't spend time tracking down a man that didn't want to be found. He sat there behind the wheel wondering where to go next.

Sudden motion in the rearview mirror made him flinch and reach for his pistol.

"Don't do it." And the sound of a gun cocking.

David put his hands on the steering wheel. "I won't."

"I don't want to shoot you," the man said from the backseat. "But I'll just keep this gun pointed at the back of your head anyway. Just as a matter of routine, you understand."

"I understand."

David's eyes shifted back to the rearview mirror.

Calvin Pope looked grayer than the last time David had seen him, his skin hung slack and sallow, red eyes sunken back in his head. Dark circles, hair greasy and matted. He was a wreck. A man at the end of his rope.

"University of Maryland."

David blinked. "What?"

"I didn't go to Annapolis," Pope said. "I went to Maryland. I spilled coffee down my front that morning in Frankfurt. I had a spare shirt but not another tie. An Envoy pal of mine was a Navy man. He lent me the tie."

"That explains it," David said.

Pope plucked a cigarette from the pack with his lips, then lit it with a cheap disposable. He puffed it. "I like your car."

"At least it's paid for."

Pope grinned, puffed his cigarette.

"I thought you'd quit," David said.

"Yeah, I quit the unfiltered ones." Pope took a long drag on the cigarette, let a plume of gray smoke out slowly. "Those fuckers will kill you."

"Mr. Pope," David said. "The flash drive shows all the men you've relocated and where."

"Yes."

"And the bribes you took."

Pope took another long drag on the cigarette. "Yes."

"Maybe you'd like to tell me what's going on," David suggested.

Pope smoked some more, thinking it over. David figured he was gathering it all in, putting it in some kind of order so he could make a story out of it and looking for a place to start.

"The thing is . . . I wanted the money," Pope said. "I have no wife or family. I had twenty-two years with Uncle Sam. What was that? What did it mean? So Dante Payne offered me money, and I took it. I didn't stop to think what would happen next. You know, I still have no idea. What happens next, I mean. Payne gave me a lot of money, but my life was still my life."

"You had a job to do like the rest of us." David wasn't sure what he'd meant to accomplish by that comment. Maybe the idea that Pope felt sorry for himself hit too close to home.

"You know what I think about that job?" Pope said. "Let me ask you a question. They'd drop you behind enemy lines and tell you to find somebody and bring them out, right?"

"Sometimes."

"You locate your target," Pope said, "but if you can't bring him out. What do you do?"

"Usually the order is to terminate," David said. "To keep certain information from being compromised."

"So my question is," Pope said. "Why not skip right to the termination? These people are the worst scum of the Earth, and we feel we owe them something because they sold out their pals or provided information on some shit bags who are also scum of the Earth. But we owe them, so we relocate them to our soil."

David said nothing. Whatever Pope wanted to say, he didn't need prompting.

"Because we're America," Pope said. "We're supposed to be the good guys, so we remember who helps us. Even if they're evil or murderers or rapists. We're the good guys. What a bunch of shit. So here we are drowning in our own good intentions. We're bringing these people over here and then what? Like we don't have enough of our own criminals."

"So your taking bribes from Payne squares that how?" David asked.

Pope chuckled, but it sounded hollow. "I didn't mean to imply that I was trying to help, just that I was disillusioned."

"The flash drive," David said. "Why?"

"Insurance," Pope said. "Against Payne. If I went down or if something happened to me then it happened to him, too. Turns out I was too clever for my own good."

"Who was it that came to my house?" David asked.

"What?"

"That first night," David said. "The man who broke into my house. He wanted the flash drive, and he wasn't one of Payne's run-of-the-mill hoods."

Pope rolled down the back window three inches and flicked his cigarette butt out of it. He immediately lit another one and puffed it.

"I'm sorry about that," Pope said at last. "I thought I was doing something good when I slipped the flash drive in with the rest of the evidence. Helping maybe. It didn't occur to me it would make your wife a target. It should have. I should have thought more clearly about it."

David cleared his throat. "Who?"

"NSA," Pope said. "Or FBI."

"Jesus."

"Probably NSA," Pope said. "They want to cover it up."

"Slow down," David said. "Walk me through it."

"If this mess gets into the newspapers, it will embarrass the administration, and that's with midterm elections on the horizon," Pope said. "So they set the NSA on me. Oh, I can't *prove* who it is, but the NSA have their fingerprints all over the place. Anyway, the executive branch always sends the NSA. They have a proud history of sweeping troublemakers under the rug. Fucking lapdogs."

That would explain it, David thought. *The man who broke into the house was good. He almost had me. An NSA spook would make sense.*

David watched Pope in the rearview mirror. The man had gone quiet, puffed his cigarette thoughtfully. He was looking out the window, and for the moment he wasn't in the backseat of the Dodge. He was a thousand miles away, or maybe a decade away, maybe replaying the choices in his life that had brought him to this point.

Or maybe he was just tired and smoking a cigarette.

"The FBI," David prompted.

Pope's eyes met David's in the mirror. "What?"

"You said the FBI was after you, too."

"Oh, yeah," Pope said. "That's a little different. They want to bring me in alive and make me talk. Seems there's a prominent senator on the Intelligence Committee looking to make a run at the White House. She'd just love to put on a show to make the current administration look bad, and dragging me in front of the committee to testify would fit the bill nicely. Lots of pointed questions about foreign murderers moving in next door to your friends and neighbors."

"I can see how that might grab a few headlines," David admitted.

"They'd make a real circus out of it," Pope said.

"Seems turning yourself into the FBI is the obvious choice," David suggested.

"Is it?" There was nothing amused in Pope's weak smile. "Tell me, Major Sparrow, when they drop you behind enemy lines, who do you turn yourself into?"

"That's not the same."

"Feels the same to me," Pope said. "Every place I go I'm behind enemy lines, okay? Why don't you turn *yourself* in? Go to the police and tell your story and let them work it out for you."

David didn't reply.

"That's right," Pope said. "You turn yourself in and then you can't undo it, can you? You're caught, trapped. And that goes against every instinct men like us have. You especially, I bet."

David found himself nodding without meaning to.

"And once they have you, they can do whatever they want. It's out of your control. And control is everything."

Control is everything.

And even as David found himself agreeing, it occurred to him that men like Dante Payne probably lived by the same creed.

"Why did you want my wife to have the flash drive?" David asked. "Was it just to incriminate Payne?"

"I thought I might work a deal," Pope said. "I don't trust the Feds, but your wife . . . I thought the DA could protect me in trade for testimony or something. Stupid. That was back at the grasping-at-straws stage. I've moved on to acceptance."

He paused to flick the second cigarette butt out the window. He stuck another one in the corner of his mouth but didn't light it. His head was down, shoulders slumped, some weight squashing him down a little at a time.

"Something else, another reason," Pope continued. "I guess . . . maybe I wanted to make amends or something."

They sat for a few seconds.

"What do I do about Payne?" David asked.

"You mean to kill him?"

"Yes."

"Then you already know what to do," Pope said.

"Anything you could tell me would help."

"He has buttons. You can push them," Pope said. "He's proud. Arrogant. He's smart, but if he thinks he's been insulted, he might act rashly. It's not much. I'm sorry."

No. It wasn't much.

David sensed Pope was winding down but wanted to keep him talking. "The flash drive. You said you were trying to help."

Pope lit the cigarette in his mouth. "Tell you what. I'm going to smoke one last cigarette, and then I'm going."

"You said you wanted to help," David pressed. "What did you mean?"

Pope sighed out a gray cloud. "Whatever Payne is . . . I helped make him. There was this time . . ."

Pope trailed off, and for a moment David thought he'd lost him.

"There was this time," Pope began again, "when Payne was first starting out. In order to set himself up, he had to clear away the competition. He was going up against the Russians. It had gotten bloody and Payne and the leader of the Russians reached some kind of truce, but it was bullshit. It was just Payne's way of lulling the Russian into letting his guard down."

David thought he heard Pope's voice catch.

Pope cleared his throat, rubbed his red eyes with a knuckle. "So one night Payne and his men burned that Russian's house right down to the fucking ground. With the Russian inside. And the Russian's three kids and his wife and his eighty-one-year-old mother-in-law. But he couldn't have done it without me. I provided his foot soldiers. I opened the gates and let the barbarians inside."

Pope blew out a stream of gray smoke. "I don't know your wife, but she seemed honest. Didn't seem like she'd take a bribe or be intimidated. She'd keep going until she nailed Payne to the wall. But that turned out to be a mistake, too."

"What do you mean?"

"I mean putting Payne in prison wouldn't solve anything," Pope said. "He'd hired a hundred lawyers to work around the clock to get him out. Or if he didn't get out, he'd still send messages to his people, and they'd come after your wife and you and your family. You've got to kill him. But you already know that. It doesn't end unless Dante Payne dies."

David considered Pope's story about the Russian and his wife and kids.

"My wife was upstairs when the break-in happened," David said. "My kids. Sleeping in bed. I don't care about senators or the administration or who slipped up at the State Department. I just care about my family."

"Yeah."

And with that single word, David now clearly heard the strain in the man's voice. How long had he been on the run, living on the edge?

"Well." Pope flicked the half-finished cigarette out the window. "My last smoke. I said I'd have one more then go. So . . . I guess . . . I guess I'll go now."

In the rearview mirror, David saw Pope stick his pistol in his mouth. David opened his mouth to shout—

The gunshot rocked the car. Brains exploded out the back of Pope's head and splattered across the rear window.

David flung the car door open and staggered from the vehicle, ears ringing. He braced himself against the hood and bent over, the urge to gag rising. For a second, he thought he'd vomit, but the feeling subsided. He spit, trying to get the bitter taste out of his mouth.

He went back to the rear car window and looked in at the body.

Calvin Pope lay all crumpled on top of himself, one arm bent at an odd angle beneath his body, the other hand still gripping the pistol. His eyes were wide and glassy. Blood leaked from the back of his head and spread across the seat.

David took what he needed out of the Dodge. He couldn't drive it around in this condition and didn't have time to clean it up. He had his guns and Gina's logbook and the cell phone he'd taken off Payne's man.

He took a last look at Calvin Pope. Charlie had told David that the information on Pope's flash drive had read like a confession.

He'd been right.

CHAPTER TWENTY-SIX

Larry Meadows was having one of those nights.

He'd had to straight-up lie to the police. David Sparrow? Who? What? Huh? If Larry hadn't known for a fact that David was rock solid, he'd be feeling pretty anxious right about now. The police had surrounded David's Escalade with yellow tape and had shut down the parking garage for over an hour.

This was not a night Larry needed extra hassles.

The Shriners were good guests, but this was the final night of the convention, and they were bringing the party strong. Larry had called in every bartender and waiter he could get to answer the phone. All hands on deck.

During almost every minute of the day something was going wrong—broken ice machines, clogged toilets, problems in the kitchens, missing luggage, and any of a hundred other things. Larry would be lost without a small army of assistant managers, bell captains, and desk clerks who stood the front lines between him and a never-ending flow of needy guests. A problem had to be fairly significant to demand Larry Meadows's personal attention.

Like when the police wanted to search your hotel for a missing fugitive.

Fortunately, a parking valet had identified David fleeing the scene, negating the need for a room-to-room search.

And, man, what a huge pain in the ass that would have been. The guests would have definitely bitched about it to no end.

The police had gone, and for now, everything in the hotel seemed to be running smoothly. Only a temporary situation to be sure, but Larry took advantage of the lull to keep a promise. He'd told David he'd check in on his wife. Probably not strictly necessary, but it might ease her stress to see a friendly face for a few minutes. Larry didn't know the woman, but he imagined she might be feeling all alone up there.

Larry didn't want to arrive empty-handed, so he headed back to the kitchens and flagged down one of the chefs.

"Brenda, you have any of that good strawberry cheesecake left by any chance?"

"Just made another one."

"Slice me a double-size piece, would you?" Larry asked.

Brenda raised an eyebrow.

"Don't look at me like that."

"You know what your wife said," Brenda reminded him. "Diet."

"It's not for *me*," Larry said. "It's for a special guest."

She sliced it for him, put the dish on a tray, and covered it with a little silver dome. Larry thanked her, took the cake to the elevator, and headed up to the top floor.

Larry knocked, and a moment later, Amy opened the door. "Mr. Meadows."

"I know the kitchen up here is fully stocked," Larry said. "But this is the dessert chef's specialty. You won't get this anyplace else."

Amy smiled politely and stepped aside to allow Larry to enter. "What is it?"

"Strawberry cheesecake." Larry took the tray into the kitchen and set it on the counter. "It's good stuff. Just stick it in the refrigerator if you want to save it for later."

"That's kind of you," Amy said. "But please don't go to any trouble. You've done enough already, and I know you have a hotel to run."

"The cheesecake was just an excuse, ma'am," Larry admitted. "Fact is I told David I'd look in on you. He's worried."

Amy sighed. "He's worried about *me*? I keep checking my phone for a text every ten seconds hoping to get word from him."

"Ma'am, this probably won't help, but please believe me. David knows what he's doing. He's good at what he does. Maybe the best there is."

Amy summoned a wan smile, nodded absently.

"You need anything, just pick up the phone," Larry said. "Army people look after one another. That extends to families, too."

"Thank you, Mr. Meadows," Amy said. "But all I want is sleep. I don't think I've ever been this tired in my life."

"I can imagine," Larry said. "So I won't keep you. Just remember, I'm a phone call away."

On his way back to the elevator, Larry Meadows envied the notion of a good night's sleep, but there would be no rest for the hotel manager until every last Shriner had been tucked safely into bed.

A short time later, Amy sat up in bed, feeling foolish. The notion she could sleep was idiotic. How many times had she texted David without a reply?

She knew the answer. Nine times.

She turned on the nightstand lamp and swung her legs over the side of the bed. She wore only white cotton panties and a Jets T-shirt. She grabbed the pair of jeans from the floor where she'd kicked them off earlier. That made her laugh. An article of clothing lasted about ten seconds on the floor with David around.

She missed him. She missed when she'd come home from a long day, tossing off her work cloths, David following her around the bedroom picking them up and carrying them to the clothes hamper.

Nine times she'd texted him.

She wriggled into the jeans, zipped them up. They were tight and she felt an irrational stab of anger at the fact. All the damn hours on the elliptical. But they were still too tight.

Nine times.

She left the bedroom and walked out into the living room, turning her head and taking in the place again. It was nice. A rich man's getaway.

A pair of French doors led out to a balcony. She hadn't been out there again and decided to take a look. There was a breeze. A good view, the lights of the city glittering. She looked down. The hotel's pool and spa were illuminated ten floors below on the roof of the annex.

It was a great place for a getaway. She imagined a weekend here with David. Drop the kids off at her sister's, a nice dinner and take in a show, retire early. Champagne.

But all it was really was a fancy place to hide.

Nine times.

She grabbed her makeup bag and headed into the bathroom. Why she'd grabbed her makeup bag when her husband had declared an emergency and told her they needed to flee the house was something best left for some future time of self-examination. Everyone had a different definition of *essentials*. For now she was glad for the distraction.

She pulled a stool up to the bathroom's makeup vanity and turned on the mirror lights. She'd start with her nails. The ritual of carefully painting each nail one at a time with the tiny brush was something she found calming. She selected a color called Neon Mango.

She methodically applied the polish to her first fingernail.

Amy had texted David nine times because ten times was one of those nice round numbers. If she texted him a tenth time, and he didn't answer, then that meant she'd have to do something. And Amy had no idea what that might be. She'd have to go somewhere or call somebody. Every time she started to think about it, she stopped herself.

She blew on the freshly polished fingernail, squinted at it, and determined she'd done a satisfactory job.

Nine more to go.

Dante Payne poured himself another Scotch in the back of his limousine. They had aimlessly been circling Midtown, waiting for a call. A holding pattern. Payne grew impatient.

The phone rang at last and Payne answered it. "Talk."

"I think I know where the woman is." Yousef's voice. "The attorney."

"Where?"

"A hotel called the Royal Empire," Yousef said.

"Then go kill her," Payne said.

"We need to wait," Yousef cautioned. "The husband isn't there yet. If we move too fast we might only get one or none at all. If we scare them and they run, we'll just have to track them down all over again."

"I will take the men I have with me and go over there," Payne said.

"No. I've sent Reagan and some of your other men to watch all of the entrances," Yousef told him. "As soon as Sparrow enters the building, I'll know. And then we'll close in on him."

"And what would you have me do in the meantime?" Payne asked.

"Wait."

More waiting! Payne bit off a curse and hung up the phone.

Yousef chastised himself. He should have been gentler with Payne. The man was proud and unaccustomed to being told to wait, even more unaccustomed to letting a situation get out of his control.

Yousef had a job to do and little time for diplomacy.

But it was more than that, wasn't it? Not just a job.

It was revenge. Yousef had taken Payne's offer for one reason only. Well, yes, there was the money. One could never have too much of that. But his primary motivation was crystal clear.

Yousef would have David Sparrow's head.

First, business.

He dialed Reagan.

The Chechen answered after the first ring. "Yes?"

"You and the others are in position?" Yousef asked.

"We are," Reagan said. "He won't get into the hotel without our seeing him."

"Do *not* engage if you see him," Yousef said. "Call and tell me and we'll all take him together."

A pause.

"Do you hear me?" Yousef asked, a slight edge in his voice.

"Yes," Reagan said. "We'll call you immediately."

"Good." Yousef hung up.

His thoughts returned to his revenge upon Sparrow. There is a difference between revenge and justice, Yousef knew. And while there would be an element of justice in Sparrow's demise, simply killing him would not constitute revenge.

Sparrow must know who is responsible. He must know it is me who is killing him.

Yousef dialed another number and rehearsed in his mind what he would say.

CHAPTER TWENTY-SEVEN

David was about to head down into the subway when the phone vibrated in his pocket. He stepped to the side and looked at the screen, saw an unfamiliar number but no name. He didn't answer.

A moment later he got a text:

Talk to me, Sparrow.

Somebody knew David had the phone.

It rang again. What could he gain by answering? Then again, what did he have to lose?

He answered after the fourth ring. "Hello."

"Do you know who this is, Sparrow?"

The lightly accented voice did sound vaguely familiar, but David was clueless. "No."

"How disappointing," said the man on the other end of the phone. "But you are smart. I'm sure if you thought about it, you would remember me from Syria, government man."

A sharp, sudden memory hit David upon hearing the

words *government man*. He remembered the man who'd called him that, remembered they hadn't parted on the best of terms. "Yousef Haddad."

"Ah, see that wasn't so hard, was it?" Yousef said. "I'm flattered you remember me. Especially since I remember you so well. I remember you as the man who promised me that my wife and daughters would be safe. Do you remember that, government man, or do I need to jog your memory?"

There was a brief temptation to tell the man that it couldn't be helped or that he was sorry or that they'd tried their best for his family, but David knew instinctively none of that would matter. "I remember."

"In a perfect world, I would kill you last," Yousef said. "So you would know vividly and in detail what had befallen your wife and children before you died. I must content myself with simply telling you that we will get around to them eventually."

David's mind raced. Yousef Haddad must have been one of Pope's relocation projects. The man was a ruthless killer and motivated beyond money to see David and his family dead. His task to eliminate Payne had just become ten times more dangerous.

"You've gone quiet, my friend," Yousef said. "You're thinking fast. Let me give you something further to think about."

There was a muted beep in the phone's earpiece.

"I've texted you a little present, government man. Take a look and see if it amuses you as much as it does me."

David switched over to his text in-box. Yousef had sent him a photo. David looked at it and winced.

He almost didn't recognize Gina at first. She was still

wearing the thin dress David had seen on her in the apartment over at Jerry's but it was ripped down the front revealing one of her breasts. In the photo, she sprawled on the floor, head to the side, eyes open but lifeless. Her lips were swollen and bloody, a purple bruise around one eye.

David put the phone back to his ear. "Was that really necessary?"

"Necessary to illustrate a point," Yousef said. "There was not time for a rape, and to be honest I'm not generally inclined for such a thing, but we will make an exception for your wife. Don't worry, we'll take our time and do it properly."

What to say when somebody announces his plan to rape and kill your wife and murder your family? A wisecrack, a threat? Reason with the man?

All options seemed equally futile.

"I took her to the airport hours ago," David said. "She's a thousand miles away by now, protected by good people."

"Truly?" Yousef asked. "She's no longer at the Royal Empire Hotel?"

The breath left David's body.

"I'm sure you wouldn't lie to me," Yousef said. "But one mustn't leave stones unturned. I suppose I should stop by the Royal Empire and just see for myself if—"

David hung up the phone and ran into the street, waving his arms to flag down a taxi. Horns blared at him and tires squealed. The first taxi sped past him, the driver making a rude gesture.

The next taxi stopped for him, and he jumped in and slammed the door closed behind him.

"Royal Empire Hotel in Midtown." David opened his

wallet, took out all the cash he had, and tossed it through the window into the seat next to the driver. "Run the red lights."

"Easy, buddy," the driver said. "Might not be the best idea."

David pulled the Browning from his waistband and stuck it through the window. "How about now?"

The driver stomped the accelerator, and the taxi shot through the intersection just as the light turned red, the blare of horns chasing them to the other side.

They got lucky most of the way to Midtown, and had to run only two more red lights. No cops around to see it. Whatever the speed record was from Chinatown to Midtown, David was pretty sure the cabbie shattered it. David told him to pull down the side street next to the hotel and let him off.

The cabbie pulled over.

"Sorry about the gun. I wasn't going to shoot you," David told him. "Keep the money."

The cabbie scoffed. "Damn right I'm keeping the money."

David got out and the taxi pulled away.

He didn't want to risk the front entrance of the hotel again. Likewise, going through the parking garage where the police had already discovered his Escalade also seemed like a bad bet. That left a side entrance that took him in near the convention halls.

David took a quick look around, pretended not to see the man watching from the deli window across the street, and went into the hotel.

———

Reagan dialed Yousef the second he saw Sparrow enter the Royal Empire.

"He's here," Reagan said.

"Excellent," Yousef said. "I thought he might arrive soon. Keep watching that entrance. Tell the others to keep watch on the other exits and to sing out if they see him. I'm on my way."

"A lot can happen by the time you get here," Reagan said. "He's right in there. It would be easy."

"Was it so easy on the boat?"

"That was different."

"It's always different," Yousef said. "Wait for me to get there."

Reagan formed a cutting response but swallowed it. "Fine."

He hung up.

This was ridiculous. Reagan was a professional. If he moved fast, he could catch up with Sparrow and end this now. He tossed back the tepid coffee he'd been nursing and tossed the paper cup into the trash on the way out of the deli.

Reagan crossed the street and went through the same entrance Sparrow had. He found himself in a quiet part of the hotel, deserted meeting rooms and convention halls. Sounds of a party emanated from somewhere deeper inside, laughter and boisterous conversation and the clink of ice in glasses.

Reagan needed to determine which way Sparrow might have gone. If he had a room in the hotel then he would have gone along the main hall toward the elevators and—

In his peripheral vision, Reagan saw the gun swinging for his face. He flinched away and took the hit on the shoulder, spun back, his fist coming up to block Sparrow's attempt to bring the pistol around for a shot. He blocked Sparrow at the wrist and punched with his other hand, but Sparrow caught his arm and tried to pin it against his body. Sparrow came in for a head butt, but like last time Sparrow tried that move, Reagan lowered his head to avoid taking it in the face.

The head butt never came.

Reagan felt Sparrow's knee come up hard into his balls.

The air whooshed out of him, and a wave of nausea flashed through his gut. He gulped air to recover and twisted out of Sparrow's grip. He tried to turn back for a punch but something hard slapped across his face. He felt his cheekbone crack. Stars went off in front of his eyes.

Reagan stepped back and kept stepping back, trying to get out of Sparrow's reach and blink his eyes clear. Pain throbbed through every part of him.

When his vision cleared, he saw Sparrow advancing with a blackjack in his hand. Sparrow brought it down hard, aiming for Reagan's head. Reagan brought up a forearm to fend it off and took the blow across the hand.

Reagan screamed as multiple small bones broke.

He took another strike on the collarbone and another on the other shoulder.

The hall blurred and the floor came up to hit him hard in the side of the face.

Reagan tried to push himself up, but his arms went watery and he kissed the carpet again. He shifted his gaze to see Sparrow standing over him.

Sparrow looked down at him a moment, face blank.

"Hey . . ." Reagan panted, feeling sick. "Hey . . . let's . . . let's talk a minute."

Sparrow glared down at him, eyes like bright stones.

Reagan gulped for air again. "Let's . . . work something out."

He watched Sparrow raise the blackjack, pause a moment, and then bring the blackjack down fast on his face before the world went dark.

CHAPTER TWENTY-EIGHT

David dragged the body into an unused convention room and rolled him under a banquet table. The tablecloth hung low enough to hide him. As David suspected when he spotted him in the deli window, it was the same man he'd fought on Payne's yacht.

Is it just him? Was he here watching for me? Or maybe Haddad is here, too. How many? Have they found Amy?

David needed information. He headed back down the convention hallway toward the lobby of the hotel. He paused at a house phone hanging on the wall and dialed zero. He didn't like this, didn't like standing out in the open in the hotel hallway, but he had to know.

The hotel operator answered, and David asked for Larry Meadows's office.

"Manager's office," Larry answered.

"It's me."

"I was wondering when you'd turn up."

"Larry, I've been a little out of the loop. Is everything okay?"

"Well, some crazy guy led a pair of cops on a merry chase through my hotel . . . ," Larry said.

"I mean Amy. Is she okay?"

"Yes," Larry said. "Nobody's gone up there, and she hasn't come down. As far as I know, we're cool."

"Where are you?" David asked.

"My office."

"Is that the room with all the monitors?"

"That's the security office."

"Can you hang out in there for a while?" David asked.

"What's up?"

"I'm going to give you a phone number," David said. "If you can watch those monitors and give me a heads-up. You know the sort of men we're watching out for, right?"

"Give me two minutes, and I'll get set up."

"Thanks, Larry." David gave him the number, then hung up.

He walked fast toward the elevators, dodging Shriners in little hats and holding drinks in their hands. David hit the elevator call button and stood there for an eternity waiting. Finally an elevator arrived, and he took it to the top.

When the elevator doors opened, he stepped out, the Browning in his hand. He stood, listened. Had anyone been up here? What if he was too late? What if Yousef had already—

No. Stay professional. Larry had said everything was fine.

David tried the knob. Locked.

He knocked.

Long seconds passed, and he almost knocked again when the door abruptly swung inward.

Amy gaped at him a moment, eyes wide as if she couldn't believe who she was looking at. Then she flung herself on him, arms going tightly around his neck. She mashed her mouth so hard into his that it hurt his lip against his teeth.

He didn't care. David kissed her back, wrapped his arms around her and lifted her up.

When she finally pulled away from him, she said, "You asshole. You look like hell." She wiped at her eyes with the back of her hand. "Do you know how many times I texted you?"

"Nine times?"

"I . . . how did you know?"

"Because ten is a good round number."

She kissed him again.

He ushered her inside and locked the door behind them.

"We've got to get out of here," David said.

"Why?" Her happiness at seeing him evaporated. "What's wrong? Did Payne . . . did you . . . ?"

"I failed," David said. "And we're out of time. Somehow, Payne's men know we're here. We need to go. Grab your things, just the important stuff, nothing else. The police found the Escalade, but we can get a cab and then—"

And then what?

David thought it through. Amy had friends. They could call them, flood the hotel with police and be escorted safely away. But the police were already looking for him because of the shooting at his house. David would spend time in a cell while they sorted it out. Payne could bribe anyone to get at him in jail. And who would protect Amy while he was locked up? Who could she trust in her own office? Payne would surround himself with lawyers. Nothing would get solved. None of them would be safe.

"This isn't going to work," David said quietly.

Amy looked at him, concern in her eyes.

No, not concern. Fear. She's afraid.

"What do you mean?" Amy asked.

"If we don't end this now," David said, "then we're back to square one. Worse than square one actually because we won't have any advantages at all."

"Advantages?" Amy said. "What advantages?"

"Payne and his men are coming to us," David said. "And I know it, and I can be ready for them."

"David, let's just go," Amy said. "We'll figure something else out. We'll find another safe place and—"

"And what? Amy, how long can your sister and brother-in-law hide our children for us? How long do we live in fear in our own homes waiting for Dante Payne to send somebody to kill us while he hides behind his lawyers?"

Amy opened her mouth to say something, then shut it again. She thought about it. A second later, she asked, "What do you need from me?"

"I need you to do something brave," David said. "I need you to stay. I need you to hang tough right here like you're still hiding out and everything is normal."

"And what will *you* be doing?" she asked.

David smiled. "Finishing it."

Amy looked at him, searching his face, deciding.

She kissed him again. "Do what you need to do."

"I love you," he said.

"I love you, too."

David's phone rang, and he answered it. "Hello."

"Three men just walked in the main entrance," Larry Meadows said. "I'm watching them on the security monitor. Could be nobody at all, but they're putting out a pretty strong badass vibe."

David described Yousef Haddad.

"I think we have a match," Larry said.

"I'm sorry this has to happen in your hotel, Larry."

"Hey, you're the good guy and they're the bad guys," Larry said. "Just make it worth it."

"Right."

David hung up the phone and turned back to his wife. He reached into his pocket and came out with the little automatic he'd taken from Gina.

He handed it to Amy. "It's not much."

She took it. "It looks like a toy."

"If you need to use it, get in close," David said.

"God help me if I need to use it."

David gathered her in his arms and kissed her. "We're almost at the end. Don't open the door for anyone but me."

"Okay."

He looked deep in her eyes and tried to think of something to say, something perfect that would ease her mind.

David kissed her again and left.

CHAPTER TWENTY-NINE

Yousef's annoyance had grown to epic proportions by the time he reached the Royal Empire Hotel. Dante Payne had called three times, demanding progress reports. The slur in his voice was quite distinct on the third call, and Yousef suspected he was taking out his impatience on the bar in his limousine.

Then he called the Royal Empire Hotel and asked the operator to connect him with Amy Sparrow's room. The operator had reported that no such guest existed. Yousef hadn't really expected pinpointing the woman to be easy, but it would have been nice for something to be simple for a change.

The fact that Yousef couldn't get Reagan on the phone annoyed him most of all. He had explicitly ordered the Chechen to stand down until Yousef had arrived.

I am surrounded by idiots.

Yousef entered the hotel with two of Payne's flunkies. As foot soldiers, they were third rate but better than nothing. He told one to station himself in the lobby and keep an eye on who got on and off of the elevator.

Sparrow and his woman were in this hotel somewhere. Yousef could feel it.

He told Payne's other flunky to follow him.

They looked for the hotel manager in his office, but he wasn't there. They found a door marked security and entered.

Two men were there. They sat in swivel chairs looking at monitors that showed various locations around the hotel and convention center. The men swiveled around to look at Yousef. One was a black man in a sports coat, the coat of arms of the hotel over the pocket. The other wore a khaki security guard's uniform.

The security guard rose casually from his chair. "I'm sorry, gentlemen, but this is a restricted area."

Yousef motioned to Payne's flunky.

The flunky pulled a knife from his belt, stepped forward, and brought it up hard under the security guard's rib cage. The guard went stiff a moment and then fell forward. The flunky stepped out of the way and let the man fall.

The other one stood abruptly.

Yousef drew his pistol. "I don't think so."

The man froze.

"You are the manager?" Yousef asked.

"I'm Larry Meadows, the manager, yes," he said. "Whatever the problem is I'm sure we can work it out without anyone else getting hurt."

Yousef gave the manager credit. Upon first glance, he seemed competent and unflustered.

"I certainly hope so, Mr. Meadows," Yousef said. "You have an unregistered guest in your hotel. I need to find Amy Sparrow, and I'm in a bit of a hurry."

"I assure you, all guests are registered," Larry said. "If she's not in the computer then she's not here."

Yousef gave the flunky a short nod, and he punched Larry hard in the stomach. Larry grunted and bent double. The flunky punched him again across the jaw, and Larry went to the floor.

Yousef knelt and frisked the manager, found his wallet and stood again.

"This doesn't get any better for you," Yousef said. "We want the Sparrow woman."

"I . . . I don't know who that is," Larry said from the floor. He made no attempt to get up. "We have hundreds of guests. I have no idea who you're talking about."

Yousef nodded, and the flunky kicked the manager in the face. He spit blood.

The flunky drew the knife again. "I could take a thumb. That usually does it."

"I'm confident you could wear him down eventually," Yousef said. "But we are pressed for time, and I sense Mr. Meadows is made of sterner stuff than the average hotel manager."

Yousef squatted next to the manager. "Look at me, Mr. Meadows."

Larry didn't move his head, but his eyes shifted up to Yousef.

Yousef held up the wallet so Larry could see it. "Do you know what this is, Mr. Meadows?"

"My wallet."

"It *was* your wallet," Yousef said. "In my hands, it has become an instant interrogation kit. Everything I need to get what I desire is contained within." He opened the wallet and took out the driver's license. "This has your address. Now I can visit your home if I wish." He took out a picture of a handsome woman and showed it to Larry. "Is this your wife?"

Larry said nothing.

"I will presume she is." Yousef removed another picture from the wallet, a young boy, maybe nine years old. "And this good-looking young man is your son."

Yousef let the silence hang a moment.

He bent his head lower so he could speak softly right into Larry's ear. "Now, I'm going to ask you some questions. I want you to think very carefully before you answer. Your answers should be as complete and as detailed as possible. I'm asking for an attitude adjustment, really. You should *want* to help me. You should be trying hard to think of anything you can tell me that I would find helpful. All the time, consider this. Anything that I or my associate are willing to do to you, we are more than willing to do to your wife and son. More, frankly. I assure you we would take our time to do things properly."

The fear in Larry Meadows's eyes told Yousef that the hotel manager would now be more receptive to his questions.

Yousef cleared his throat. "So. Amy Sparrow."

David didn't like the idea of stepping off the elevator into a busy lobby. Payne and Haddad had probably noticed by now that one of their men had gone missing. Maybe they'd called in reinforcements. Maybe they'd be waiting for him. Maybe a hundred different things.

He got off the elevator on the second floor. No guest rooms here, instead a business center, a gym and spa, meeting rooms and more convention facilities. He stepped into a little alcove with an ATM to get out of sight. He had one more errand.

David took out the cell phone and dialed Charlie Finn.

"You shouldn't go so long between calls," Charlie said. "Mama worries."

"Calvin Pope shot himself."

"Fucking shit."

"Charlie, I'm about to get to the end of this," David said. "There's no guarantee the good guys win this one. If you don't hear from me by morning, I need a final favor."

"Name it."

David briefly related to Charlie what Pope had told him, focusing especially on the NSA's and FBI's interest in the matter. "You know the only thing I care about is my family. This isn't about politics for me. But if I don't make it, find somebody at the FBI and give them the flash drive. Do it anonymously and then step away. The ball will be in their court then."

"You have my word, man," Charlie said.

"Charlie."

"Yeah?"

"Thanks for everything. You didn't have to help me when I called, but you did."

"Good luck, Major."

David hung up and put the cell phone in his pocket. He checked his guns and spare magazines. He took a deep breath.

Go time.

Charlie felt a tightness in his gut after he hung up with David.

You didn't help him enough. You could have done more.

Even as a cooler part of his brain realized this was nonsense, the rest of him couldn't stop thinking he needed to do something better.

David had told him to contact somebody at the FBI. Maybe he could fulfill David's request in a way that would be a little more helpful than a final posthumous favor.

He pulled up his electronic Rolodex and scrolled through the names. Charlie had been meticulous about maintaining the database and keeping it as current as possible. He marked some as deceased and others retired. He also made note if the person moved from one department to another.

Charlie hit one of the filters that only scanned FBI names. One stood out, somebody who'd recently retired but probably still had some juice back in Washington.

Maybe this person could put him in touch with somebody reasonable, an agent with a head on his shoulders not too eager to shoot first and ask questions later.

It was a start.

CHAPTER THIRTY

Yousef turned the copper key over in his hand, examining it with mild curiosity. Hotels used plastic key cards now. An actual metal key seemed almost quaint.

The hotel manager had offered only token resistance before giving up the information that the Sparrow woman was in the special penthouse on the top floor. It wasn't on the key card system, and Meadows had been persuaded to hand over the spare key.

Yousef glanced up at one of the monitors and did a double take. David Sparrow hovered in the doorway of an ATM alcove, talking on a cell phone. He looked much the same as when Yousef had met the man in Syria. The monitor was labeled 2ND FLOOR MEZZANINE.

"I want *everyone*," Yousef told the flunky. "We'll converge on the second floor. That's where he is."

He considered if he should try to take the man alive. In Yousef's revenge fantasies, Sparrow had been made to suffer for endless days. This indulgence was no longer practical, and in any case, attempting to capture him alive before hadn't quite worked out.

"Tell the men to shoot him on sight," Yousef said.

The flunky gestured to the hotel manager on the floor. "What about him?"

"We don't need him anymore," Yousef said. "Kill him and follow as fast as you can."

Yousef left the office.

The flunky approached the prone hotel manager, knife blade gleaming in his hand.

When the flunky had kicked him in the head, Larry had made a show of going as limp as possible. As far as they knew, he was down for the count. His only chance would be to try to sucker them in.

The badass who did all the talking saw something on one of the monitors he didn't like. He exchanged words with the flunky then stormed out.

Good. That cut the enemy forces exactly in half. This would be Larry's best chance to make a move.

And he *did* need to make a move, not just to save his own life, but because he owed it to David. When the guy doing the talking took the picture of his wife and son out of his wallet, Larry knew it had been all over right then. Larry had faced down numerous enemies on the battlefield. Having his family threatened that way was a whole new experience. He'd told the men exactly what they'd wanted to know.

And while Larry hadn't felt he'd had any other choice, he now felt guilty about. He needed to put this man down and call the penthouse to warn Amy.

The flunky bent toward him with the knife, and Larry played possum until the last possible second. It was a test of nerves with a knife coming at him, but Larry would only have one shot at this.

When the man's knife hand was close enough, Larry moved fast and latched on to the man's wrist.

At first the flunky tried to pull away, but Larry hung on with a death grip. Then the flunky came down hard with his other fist, but Larry had been expecting it, turned his head to take the punch on top of his skull. The blow hurt, but he heard knuckles crack and the flunky grunt pain.

Larry grabbed the guy's knife arm with his other hand, too, and pulled the man's hand toward his mouth. He bit into the soft area under the guy's thumb. Hard. The flunky screamed. Blood flooded Larry's mouth, the taste of copper and salt. He didn't ease off until the flunky opened his hand and dropped the knife.

Larry let go of the man's wrist with one hand and grabbed the weapon. He drove the blade as hard as he could through the top of the man's shoe, pinning his foot to the floor.

The flunky howled like a deranged banshee.

Larry lurched to his feet and took two more punches from the man before stepping away and steadying himself. The man continued to scream in agony, jerking his foot, trying to pry it up from the floor.

Larry's hand landed on the first thing he could reach, a heavy marble ashtray on the desk. It had been leftover from the old days when smoking was allowed in the hotel.

He swung it overhand and bashed the top of the flunky's head with a muted crack. The man's body spasmed, mouth falling open for a scream that never came.

Larry swung again, the ashtray connecting hard against the side of the man's head. The flunky went limp, fell over awkwardly, his foot still pinned to the floor.

Larry dropped the ashtray, panting, head dizzy. His heart hammered away in his chest. Suddenly his legs went noodle weak as the adrenaline drained from his body. He leaned against the desk.

Amy. Warn her.

He picked up the phone and dialed zero. "Switchboard? Yeah, it's me, Ruth. I need you to connect me to—"

He turned his head and saw the other man enter the room, the one who'd taken his wallet. He lifted a pistol.

The room exploded.

And that was all.

Dante saw that it was Yousef calling in and answered by asking, "Have you killed them yet?"

"We've spotted him and are closing in," Yousef said. "I need the men with you to finish the job."

"Excellent," Payne said. "We're on our way."

"Not you," Yousef said. "Just the men. Park someplace out of the way, and wait in the car with your driver."

Payne felt his face flush hot. "Wait in the car with my—"

"The purpose of this entire enterprise is to conceal evidence that may be used against you and to silence those who've seen that evidence," Yousef said. "Having you seen at the scene of a bloodbath completely undermines all that."

Payne hung up the phone. "Take us into the hotel parking garage," he told the driver.

CHAPTER THIRTY-ONE

David Sparrow strode the broad, second-floor mezzanine, eyes sharp for trouble.

He paused and glanced over the railing at the writhing Shriner party on the convention floor below. He had vague hopes of spotting Payne's men and then maybe he could take them out one at a time.

The ground floor was his most likely hunting ground. There were three ways down that he knew of. The escalator at the opposite end of the mezzanine, the bank of elevators, or the stairs around the corner and down the hall from the elevators.

He decided on the stairs.

David walked toward the elevators just as the doors to one of the convention rooms opened and a bunch of rowdy Shriners spilled out in front of him. They talked loudly, arm-in-arm with wives and girlfriends.

On the other side of the crowd, both elevators dinged at the same time and the doors slid open. Two men emerged from each and the four of them saw David through the crowd, their hands going immediately into their jackets.

David drew the Browning and the Glock.

A woman clinging to one of the Shriners saw the guns in David's hands and screamed. Confused murmuring ran through the crowd, heads turning to see what was happening.

It was one of Payne's goons who fired first, the bullet whizzing over everyone's heads.

Chaos erupted.

People shoved over one another trying to decide which way to run. Shouts, more screams.

One of the men took a bead on David with his pistol.

David leaped on the middle-aged couple in front of him, riding them to the floor. "Get down!"

Payne's goon blazed away down the mezzanine. There was the sound like the loud slap of a leather strap, and a Shriner standing near David screamed, blood splattering from the fleshy part of his thigh. He fell hard and writhed, moaning in pain.

David rolled off the couple he'd shoved to the floor, came up on one knee and fired both pistols at the nearest attacker. Lead ripped across his chest, and he shuddered, took one halting step backward, and fell.

The other three opened fire, but David was already scrambling out of the way and dove behind a big ceramic pot that overflowed with some kind of huge fern. He drew his legs up, trying to make himself small behind the big pot. Lead struck all around him, dust and chips flying off the pot and plaster exploding on the wall above him.

David aimed his pistols over the pot, and pulled the triggers until they clicked empty.

Another of Payne's men clutched his bloody gut and toppled over.

The remaining two gunmen wised up and dove behind a leather sofa for cover. David took the opportunity to slap a new magazine into each pistol.

He evaluated the gunmen in a split second. Third-rate, not Payne's A team or else they wouldn't have tried to gun him down through a crowd of Shriners. They'd get their ducks in a row and start shooting again in a second, and anyway the ceramic pot was pretty lousy cover.

David needed to make a move.

If these guys are third rate, then they probably rattle easily, right? Well, there's one way to find out. . . .

David rose from his hiding place behind the big pot.

And ran at them.

There was a split second of paralysis while Payne's men tried to figure out what they were looking at, and David closed the distance. An instant later they started firing, but it was sloppy and undisciplined as David sprinted straight for them.

David raised his pistols as he ran, firing nonstop and not breaking stride. A bullet hissed past his ear. Another passed close enough to tug at his shirtsleeve.

David kept squeezing the triggers of both guns. Stuffing flew up from the leather sofa. The gunmen flinched, trying to return fire and stay low at the same time.

A slug caught the first man above the left eye and knocked him back, trailing an arc of blood, into the other one behind him, throwing off his aim. He tried to swing the pistol back in time for a shot, but David had arrived.

He leaped upon the sofa to fire down behind it at the

last gunman, emptying both pistols and shredding the man's chest with hot metal.

David stepped down from the sofa, replaced the magazines in his pistols and spun a slow arc, pistols raised for whatever came next.

For the moment, nobody was trying to kill him.

Moans around the mezzanine, women crying. A number of people were tentatively rising from the floor, looking at David with fear and confusion.

David raised his voice and said, "You'll be safer if you get back to your rooms and lock yourselves in."

They didn't need to be told twice, some moving toward the elevators, others back toward the escalators.

David went to the man who'd been shot in the thigh and knelt next to him. A crying woman knelt on the other side of him.

"You need to calm down," he said to her. "You're his wife?"

"Y-yes."

"Do you have a phone?"

"Yes."

"Call an ambulance right now," David said. "Tell them which hotel and that you're on the second-floor mezzanine."

"Yes, of course." She reached back for a small beaded purse behind her, took out her phone, and made the call.

David forced a smile for the wounded man's benefit. "You're going to be fine."

The man nodded, pale face clammy with sweat.

David pulled the man's tie loose. "I need this."

He used the necktie to fasten a tourniquet around the man's leg. "I don't think the shot hit anything vital."

David had no idea if that was true or not but figured it would be nice to hear.

"They're on the way," said the woman who'd called the ambulance.

"Good." And the police with them, thought David. His time was running out.

"Give me your sweater," he told her.

She took if off and handed it to him. David folded it into thirds and put it over the bullet wound. The man winced. He took the woman's hands and placed them on top of the sweater.

"Keep pressure on this until the paramedics arrive," David said. "Can somebody stay with you?"

She turned her head toward a man hovering in the background. "Dale?"

Dale came forward, a ruddy-faced man with a beer gut. He'd somehow managed to heroically retain possession of his drink throughout the gunfight. He knelt next to the wounded man and touched his shoulder. "You hang in there, Brad. I'm here. You just relax, buddy."

"I've got to go," David told the woman.

Words of gratitude chased after him as he left, but he barely paid attention. He passed the elevators at a jog and kept going until he found the stairs.

Yousef cursed as he watched Sparrow slaughter Payne's men on the security monitor. The man paused to help a wounded hotel guest and then passed out of sight. He frantically searched the other monitors until he picked him up again.

He found Sparrow again in the basement.

Yousef pulled his pistol. *If you want somebody killed right, you've got to do it yourself.*

But that didn't mean it had to be a fair fight. He dialed Dante Payne's phone number.

Dante answered the phone, frowned, and handed the phone over to the Serb. "He wants to speak to one of you."

The Serb put the phone to his ear. "Yes? Okay. I understand." He hung up and handed the phone back to Payne.

"Sparrow is in the basement of the hotel," the Serb said. "He wants us to go down there." He looked at Payne. "He says for you to stay here."

Payne snarled. "Of course. Well, go on then. Go kill the man. This has all taken far too long already."

They nodded curtly and left.

Dante Payne fixed another drink and sulked.

CHAPTER THIRTY-TWO

David needed chaos and confusion.

He passed through the hotel laundry, looking for the maintenance room and the hotel's circuit breakers.

Soon the police would arrive if they weren't here already. David would have to dodge them while searching for Payne all while avoiding getting killed by Yousef Haddad and his henchmen.

It was a tall order.

David needed some kind of advantage.

He found a locked door marked ELECTRICAL. It was far too sturdy to kick down. He aimed and shot the lock. No good. He shot it again, and this time it opened.

He scanned the room once inside. There was a small table with a couple of flashlights on it. He'd need one soon and selected a heavy Maglite.

The main breakers were housed in a large metal box closed and padlocked. He shot the padlock off and opened it.

Inside, he found the main power switches for the entire hotel. With the police helping frightened hotel guests in the dark, he hoped it would keep them off his back for a while. And as a solo operative, he liked the thought of a blind enemy.

The bonus of cutting the power would be shutting the elevators down. Anyone trying to get to Amy would be delayed.

Of course, if I need to get up there and help her, I'll be delayed, too.

And I need to stay alive for any of it to matter.

He took hold of the main power switch and yanked it down. There was a loud *fump* and then darkness.

David flipped on the Maglite and headed back through the laundry.

Shots rang out from the darkness, and David dropped low, scooting behind an industrial clothes dryer. He killed the Maglite, waited and listened.

Apparently, they were doing the same thing because David didn't hear anything. He tried to recall what was back the other way, if there were another passage or hallway, but he already knew there wasn't. Just the electrical room. The only way out was back past whomever was shooting at him.

He reached the flashlight around the side of the dryer and switched it on.

The attackers immediately shot at the light, the bullets flying past just inches away. David dropped the flashlight and yelled as if he'd been hit.

David waited. One thing you learn as a solo operative is patience, and in a situation like this, a minute or two can seem like an eternity. Breathe, listen, wait.

They almost out-waited him. David was just about to try something else when he heard a low scraping, then movement. A whispered conversation.

There's more than one.

A few seconds later, the sounds of movement came toward him. One of them was coming to confirm the kill.

When David had dropped the flashlight, he'd tried to angle it just right. He gripped the Browning and held his breath and waited.

A second later, his opponent came into range of the flashlight, casting a huge jagged shadow on a washing machine across the aisle. David made a good guess from the shadow about the man's position, stuck his head and the Browning around the side of the dryer, and fired.

He shot the man in the groin, and the guy went down screaming. He shut him up with a shot to the head.

The other one was already returning fire, lead tinging off the dryer.

David kicked the flashlight away, and the beam played wildly over the room in a jerky motion, drawing more gunfire.

All or nothing time.

David stepped out from his hiding place, drawing the Glock with his other hand, and when the other man fired again, David zeroed in on the muzzle flash.

He poured fire onto the spot with both pistols, attempting a wide spread in the hopes of catching him with at least one of the shots.

When David's pistols clicked empty, he rushed forward, scooping up the Maglite as he went and ran for the spot as fast as he could, raising the flashlight high for a strike, but it wasn't necessary. He'd hit his target twice, once high on the chest and again in the throat.

David aimed the flashlight at his face. A slightly older man, gray at the temples. He looked more like somebody's dentist than a hired killer, but that was probably an advantage sometimes.

David didn't linger, didn't want to be caught again in a dead end. He went back through the laundry room and up a different set of stairs than the ones he'd come down.

The next level up put him in the same service corridor he'd been in before when he'd fled from the two cops. One way led around the corner to the bar, and the other way led to the kitchen. Dim battery-powered emergency lighting along the floor cast just enough light to walk.

He turned the corner toward the bar—

The sharp crack of a pistol shot, and David dropped the Maglite, slapped a hand over the shallow wound on his upper arm as he ducked back around the corner. It wasn't bad, just a gash, but it stung and bled.

He ejected the magazines from his pistols and reached for spares. There was only one left for the Glock. None for the Browning.

Shit.

He tossed the Browning away, turned the corner, and blazed down the hall with the Glock.

Yousef Haddad returned fire, shots gouging the walls on all sides of David.

He returned fire until the Glock was empty and then tossed the gun away and ran in the other direction. At the end of the hall he pushed through a swinging door and into the hotel kitchen. The only light was from the gas stove. The burners had been left on and the flames cast a weak blue glow. He took a big cleaver from a set of knives and hid himself between two metal cabinets.

A second later Yousef burst through the swinging door. He stopped and scanned the darkness, pistol in hand.

"I know you're in here, government man," Yousef said. "I saw you toss down your pistol. You are getting tired and sloppy. You should not have been so careless with your bullets."

It was true. It hadn't even occurred to him to notice until Yousef had mentioned it. David was running on fumes. It had been a long night.

But it would be over soon. One way or another.

Yousef went to the stove and cranked up the burners, the flames swelling larger. It cast a little more light in the kitchen but not much.

The door to the kitchen swung open and a man wearing an apron entered. "Hey, everyone is supposed to be out of—"

Yousef turned and shot him between the eyes.

David burst from his hiding place, cleaver held high. Yousef turned back just as David brought the blade down, catching David's wrist to fend off the strike. Yousef tried to bring the pistol to bear, but David knocked it away, sent it clattering across the kitchen floor.

Yousef punched, and David was too slow to block it, took the fist in the gut. He grunted and dropped the cleaver.

Yousef moved in with a combination of punches, David blocked one and then another and then countered with a short pop to Yousef's ribs. Yousef stepped in close and brought an elbow around that rattled David's teeth.

David stumbled back, shaking the bells out of his ears. Yousef pressed his advantage and leaped at his opponent, but David got a foot up and kicked him hard in the chest. Yousef flew back.

And landed on the flaming stove top.

Yousef screamed.

David rushed forward, put a forearm against Yousef's chest to hold him in place, the flames burning his hair and licking along the flesh of his ears and his neck. The scorched smell was sickening.

Yousef tried to twist and struggle up from the stove top, but David punched him in the side to take his air away, drew back, and punched him again.

The screams that came next were so shrill with animal agony that David almost let him up. Then he remembered the picture of Gina, the promises Yousef made, what he'd do to Amy. What he would do to his son and to his daughter.

David leaned in with all his weight and held Youself flat against the fire.

Yousef's hands shot up and latched on to David's throat.

David didn't let up, kept pushing Yousef against the stove top. The hands around his throat tightened. He couldn't draw air. Tiny spots hovered before David's eyes, a cottony darkness seeping in at the edge of his vision.

Yousef squeezed harder.

David glanced up at a line of cast-iron skillets hanging from hooks over the stove. He reached, stretched, grabbed one that might have worked well for fried chicken.

He brought it down hard on Youself's forehead with a dull clang. Yousef's grip didn't ease.

The strength leaked from David. He didn't have much left, but he summoned what he could and struck Yousef again. He still wouldn't let go. David bashed him again and again, and when the grip loosened, David took hope and bashed him one more time.

Yousef let go and his arms dropped.

David backed away, gasping desperately for air. His throat was raw and ragged. It hurt to draw breath.

David didn't mind. Breathing was better than not.

Yousef's body slid off the stove top and hit the kitchen floor with a thud, where it lay smoldering.

It was the smell of human flesh that put him over the edge, and the long night and the fact he'd been strangled. All of it together.

David fell to his knees and vomited.

He gagged and dry heaved a few more times before lurching to his feet, dizzy, and pushed through the swinging kitchen door into the service corridor beyond. He followed the emergency lights to an employee restroom and entered.

He bent over the sink, turned on the cold faucet, and splashed his face. Then he scooped water into his mouth. Swallowing hurt his throat, but he scooped in several more mouthfuls.

There was a Knicks coffee mug on the edge of the sink.

God, the Knicks suck.

He realized his mind was drifting and drank more water.

When he finished drinking, David backed away from the sink until he hit the wall, then slid down into a sitting position.

He closed his eyes for a little while.

CHAPTER THIRTY-THREE

David's eyes popped open.

He took a moment to orient himself. How long had he been out? Maybe five minutes. No more.

He had one more problem.

Payne.

To come through so much, to come this far, and not get Payne. It would all be for nothing. It would be dozens of broken eggs without an omelet to show for it.

David took out the cell phone and dialed.

Dante Payne fumed in the back of his limousine.

He drank Scotch and spilled some down his front. He cursed as if it were the Scotch's fault.

They made him wait. *Him*. Payne built his organization from the ground up. In those early days, he'd gotten his hands dirty, and the men respected him for it. He had been feared.

Now he was treated like . . . what? Some delicate, milk-skinned prince? Yes, he had men to do his dirty work for him now, but to be treated like he couldn't do it . . . like he didn't have the stones . . .

His phone rang.

Payne grabbed it quickly off the car seat next to him. Maybe this was good news. Perhaps Yousef and the others had at last accomplished their mission.

He looked at the screen. It wasn't Yousef. It was one of his men.

"Ramirez, where the hell have you been?" Payne said.

"It's not Ramirez," said a different voice. "I borrowed his phone."

"Who is this?"

"David Sparrow."

A pause. Then Payne said, "You have brass ones, my friend."

"Your men are dead," Sparrow said.

He could have been lying, but something told Payne he wasn't. "I can get a hundred more men. And then you'll be dead. Just a little later. That's all."

"I know," Sparrow said. "I can't beat you."

Payne didn't know what to say to that. Was Sparrow going to beg for mercy?

"That's why I called," Sparrow continued. "I can't beat you, but maybe I can make a deal. But we finish this. Tonight."

"What kind of deal?"

"I give you the flash drive," David said. "But then you call it square. The DA's office can't prove anything without it, and there's no other evidence. You go your way, and we'll go our way, and you have my guarantee the DA doesn't bring any more charges against you. Ever. For as long as my wife works there. Otherwise you'll get us eventually. You've got power, money, influence. You're holding all the cards. A deal is our only chance."

Payne thought about it. "I suppose I'm to meet you in a dark alley, so you can give me the flash drive there."

"I know you're not going to fall for anything amateur," Sparrow said. "I'm still in the hotel. I'll leave it in a place out in the open. On the second-floor mezzanine there's a big ceramic pot with a fern in it. I'll leave the flash drive there. I'll be all the way across the hotel."

"Double-cross me, and you die," Payne said.

"I'll assume we have a deal." Sparrow hung up.

Payne opened a compartment next to his seat and pulled out a nickel-plated .45 automatic. If Sparrow planned some kind of trap, he'd be ready. Dante Payne knew how to handle himself.

Amy was so nervous, her hands shook.

The only remedy was the eyeliner pencil. Her hands *had* to stop shaking or she'd put her eye out. David had warned her repeatedly not to use the thing in the car. She could almost hear his voice.

Hit a bump and . . .

She heard the door to the room open and turned expectantly. "David!"

He was back! *Finally!* She'd been so worried that her stomach hurt.

She ran into the next room to fling her arms around her husband and—

Amy's eyes went wide, and she opened her mouth to scream.

A strong hand clapped over her mouth to prevent it. Another hand shoved an automatic pistol in her face.

CHAPTER THIRTY-FOUR

Payne entered the hotel and walked up the powerless escalator to the mezzanine as Sparrow had instructed. Paramedics were just taking a man on a gurney toward the elevators.

Payne had to move fast. The police would arrive any minute, might already be downstairs.

He spotted the large ceramic pot Sparrow had described and fast walked to it. As promised, there was a small paper bag nestled in the fern. He glanced about to make sure no one was looking and then snatched it quickly and retreated back toward the escalator.

Payne did his best to look inconspicuous as he walked back down the escalator and out to the parking garage.

On his way he opened the bag and took out what was inside.

He stopped walking.

Payne blinked at the item to make sure he was looking at what he thought he was looking at. A coffee mug that said NEW YORK KNICKS.

"Son of a bitch!"

He hurled the mug against the wall of the parking garage where it shattered.

What was the point of that? If Sparrow had meant to taunt him, it only meant the man's eventual death would be doubly painful.

Payne walked back to his limousine, spitting curses. He opened the back door to climb in and—

Lightning white pain exploded between his eyes.

Hands grabbed Payne by the jacket and yanked him into the back of the limousine. He reached for the .45 in his belt and the same hands took it away from him.

He felt something hot and sticky trickle down his nose and over his lips. He blinked his vision back, touched his forehead, and looked at the blood on his fingers.

Payne turned his head and saw David Sparrow in the next seat, pointing his own .45 at him. In his other hand he held a leather blackjack. Sparrow looked haggard, but there was something wild and lethal in his eyes.

"The hotel has a security office with cameras that monitor all the entrances. In one of the few places in the hotel that gets power from the backup generators," Sparrow said. "All I had to do was give you a reason to show yourself. By the way, Larry Meadows says hello."

Sparrow brought the blackjack down hard on Payne's kneecap. He felt it break, and fiery pain exploded down his leg. He yelled and cursed.

"I don't even know who that is," Payne said angrily.

"No, you wouldn't, would you?" Sparrow said. "You have men to handle people like Larry. So you don't get your hands soiled."

"Fuck you."

"I thought about what I was going to say to you,"

Sparrow said. "You know what I realized? I don't have anything to say to you. Not one thing. You're just something that needs to go away, so I can have my life back."

"So you'll shoot me with my own pistol? What's that supposed to be, poetic justice or something?"

"It's convenient," Sparrow said. "After I shoot you, I can put the gun in your hand and make it look like suicide."

Payne scoffed. "I shot myself. After I broke my own kneecap?"

"Shit happens."

"You're not going to kill me, and I'll tell you why," Payne said. "Because you're a smart man, and you see an opportunity sitting in front of you. I underestimated you, that much is clear. So, here I am a rich man and you—how did you put it before? You're holding all the cards. Or at least one .45 caliber card that at the moment is enough. I'm sure we can come to an agreement that would be mutually—"

Bang.

CHAPTER THIRTY-FIVE

The last flight of stairs almost killed him.

The thought made David laugh. After all he'd been through . . . to be killed by the stairs of the Royal Empire Hotel seemed an absurd injustice. His own fault for shutting off the power and killing the elevators.

He'd seen the police lights out on the street even as he left the parking garage. The cops would be busy downstairs for a while, but eventually David would have to face the music. There would be lots of questions to answer. David would do his best to take the heat off of Amy. He'd take the blame. He didn't even care anymore as long as his family was safe.

And if he could drag his bedraggled ass up just a few more stairs, he could throw his arms around her and kiss her and tell her he loved her and that she was all he needed in the entire world.

And to hell with the Army.

He opened the door to the penthouse and stepped inside. "Amy!"

David rounded the corner into the living room. "Amy, where are you? I—"

David froze, his stomach twisting into a knot.

"Hello, government man," said Yousef Haddad. His voice was a grotesque croak. "It seems we still have some unfinished business."

The front of Yousef's face was a lumpy purple mess from the beating David had given him with the skillet. One ear and one side of his head were blackened with major third-degree burns. His lips were gone from half of his mouth, exposing cracked teeth. Hair scorched and patchy.

In all of that mess, one eye looked out clear and bright with hatred.

He held Amy by the neck. In his other hand he held a Glock to the side of Amy's head.

"I'm sure I've looked better," Yousef said. "If you're curious, my entire back is burned. When the shock wears off, I imagine the pain will be excruciating. In any event, I don't expect to live."

"There's an ambulance downstairs," David ventured. "Maybe—"

"I rather think we'll all be beyond the need for an ambulance after I'm finished," Yousef said.

David swallowed hard.

"I've been hanging on waiting for you to arrive," Yousef told him. "I'm going to die, and a dying man should get a last wish, don't you think?"

David said nothing. Amy caught his eye. She had a look on her face like she was trying to get him to read her thoughts by sheer willpower.

One of her hands was very slowly moving around behind her to her back pocket.

"There's a nice balcony behind us." Yousef gestured with the Glock. "I thought to throw her off. You can watch her all the way down."

Amy's hand slowly dipped into the back pocket of her jeans.

"Listen to me, Haddad." David knew reasoning with the man was useless, but he wanted to keep Haddad's attention focused on him. "I'm the one who lied to you. I said your family would be safe. Take it out on me, okay?"

Yousef pointed the Glock at David's face. "Trust me, government man. After you've watched her die, it will be your turn for pain."

Amy's hand came quickly out of her back pocket, the little silver automatic David had taken from Gina glinting silver. She brought the gun around to take aim at Yousef.

Yousef caught her wrist.

Twisted.

There was a snap, and Amy screamed, dropping the gun.

David tensed to make a play, but Yousef brought the Glock up fast.

"Too slow, government man."

Amy's arm hung limp at her side. Her breathing came shallow, skin going ashen.

Yousef said, "I think she has more fight left in her than you do, Sparrow. Maybe she—"

Amy spun on Yousef and struck with the other hand, burying the eyeliner pencil deep into Yousef's good eye. Yousef screamed, blood spurting out over Amy's fist.

David was already moving. Yousef tried to bring the Glock around again, but David leaped and grabbed it just as Yousef pulled the trigger.

The pistol went off an inch from David's ear and the world exploded in sound. David screamed.

His momentum carried him forward and they went stumbling back out onto the balcony. David kept pushing forward until the small of Yousef's back hit the railing. David smashed Yousef in the face with a forearm, and the momentum carried Yousef over—

—and down.

David watched him hit with a crack on the cement below between the pool and the spa.

He staggered back into the penthouse suite, bells still going off in his head. He knelt next to Amy and gathered her in his arms, careful of her injury.

"Let's go," David said. "Let's get you downstairs. Get you some help."

"Is . . . is he . . . ?" Amy looked toward the balcony.

"We're all done with him," David told her.

They walked out to the hallway together, David turning them toward the stairs. The apartment had its own generator he reminded her and then explained about shutting off the hotel's power, putting the elevators out of commission.

Amy sighed. "That's a lot of stairs."

"Sorry," David said.

At that moment the lights came back on. Somebody had found the switch.

"See?" David said, escorting her onto the elevator. "Things are looking up already."

They staggered out through the main entrance of the lobby, holding each other up. The street was bathed in the red and blue lights of the emergency vehicles.

Paramedics tended the injured, and police officers took statements. Shriners hovered in the background and wondered where their convention had gone.

David took Amy to a paramedic. "Broken arm."

"Okay, man," said the paramedic. "We got this." He set Amy on the curb and began to gently prod the arm. David kissed her on top of the head, then headed for the nearest cop.

He presented himself to the officer. "Hey, I think you're looking for me." David swayed on his feet, just about to fall over.

"We're looking for a lot of people, pal," the cop said.

David explained who he was.

"Holy shit." The cop turned to his partner. "It's that fucking guy. The one from TV."

There was a brief discussion about whether David should see one of the paramedics or be handcuffed first.

A man in a dark blue suit pushed his way through the crowd. He looked so clean and so groomed and so well pressed that David thought he might be computer generated.

"I think I can handle this for you, officer," the man in the suit said.

"Oh, yeah? Who the hell are you?"

"Agent Joseph Armand." He flashed his ID. "FBI."

"Shit," the cop said. "Fine. He's all yours." The cop stomped away looking half pissed and half relieved.

"You look like you've had quite a night, Mr. Sparrow," Armand said.

David turned his head, pointed at his good ear. "Talk into this one."

"A friend of yours named Charlie Finn said we might be of assistance to each other," the FBI man explained. "Would it be all right if we had a conversation?"

David grinned. "As long as we can do it sitting down."

EPILOGUE

"Mommy!"

Anna ran up the driveway and threw herself at Amy.

"Watch the arm!" Amy said.

They hugged, and Brent joined in a second later, squeezing her tight. Both children were pink. They'd gotten some sun out by the pool according to Amy's sister.

"How about me?" David asked.

Anna and Brent launched themselves at David, hugging him tightly around the neck. Anna kissed his cheek.

Then she pointed at the cast on Amy's arm. "I know why you sent us to Disney," Anna said. "It was so you could go on your own vacation. You went skiing, didn't you? Brent says people break all their arms and legs when they go skiing."

Amy laughed. "What?"

"I'll let you handle this," David said. "I'll help with the bags."

He paused to give Amy's sister a hug and then found Jeff unloading the luggage.

"Hey, David."

"Welcome back, Jeff."

Jeff rubbed the back of his neck and shuffled his feet, embarrassed. "I hate to say it, David, but I guess I better give you the heads-up. We charged a *lot* of stuff to the room. Just didn't want you to have a heart attack when the credit card bill came in."

David offered his hand, and they shook.

"Thank you. Thank you for taking my children away from danger. And for bringing them back in one piece."

A lot happened the next few weeks, most of it good.

Between the FBI's intervention and Bert's full confession as part of his plea bargain, David and Amy were cleared of any wrongdoing in an expedited fashion. The FBI seemed especially pleased to get their hands on Calvin Pope's flash drive. David didn't ask what they planned to do with it but guessed multiple political careers would soon be destroyed or made depending on how well Washington's power brokers could work the spin machine.

David really didn't give a damn.

The doctor told David his damaged eardrum would heal, loss of hearing would be minimal.

David arranged for a repairman to come out to the house and fix the garage door.

The Escalade had been declared a complete write-off. David thought maybe a minivan next. Is that what stay-at-home dads drove these days? More study was needed. He wondered idly if the dealership offered armor and bulletproof glass as options.

On a rainy Sunday morning, David Sparrow served as a pallbearer at Larry Meadows's funeral. The somber event was the single moment of gloom in a time of relative optimism.

David Sparrow had his family back. They were safe.

Very gradually life began to seem normal again, and on the Saturday Amy got the cast off her arm, David dragged the charcoal grill into the backyard for hamburgers, and they ate outside at the picnic table.

"My hamburger is still all red on the inside," Anna said.

"Mine is red on the inside but hard and black on the outside," Brent said.

"That just means you need more ketchup," David told him.

David took everything the day would give him, throwing a football with Brent, blowing bubbles with Anna. The way the hazy orange of the setting sun made Amy's skin glow and lit her hair, creating a halo around her head, reminded David how in love he was with her. The four of them had a life, something good and solid and it took almost losing all of that to remind him he was a lucky man.

He wouldn't take it for granted. Not ever again.

That night, after David tucked the children into bed, he returned to his own bedroom to find Amy already curled under the covers, wearing her circus tent flannel, the covers pulled up to her chin.

David slipped into bed next to her, put an arm around her and pulled her close. "What are you doing tomorrow?"

"Catching up on briefs," she said. "You?"

"Nothing. I thought I'd take the kids to the park."

"I thought you were having lunch with Charlie Finn," she said. "You were going to buy him Chinese food, and he was going to tell you about his new FBI job."

"That's Monday."

David buried his face in her hair and smelled her shampoo. He yawned and said, "You want to fool around?"

"Yeah, baby. Rock my world."

David began to snore lightly, but Amy didn't hear it because she was already asleep.